GILMAN'S PARALLEL

The French King

Robert W. Boyer

Robin Peter Gilman has never seen proof of the Holy Grail. But all of that changes in Llangollen, Wales, when a fairy mysteriously appears in his life and shows him the existence of a parallel universe and a destiny he never could have imagined. He finds new friends and powerful allies. Nothing happens without reason, however. Robin is the future king of the two parallel worlds but so is Peter Robyn, his own parallel life. Only one will exist when the two worlds merge, only one will be left to rule with good or evil intent, and only one can be the Mabus.

Copyright © 2009 by Robert W. Boyer

All rights reserved. No part of this book, in part or in whole, may be reproduced, transmitted or utilized in any form or by any means, electronic, photographic or mechanical, including photocopying, recording, or by any information storage and retrieval system without permission in writing from the author.

LCCN: 2009903631
ISBN: 1-4392-3701-8
ISBN-13: 9781439237014

Visit www.booksurge.com to order additional copies.

For Rose, who gave me strength.
For Jon, who taught me love is unconditional.
For Gwyneth, who taught me life is worth it all.
For Maggie, who told me I can't afford not to write this story.
For Robin Ireland, my first editor.
For Frances Dayee, who helped me develop my craft.

⌘ ⌘ ⌘

This is a work of fiction. Names, characters, places, business establishments and incidents either are the product of the author's imagination or are used fictitiously, and any resemblance to actual persons, living or dead, business and educational establishments, events, or locales is entirely coincidental.

CONTENTS

ONE
The Beginning........1

TWO
Castell Dinas Bran........15

THREE
The Mirror........27

FOUR
Myrddin........39

FIVE
Earth Changes........47

SIX
The Holy Grail........61

SEVEN
The Sikorsky Sea King........75

EIGHT
Genetic Engineering........83

NINE
Crossing Over........97

TEN
Good-byes........103

ELEVEN
Princes Du Sang........ 111

TWELVE
The Nephilim........ 123

THIRTEEN
The Clue........ 131

FOURTEEN
The Dragon Revealed........ 141

FIFTEEN
Blood Oaths and Consequence........ 155

SIXTEEN
The Confrontation........ 167

SEVENTEEN
A Battle Joined, a Plot Revealed........ 181

EIGHTEEN
The Wonder in Heaven........ 189

NINETEEN
The Choosing........ 197

TWENTY
The War in Heaven........ 207

TWENTY-ONE
The Kingdom of Magic........ 227

Chapter 1
THE BEGINNING

Robin dreamed about flying. He soared high above the clouds, close to the sun, where it was warm. The people below him in the old castle ruins called out to him that it was nonsense to fly, but they didn't know what it was like. They had never flown.

Robin spied another boy, waving frantically at him. *He seems so desperate to talk to me*, thought Robin, *maybe I should*. Robin wheeled in a graceful arc, flew around a flock of geese, and drew near.

As Robin approached, he could hear the other boy's voice but couldn't understand what he was shouting. An astonishing idea came unbidden into Robin's brain. It wasn't that it was abnormal for Robin to have ideas, but it was the way it appeared in his thoughts. This boy wanted him to go away, and now Robin was close enough to understand his words.

"Go away!" the boy shouted. "You can't be here. It's against the rules. Go away!"

What rules did I break, Robin puzzled? He flew back up toward the sun. He looked down through a thin cloud and thought he recognized a landmark. It was the crumbling walls of Castell Dinas Bran. He turned and saw the Dee River below, and way off in the distance, he thought maybe he could make Colwyn Bay out to the northwest.

That's when he saw them. They looked like a swarm of angry bees, and they were coming straight at him. He completely forgot about the other boy and was about to fly away when another thought entered his brain.

"Fear not. We mean you no harm," it said.

And then the small creatures were upon him in a cloud of golden dust. They laughed, and some sang in tiny voices that infected him with their glee and joy of life. They lifted him, and he could feel the currents of air created by their tiny wings. It was wonderful.

Robin surrendered his flight to them as they propelled him in a single direction. One of the tiny creatures flew in front of him and faced him while she flew backwards. She turned her head and gave him a curious look and smile.

She had almond-shaped eyes the color of green grass and golden hair streaked with red that reached to her feet. She wore forest green leggings and a diaphanous tunic that had every hue of the rainbow and changed with whatever aspect of light it was exposed to. An ornate belt made of interlacing silver links inset with turquoise held the tunic at the waist. A jewel-encrusted scabbard held a sword that hung from the belt. She carried a shield decorated with the image of three black cats in a circle, with each cat grasping the tail of the next in its respective teeth. The cats' baleful yellow eyes followed Robin wherever he was as if they were alive and watching him. Robin thought she was very pretty.

"Bendith y Mamau," she said.

"Excuse me?" Robin said.

"Bendith y Mamau. It means 'Mother's blessing.'"

"Are you...fairies?"

The tiny creature put her hand over her mouth and laughed. "We are indeed. We are the Ellyllon Tylwyth Teg of Glamorgan."

"Could I ask where you are taking me?"

"To meet someone who wishes to speak with you. Do you not wish to go?" she said.

"No...er, I mean, yes. I do wish to go. It's only a dream, anyway, and this makes me happy, you see. Who are we going to visit?"

"But we thought you knew by now."

The entire troop of fairies stopped abruptly. The tiny fairy flew close to Robin's face so that she was almost touching his nose, and stared at him for a moment.

"Knew what?" he asked.

"This is not a dream; this is reality."

At that moment, he fell.

He yelled out just as he hit the floor beside his bed. He lay for a moment on the hardwood floor and tried to collect his thoughts. His heart hammered in his chest, and his hazel eyes stared wide open as he tried to see into the darkness. His head hurt where he had bumped it, and he rubbed the spot, which only made it hurt more. He brushed his dark brown hair back as he picked himself up. The room spun when he stood, and he dizzily fell back into bed and pulled up his quilt.

Oppressive silence filled the night. It weighed down on him as if to flatten him into his mattress until he disappeared. He shivered with the thought of becoming part of his bed, unable to free himself, lost under the covers for all time.

The room was dark, save for the moonlight coming in his window. He watched the light filter through his curtains…not curtains he would have chosen, but his mother had liked their frill and lace. He would have preferred curtains that were simple—blue, perhaps dark indigo blue—and a design of the heavens at night. That would be nice.

He thought about calling out, but it was April, and his mother had died in December. His father was probably asleep in the easy chair from too much drinking. His dad did that a lot lately. Robin wished he could be transported to another place, another time, away from all the grief that consumed him and that was made worse by his uncaring father.

Unfair, that's what it was. He wanted to talk to his father, not watch him get drunk every night. He didn't want to be ignored like he didn't exist while his father lost himself in his own sorrow.

Robin's thoughts turned automatically to his mother. She was healthy enough, when first they arrived in Llangollen, Wales. She was happy as she set up their new home. But a few days after Robin began the school term, she fell ill. It wasn't long before a visiting nurse was needed, and not long after, a doctor began making daily house calls.

Robin's father didn't cope well with the situation and was often cross with him, especially when Robin would ask what was wrong. His father never answered his questions fully, so Robin took to eavesdropping in on the conversations between the doctor and his father. He became so good at eavesdropping that he could soon hear conversations downstairs from his upstairs bedroom. Then he began to hear the neighbors, and next their neighbors. He decided that it was some sort of telepathy rather than good hearing.

Robin felt the ground fall away from him one day, when he overheard the words "inoperable cancer," "metastasized," and "hopeless" all in the same sentence. He cried himself to sleep that night.

Robin thought of asking his mother what was wrong but knew he wouldn't be able to keep from breaking down, which would only upset her more. She was in so much pain the doctor had to give her medicine that made her sleep most of the time. Even if he had asked, she was incoherent when she was awake. He wished now he had found the courage to speak to her.

School was out for the Christmas break when his mother died, and not many of his school acquaintances ever knew anything unpleasant had occurred in his life. After the holidays, school resumed as usual, and everyone treated Robin as if nothing had happened, making him feel as if his mother's death didn't matter any more than anything else.

His father grew withdrawn and took to staying out late at night, making it difficult for Robin to speak with him when needed to. His grandmother arrived next. After an argument with his father about his constant carousing and who was in charge of the household activities, she went back to Redmond, Washington. Robin found he liked it better without her. But now that he was thinking about her, he remembered his mother had told him it was grandmother who had chosen his name. He figured there must have been a grand argument over his naming.

Robin didn't particularly like his name. It wasn't like he had a choice in the matter, but he supposed it was better than his middle name, Peter, which was always a great source of fun for the local bullies at school. Robin Peter Gilman, what a mixed bag of names; what a load of...

"Robin!" his father called.

Robin lay still in his bed, hoping his father would think he was asleep. He must have woken up angry about something. Robin tried to think of what it was he could have possibly done to annoy him. Maybe a neglected chore, a light left on, the water running, or any number of things. It didn't take much to set his father off anymore. Nothing came to mind. He waited, but his father didn't call out again. Sleep began to overtake Robin's mind once more.

"Robin! Get down here, right now! Don't keep me waiting, young man!"

"What, Dad?" Robin called back in his most innocent voice. "Is something wrong?"

"Robin!"

"Yes, sir."

His throat tightened and his stomach began to hurt as he swung his feet out of bed. He put his robe on and steeled himself against his father's verbal abuse, or perhaps worse. If his father reached for his leather belt, Robin decided to remind him he was almost thirteen and too old to be spanked anymore. He wasn't sure if he could muster the courage to carry out his plan, though, without showing fear. Worry gnawed at his insides.

A voice! He heard another voice! A woman's voice! Not soft, but harsh. It sounded as if it were used too often and older than it ought to.

"Will, don't yeh 'ave any guest towels in this bloody place?" the woman asked his father.

"Look in the closet behind the bathroom door, and hurry up. You're on the clock, you know." Then under his breath, "What the hell does she think this is? The bloody Ritz?"

Robin stopped at the foot of the stairs and tried to make sense of what he was hearing and seeing. His father had left him alone, and now he had brought a strange woman into the house. Who was this woman and why wasn't she dressed in warmer clothes? She looked cold.

"Look at yeh," the woman said when she spied him on the lower step. "Yer almost cute 'nough to eat. Yeh didn't tell me yer kid was so 'andsome, Will. 'E's got yer 'awk nose. 'E's delicious." Then she leaned closer to Robin, close enough so he could smell her alcohol breath, and whispered, "Fancy a go with me, love? It's free for a first timer, yeh know."

Robin, confused, looked directly into her face. It was as if all the life had gone from her eyes and she merely existed on borrowed time.

"What are you doing here?" he asked.

"Makin' a livin', love, makin' a livin'."

"You're not being rude to my guest, are you, young man? Well? Answer me!"

Anger welled up inside Robin. He wasn't sure what was happening, but he was sure he didn't like this woman. And he was sure he didn't want her in their house anymore. He knew his mother would have been very unhappy about this.

"No!" Robin fumed, "but she was rude to me! She asked me if I wanted a 'go' and I don't know what that means, but it sounds rude!"

"Where," William said to his son, "do you get off speaking to me that way?" Then his voice became dangerously quiet as he leaned closer to where Robin stood at the foot of the stairs. "I am getting tired of the way you've been acting ever since your mother died and have come to the end of my patience. You will apologize to our guest immediately!"

Stung, fighting back tears he wished were not there, Robin angrily retorted, "You can't just go out and leave me alone, bringing strange women home and drinking all night! You know Mom wouldn't like it!"

"What did you say?"

"I said, *Mom wouldn't like this!*"

Robin's defiant words hung in the air. He knew he couldn't take them back, but oh, how he regretted them when he saw the blazing rage in his father's eyes. A shiver ran through him as he watched his father raise his right hand, as if in slow motion, across his chin to just above his left ear and then back across toward Robin's face. The blow landed and knocked him backward, forcing him to sit down hard, bruising his tail bone. Now there was no stopping the tears.

"*I hate you!*"

As Robin ran back up the stairs, he heard the strange woman laughing while William called to him, "Robin, wait! I didn't mean it! Please, son, wait!"

William started up the stairs. "Robin, please, you've got to listen to me...will you shut your hole, bitch?" The woman ceased her derisive laughter, as if she had been the one slapped.

"Well," she said, "that went rather nasty, if yeh ask me. Yer certainly no fun anymore."

"Here! Here is what I owe you and enough for the rail! Take it and get out of my house!"

"Oy, come on love. We can still 'ave a good time, and if yer still in the mood, I likes it rough sometimes."

"*Get out!*" Robin heard her call his father a four-letter name as she slammed the door.

Once she was outside and unseen by anyone in the house, a man stepped out of the car parked in the Gilman carport and seized the woman by the arm. His hand clamped down over her mouth before she could scream, and he thrust her into the back seat. The man's eyelids were grown together over his empty sockets, and, though unseen by him, the woman's reaction was one he was all too familiar with. He leaned into the light where she could see him and grinned at her as her voice failed. She froze in terror, mouthing her silent scream.

"Keep her quiet," the second man said from the front seat. "I'm going inside."

Robin wiped his eyes to get rid of his tears and lay down on his bed. There was the sound of a door lock as someone walked quietly into the Gilman house. Robin strained to hear even the smallest sound for a clue as to what was going on downstairs. The conversation drifted upstairs in muffled tones, but Robin listened with his mind to catch the words.

"What are you doing here?" William asked.

"Cleaning up your mess," the new voice hissed.

"I kicked her out. There's nothing left for you to do."

"Didn't we discuss this?"

"What do you care what I do?"

"I don't, but your subjects will, and your son. Right in front of him. And what were you thinking when you hit the boy? He must at least think you care."

"The king doesn't always take advice from his adviser; he only must hear it. Besides, you said I could do anything I—"

"Not in front of the boy!" A moment of silence followed, and then the hissing voice continued. "I'll say it again. The boy must have a father who sets both a moral and ethical example beyond reproach. He must not only be taught these values, as prescribed by the true church; he must also have someone he looks up to who has the visible if not actual integrity to live these values. What you do out of his sight and away from public view is the king's business and only the king's business."

"In other words, don't get caught?"

"Don't be seen! You are most correct that the king only has to hear his adviser, but you would do well to consider that the advisor does not always have to give advice."

"That's not what we agreed to. What are you planning to do when he comes of age? Eliminate me as you did Cerridwen?"

"How perfectly astute of you. You are fortunate the adviser, to fulfill his ends, needs the king's participation."

"Good. As long as we understand one another."

"You are a blind man, William Gilman. It is your greed and desire for power that makes it so. Be warned: if I find a way to reach my ends without you, our relationship will be terminated."

"That's an empty threat. You and I both know there's no other way."

Robin heard his father choke. Then the picture of his father dangling in midair, held by unseen hands and clutching his throat, appeared in his mind's eye.

"Woe unto him who underestimates me. He is the Mabus...not you. I must now discreetly dispose of the problem you brought into your house and paraded so salaciously in front of the boy. Be ready to go when I return."

Robin shivered as he wrestled with his mixed emotions. Part of him was glad that this strange man could terrify his father, but part of him was truly scared that this same person could come after him next. He was wishing he could see the man's face when he heard a thump and his father gasping for air. The door slammed next, and then he heard a buzzing sound. He looked up and saw the same tiny fairies from his dream. The fairy who had spoken with him earlier flew in front of his nose, turned her head, and gave a curious look. Robin couldn't help but notice how penetrating her stare was.

"Bendith y Mamau. She is waiting," she said.

"Who is waiting?" Robin asked her.

"Promise me one thing," she said.

"Promise what?"

"Promise you will control yourself when we tell you the truth. Last time, we nearly dropped you, and for a fairy, that is most unforgivable."

"Then this is real and not a dream? That means what I heard is the truth! My father's a king and my mother was...my dad's in trouble!"

"We mean you no harm, and where we are taking you will do you no harm. It is you who are in trouble, Robin. Your father must take care of himself."

"But he needs my help!"

"Promise me!" Tiny tears formed in her eyes like miniature crystalline diamonds.

"Please don't cry," said Robin, suddenly contrite. "I've done enough crying as it is. I promise I won't do anything to make you drop me."

"Lilith."

"Excuse me?"

"Lilith. You asked for a name. It is Lilith."

"Oh, where you are taking me. That's the name of the person who wishes to speak with me, then?"

"Patience, Robin. You will see."

The fairies bore him aloft and controlled the direction of his flight. He looked for any landmarks he could recognize, but there were clouds below, and it was difficult to determine where he was. He looked back at the fairy before him. She was laughing and flying backwards without so much as a glance in the direction they were going.

"Hang on...how did you know my name? I never told you. I don't know your name, either, come to think of it. I'll wager it's a brilliant name, just like you are. Would you tell me, then?"

All the fairies laughed at his question. There were tears in the eyes of his tiny host again, but this time of mirth and not sadness like before. When her laughter subsided, she put her hands on her hips and flew up next to his nose so that he had to cross his eyes to see her properly.

"You may call me Kat-sidhe. You may call for me at any time, and I will appear before you, here in this universe as well as in your own."

"Yes," he said, "thank you for that."

"You are most welcome, Robin. We have been aware of your name for some time. It was foretold to us, and we have been looking for you ever since. But Lilith will explain more to you. Ah, we are here. By the way, when you call for me, if you think of it intentionally, I will hear it just the same as if you spoke it out loud."

They landed in a small glade surrounded by thick forest. In the center of the glade was a single tree surrounded by springs and several wells. It was the largest tree he had ever seen. Kat-sidhe set him down at its base and joined the other fairies in a circle that surrounded both him and the tree.

"Wait here," Kat-sidhe said. "She is coming. Remove your shoes, for the ground upon which you walk is holy, and you are about to enter a hallowed state. When she arrives, follow our lead."

Robin felt the hair on the back of his neck rise up, and he shivered as if something unseen had brushed up against him. A mist formed in front of him and rapidly took form. All of the fairies fell silent.

There she stood, clothed in raiment made from the light of the sun and the moon, and upon her head was a crown made of twelve stars. She had wings that were fourteen feet across when they were fully open, and she was as tall as her wingspan was wide. She had substance and yet no substance at all. Robin could see her every detail and could also make out every detail of the landscape directly behind and through her. The fairies bowed before her, and Robin immediately dropped to one knee and bowed his head in reverence, just as the fairies did.

Then the fairies sang in their tiny voices:

Welcome, reverend mother.
Welcome, goddess mother.
Welcome, nature's mother.
We all sisters, brothers.
Welcome, Azna mother.
All creatures welcome mother.
Welcome, holy mother.

"Gather round, children. Come and gather round," she said. "And you may rise up, young Robin. I would speak with you."

Robin realized that before him stood the very essence of all things beautiful and powerful. She had requested an audience with him. He struggled to compose himself, to conquer his fear, and rose up as she bade. His knees shook. He knew his voice would quaver when he tried to use it.

"Are you an angel?" he asked.

Her laughter filled the glade. "No, Robin, I am not," she said. "I am called Lilith. I am the mother of all magical creatures great and small. I am the mother of all the beasts in the field that would be the totems of mankind, and I am the mother of the earth, both in this universe and in yours. I am the comforter."

"What should I call you?" he asked her.

"You may call me Mother Azna, if you like. Or perhaps Mother Lilith, if you would. That is my favorite. Now, as to my purpose for bringing you here, I have a request to make of you. Will you listen to my plea?"

"How may I serve you?" Robin asked.

"You are a most polite boy. I am pleased by your manner and wish you to know that you need not fear me as much as you do. I will not harm you. Please sit down and be at ease. Relax; be comforted. You are trying to carry too much on your shoulders."

Robin sat down beneath the huge tree and looked up at Lilith with expectation in his eyes. Her voice was stunning, both loud and magnificent. It was like a song of the angels, and it soothed away the uneasiness he had been feeling. He was no longer afraid and felt miraculously at ease with himself and with everything around him. It was as if a terrible burden had been lifted away from his heart.

"Do you know the name of this tree, Robin?" Lilith asked him. "It is called Yggdrasil, and it is a giant ash. Some call it the Tree of Knowledge, some the Tree of Fate, and some the Tree of the Universe. It is most correctly known as the World Tree. It connects all of the known universes, and you would be surprised how many there are. It is here that your journey begins, if you will accept it. This is the gateway to the universes that will concern you in both your future and in ours. This is the gateway to your soul."

This wasn't like any classroom Robin had ever been in. He didn't even have to struggle to concentrate on what was being taught like he did at his school in Llangollen. What Mother Lilith said spoke to his soul, enlarging it as if this was the very food it had needed all of his life.

"What must I do?" he asked.

"Do nothing. Be." Lilith replied. "Live your life both here and in your universe. By living, you will teach the others. However, you must also be taught about your mystical abilities. Will you learn?"

"I'm not sure I could teach anyone anything but, yes, I do want to learn. Is it you that will teach me, Mother Lilith?"

"Yes, but you will be sent other teachers, as well. You must learn certain aspects and receive certain knowledge of coming events. What I tell you now is most important. You are in line to inherit a throne that rules no country, but there are certain tasks you must accomplish before you can be crowned."

"I'm...I'm a king? No, that can't be right, can it?"

"I know this must be difficult for you to accept but, yes, you are a king. To be crowned, you must prove your lineage and must, therefore, first find the Holy Grail. There is an enemy who will try to find the Holy Grail before you and use it for evil. Will you do this?"

"But I don't even know where to begin looking. I don't even know what it is."

"The Holy Grail in legend is the cup Christ drank from at the last supper. In reality, it holds a record of your ancestors and proof of your right to be king. You shall receive help, and it will be more than you think. You will also discover magical abilities along the way, and you must use them for good."

"But, my dad! I heard someone say he was a king! Are we both kings?"

"I know this someone. What he said is true. You are the son of the king and the heir apparent. It is your lineage you must prove. That means you must prove whom you are related to. You will find the records of your bloodline in the Holy Grail. It is why you must find it and protect it."

"But wouldn't my dad know about this?"

"He is not the one to ask. Do you understand why he is not the one to ask?"

"He...hit me. Why would he do that? He said my mom was...doesn't he love me?"

"What did your mother say to you the night before she passed on?"

"She said I was someone special. Someone who could change things. She called me her prince...her...hang on...how do you know she said something to me that night?"

"Do you remember being bathed in golden light that night? Do you see that golden light now? I was there, though you did not see me."

"None of this is making sense. My dad said something about my mom to that man. Something about getting rid of her."

"Your father made a concordat with the church to be a king in name only. Your mother, Cerridwen, found out the details of this agreement conceived by a highly placed cardinal. She stood in the way of his most evil plans."

"Then it's true. She's dead because..."

"Because she loved you. If the Holy Grail falls into the wrong hands, it will be used for evil. Your father wants the Holy Grail to prove he is king in more than name and is plotting to prevent your ascension to the throne. I know this is difficult to hear, beloved one, but know your mother's love lives on whether your father loves power more than you or not."

"Does this cardinal guy know where the Holy Grail is?"

"The evil one is using your father, and it is difficult to see the answer to what you ask. It is the shadow of his presence in your world that prevents those who would stand against him from seeing what is afoot."

"You don't know?"

"Not yet, but it would be better if you found the Holy Grail before your father."

"Is Dad...would he try to...to...kill me?"

"This is what I know. It is you the evil one wants to be king and not your father. Your father is aware of this but is jealous. He secretly plots to thwart the evil one and become king in your place. Find the Holy Grail, Prince Robin; it is your only hope."

"Oh, wow. Oh, wow! I'm just a kid. Why me?"

"Because you agreed it would be so before you were even born. Now it is time to go. Rest for you is most important. Princess Kat-sidhe will escort you back to your universe."

"As you wish, my mother," Kat-sidhe said. She had approached from behind Robin, startling him when she spoke.

He turned to look at the tiny fairy, and then he turned around to face Lilith once more and to make his good-byes. When he did, she was nowhere to be seen. All that remained were wisps of mist floating in the air. She had simply evaporated.

"Wait...wait...where can I find you?"

"I am always here, at Yggdrasil," Lilith's disembodied voice said. "Kat-sidhe will bring you when you need or until you learn to come here on your own."

"I didn't know you were a princess," Robin said. "Why didn't you tell me?"

"You never asked," Kat-sidhe said. "I am one of the nine cat fairies."

"Oh, well, I was wondering if I should call 'your majesty" or something of that sort? And if you are a princess, is there a queen?"

"I am Kat-sidhe first and a princess next. There is a queen, and you have just met her. For us, the title of princess is a ranking in our hierarchy and not so much to do with the right of inheritance. You may address me as 'my lady,' if you like, but I would prefer less formality. It is time to go."

Kat-sidhe and the fairies flew him back to his own bedroom. He watched in awe as his covers magically turned down and then unfolded back over him. Kat-sidhe flew to his face and kissed him directly in the center of his forehead. Golden sparks fell all around as if they were dust caught in the sun.

"All humans have an invisible eye," she said, "and by my kiss and by my intent, I have allowed yours to open for the first time. Most humans never open this eye and never see within, for this is where this eye gazes. It also gazes at things not normally seen in your third dimension, things that are not physical."

Robin did not understand, but since he was becoming very sleepy, he decided not to ask any more questions.

"Thank you," he said.

"You are welcome. Good night, Robin."

"Good night," Robin mumbled.

Chapter 2
CASTELL DINAS BRAN

Robin woke and lay for a moment, letting his thoughts race through his brain. Not able to sleep anymore, he rose and went to the bathroom mirror. His cheek was swollen and bruised beneath his eye, where his father had hit him.

Still in his pajamas, he crept down the stairs toward the kitchen. He looked into his father's bedroom on the way. The annoying smell of liquor clung in the air around his sleeping father. As long as he didn't wake him, Robin knew he would sleep most of the day away, oblivious to any noise around him. *Why does Dad have to drink so much?* he wondered.

Once in the kitchen, he opened the freezer compartment and got the ice out. He sat down at the table and thought about the night's events. He iced his cheek until he noticed the April morning sun filtering in through the window. At least it was Saturday and that meant no school.

He opened the kitchen door and walked out into the carport. The chill of the air made him wish he had put his robe on, but his intent was only to take a quick look and then go back inside. His heart sank when he saw his mountain bike in the hands of Dewey and Fred Wilkins, the two local bullies.

"Hey, that's mine. Give it back," Robin said.

Grinning maliciously, Fred walked toward him. Dewey, still holding the bike, silently watched his younger brother. Then, Fred broke into a run and grabbed Robin by the arm, closing the distance too soon for him to get away. Fred shoved him, and Robin scraped his knees and hands while trying to break his own fall. Then they were on him. They stood him up. Fred held his arms from behind.

"Perfect, Fred. 'Old 'im just like that," Dewey said. "Hey, Peter breath. 'Ow 'bout a ride on your bike?"

"Leave me alone!"

"I thought all this time you were our friend. It's not very nice of you to refuse us, really."

"We're not friends. Now leave me alone!"

"Your funeral," Dewey said with a shrug.

"Hey, Dewey," Fred taunted, "show 'im 'ow we treat someone who won't be our friend."

Dewey grinned and kneed him between the legs before Robin could guard against it. Fred let go, and Robin fell forward, holding himself. His body crashed into Dewey, causing the bully to step back, tripping over Robin's bike.

"Just for that," Dewey growled, "We're gonna' take your bike for a spin. We might bring it back if you're lucky, but I'm not gonna' guarantee it'll be in one piece."

Robin watched them as they took his bicycle away. He groaned and closed his eyes. Why had they ever moved to Llangollen in the first place? What was so special about Wales, anyway? Even if it was true his father was born in Wales, couldn't his dad have stayed in Seattle and run the business he owned and been just as comfortable in the United States? He wished he was back in Redmond, Washington, with all of his friends and no bullies to pick on him because he was smaller than everyone else or from another country. But that was halfway around the world.

When his pain had finally subsided enough for him to move, he gingerly stood and walked toward the kitchen door. He had never felt as humiliated as he did at that very moment.

"Aren't you cold?" said a voice.

It was Gwyneth, the girl next door. She was in his same year at school. She flipped her long blond hair away from her face and stared at him, obviously expecting an answer. Her ice-blue eyes seemed to penetrate Robin. It was almost as if she could see right through him. It made him uncomfortable.

"A little," he admitted, "but I shan't be out here much longer anyway. What about you? You need your robe on, too."

"Well, that's me, too. I only came out because I saw you. All right?"

"Yeah, I guess. And you?"

"That's a nasty bruise," she observed, looking at his face where his father had hit him. "You want to tell me about it?"

"Not really. There's not much to tell, anyway. Just an accident."

Gwyneth, silent for a moment, said, "You sure you wouldn't like a go at it?"

"What did you say?"

"Don't you think I'll understand?"

"Not that it's any of your business," he began, "and I'm not trying to be rude, but it's a very private matter between me and my dad. I think I can solve it myself. Still, maybe I could tell you about it. It's just...well...we had a small argument, and our guest thought we were being rude, so she left, and I was kind of upset and accidentally walked into the bathroom door, and Dad was tired and shouted at me for being so clumsy, as it was my own fault anyway."

"I don't believe any such thing, Robin Gilman," Gwyneth said. "You're not a very good liar, you know. I can see the landing of your stairs from my bedroom window. You need to tell someone about this, before it starts to get any worse."

"You've been snooping!" Robin accused.

"I was not! I was concerned!"

"Er, it's cold. I need to go back inside, and that wasn't a lie."

Gwyneth, avoiding Robin's eyes, said, "Well, it is rather cold, but if you want to talk...well, I will listen, you know. And, Robin?"

"What?"

"I was wrong about you not being a very good liar, you know. You are simply dreadful at it." Gwyneth turned around and went inside her house without once looking back.

Robin closed his mouth and then went inside. He sneaked back up the stairs to look at his face in the mirror again. The bruising was just below his right eye and was spreading down his jaw line. It looked suspiciously like a hand print. *Gwyneth was right*, he thought to himself. *I'm not a very good liar.*

All he wanted to do just now was to go someplace for the rest of the day that would keep him out of his dad's way and away from the neighbors' prying eyes. Maybe he could sneak out and go look at the Eisteddfod Pavilion at the Penddol site. The Clwyd County Council had hired his father's engineering firm to renovate it for the upcoming July Eisteddfod Music Festival, and the project was almost finished. The pavilion would be used for the boys' choir competition and the Columbia Boys' Choir, from Washington, would be there. Robin had friends in the choir, and he could scarcely wait for July.

The morning sun blazed in the cloudless sky. Just for a moment, he considered leaving a note, but decided not to. *Besides*, he thought, *why would Dad care where I go?* He was dressed and soon outside without waking his father.

"Off somewhere?" Gwyneth stood in the carport, studying him with her same penetrating stare.

"Maybe. I thought I would go to the Penddol site to see how far along my dad's gotten."

"Oh," she said. "You know, I bet one could see it from Dinas Bran, if one felt up to an early morning climb."

"That's not a short trip on foot."

"We better get going, then," she said.

"We?" Robin said as he looked down at her feet. She had hiking shoes on.

"Sure, I was going anyway. Thought you'd come with, unless you've some place you'd rather go."

"Not really. You know the way, then? I've never been. Hang on, you haven't been planning this? I mean, not that it isn't a good idea...er... I mean..."

"So what if I have? Besides, you need a better story about your face than what you told me, and I thought I could help. You know, two heads better than one, you see."

"Oh," Robin said. "All right, partners in crime, then?" Gwyneth smiled, and Robin found himself considering how pretty she was, standing there in the sunlight.

"Partners in crime sounds fun," she said. "Let's go."

They made their way to Berwyn Street and turned left onto Castle Street until they came to the Dee River. Before they crossed over on the bridge, they took a quick trip to a nearby park. Even as early as it was, the tennis courts were in use, and several pushcarts were already open for business. Robin and Gwyneth bought meat pies called pasties with their pocket money and then headed off in the direction of Dinas Bran. They soon found themselves walking in a northerly direction along the Wern Road.

"How far do we have to walk?" Robin asked.

"It's two kilometers, one way," Gwyneth answered.

"Let me think. That's a little over a mile and about two and a half miles round trip. I'm still not used to the metric system here, you know, being from Seattle."

"What is Seattle like?" Gwyneth asked.

"A bit like this, actually. Well, really it's a lot like this except there are mountains all around. They're called the Cascades. You should see them in winter, all white with snow, loads of fun skiing or snowboarding. Different pace, though, and I'm really from Redmond, across Lake Washington and east of Seattle."

"Redmond. That's where Microsoft is, isn't it?"

"Yes, actually, but that's in the Overlake area, and I live near Novelty Hill. It used to be a huge watershed, and the watershed is still there, but now the land has been cleared of almost all the trees. Houses have been built everywhere, and my dad says the water tables are liable to go down, now that most of the trees are gone. I wish it was back the way it was."

"Your dad knows about those sorts of things, does he?"

"Well," Robin said as he stopped walking. "Yeah, see, he studied hydrology when he got his engineering degree. At least that's what he told me."

"Sounds like you and your dad used to do a lot of talking."

"A bit. Not like now. When he's not working, he's always out drinking." Suddenly, Robin felt a twinge of guilt for having revealed one of his dad's problems.

"Is that since your mum died?" Gwyneth pressed on.

"You know," Robin said, "maybe I've said a bit much already. Would you mind very much if we talked about something else, please?"

"I understand," she said. Then she quickly changed the subject. "We better get going if we're going to get to Dinas Bran before noon."

Soon, they were on their way up the tor. When the sun was directly overhead, they reached the top. Tired and sweaty from the exertion, they sat down to regain their breath.

"Wow!" Robin said. "I didn't know you could see so far from up here. This is really cool. It looks familiar, too. Almost like an old castle I saw in a dream."

"It's called Dinas Bran, but it's also known as Crow's Nest." Gwyneth said, "That's because of the crows that keep watch here. They say that if they land on the ground, there's danger coming."

"Looks like we're safe then." Robin looked up at the crows flying overhead. "What are they guarding?"

"The Holy Grail."

"The Holy Grail...here? How do you..."

"Legend has it that this is its magical resting place," Gwyneth said with quite a lot of self-assurance.

"Wow, this is a lot like a dream I had."

"Tell me."

"Nah, you wouldn't want to hear that."

"I would. Please?"

"Well, it's just...it's kind of embarrassing."

"I won't tell anyone. I promise."

"There were fairies."

"That's what embarrasses you?"

"Guys don't dream about fairies, and if they do, they don't say."

"You are a right git, Robin."

"What's a git?"

"To find the answer to that," she said with a twinkle in her eye, "look in the mirror when you get home."

"Ah, that's not nice."

"Well, finish your dream, then."

"The fairies took me to...it was a tree. A really big tree. It was kind of spooky. I met someone. Lilith."

"She's the queen of the fairies!"

"Yeah, I know. Anyway, she told me I had to find the Holy Grail."

"It's just a dream. It's not like it's real."

"That's not what they told me."

"Who?"

"The fairies. Well, one fairy. She said it was real and not a dream."

"What was her name?"

"It was Kat-sidhe."

"You believe it! I believe it. It's not fair. I go out in Mum's garden every chance I get but I've never seen a fairy. Not one! But you've seen...how many?"

"Loads, and you know what? I bet I know why no one's seen a fairy. From a distance they look like a swarm of bees. Who'd be crazy enough to go near a swarm of bees?"

"Except a beekeeper! But, sooner or later, they'd tell!"

"Maybe, unless they were sworn to secrecy or because of some magic."

"It's not fair! You spoke with their queen, she gave you a quest, and you're embarrassed? You really are a git!"

"Hey, no name calling! I didn't ask for this! I didn't ask for a lot of things. Hang on...you said the Holy Grail was here?"

"Dinas Bran is supposed to be the magical resting place for it. But I think you probably need magic to find it."

"Right, well, then maybe I have to find magic first. That way I'll know how to find it."

"See that oak?" Gwyneth pointed to an ancient oak in the middle of the castle ruins. "Oaks have magic in them."

"How can a tree have magic?"

"Druids. Myrddin was a druid. Mum says she's related to him and lets me read about druids all the time. All trees have magic...just depends what sort you need."

"Gwyneth, if you read about druids, then maybe you know a way to get the magic from the tree."

"I don't know about that. At least I've never read about it."

"You must know something."

"I wish I did. Now, if Myrddin were here, he'd show you how."

"That'll never happen. Hey, I know. If the tree is magic maybe that's where the Holy Grail is. Come on, let's go see."

"Oh, yes, let's," Gwyneth gushed.

They both ran to the tree and looked all around the bole but found nothing. They explored the ancient crumbling walls of Dinas Bran next, looking through what was left of every window and every doorway. Tired of searching for something they probably wouldn't find anyway, they started a game where they would identify different landmarks and, at last, looked in the direction of their houses.

"They are over there, just behind that line of trees," Gwyneth called out from one of the windows.

"No, they're not," Robin answered from the next window. "Look to your left more. Hang on, look at that! Flashing blue lights near Wern Road. You don't suppose there's been an accident?"

"*That's it!*" Gwyneth cried.

"Excuse me, what's it?" Robin said, nearly losing his balance.

"Your cover story! You know, how you got that bruise on your face!"

"Huh?"

"Oh, Robin, don't you see? You can say you had an accident on your bike and you fell on your face."

"Perfect! So when someone asks, I can say, 'Oh, yeh, I fell on muh face and had a accident.'"

"I'm being serious, you know."

"Well, it might work. I've already got skinned knees and scraped up hands, too. But I don't know. Dewey and Fred already know something about that. Maybe no one would ask them anything, so it might work. Thanks, Gwyneth."

"Dewey and Fred? Those two idiots? What have they got to do with this?"

"Didn't you see? They nicked my bike this morning."

"Was that why you were outside? Did they beat you up?"

"So what if they did? There were two of them, you know."

"I'm sorry. I must have come out just after."

"Yeah, how lucky you missed it all." Robin sighed. "Maybe we better head back; it's getting late."

Retracing their steps, they soon found themselves near their homes. It was then that Robin saw Dewey and Fred walking toward them in animated conversation. Quickly, Robin grabbed Gwyneth by the arm and propelled her behind a privet hedge in their neighbor's yard.

"What are you playing at?" Gwyneth cried out.

She stood and brushed herself off. Robin quickly seized her arm again and sat her back down. His gaze was intent on the approaching brothers.

"*Oy!*"

"Shush!" Robin whispered. "They'll spot us!"

"Who?" she whispered back.

"Dewey and Fred, that's who! I want the rest of the weekend to be Dewey and Fred free, thank you. Now shush, they're getting nearer."

Soon after he spoke the words, bits and pieces of the brothers' conversation reached them. Then, just on the other side of the privet hedge, every word of the conversation could be heard.

"Did yeh see the look on 'is face before I got 'im, Fred?" Dewey asked.

"No, I was 'oldin' 'im, remember? Next time you gots to 'old 'im, okay? We are gonna get 'im again aren't we, Dew?"

"Too right! I only wish 'e 'ad another bike." They started laughing, and the sound of it rekindled Robin's anger toward them.

Their voices drifted away, and Robin stood up, thinking it was safe. His eyes grew wide when he saw them still standing on the corner. They stared right at him and then ran toward him and Gwyneth.

"Ah, no!" Robin said. "What are we going to do? Do you think you could outrun them?"

"I don't know," Gwyneth said as she gave an involuntary shudder.

"Then run. I mean to face them while you get away."

"Oh, no, you mustn't! There are two of them, and they are bigger than you even if there was only one of them. You just simply can't!"

"Run!" Robin said as he gave her a shove.

Fred was the faster of the two, and probably the fastest boy in all of Llangollen. But Robin wasn't astonished so much by his speed as he was surprised by his target. In no time at all, he closed the distance and seized Gwyneth from behind before she could run two steps.

Gwyneth frantically tried to step on his feet, but Fred kept his feet away from harm. Dewey coolly made his approach, taking his time. Robin set his jaw and waited for the bully to come. There was no way he could leave Gwyneth alone against these two.

"Hello, Peter breath!" Dewey said with a twisted grin. "Who's your new girl?"

"What do you want, Dewey?" Robin asked.

"Just to talk is all."

"If it's me you want, let her go."

"S'pose I don't want to? What if we decide to mix it up with both of you?"

"Look," Robin began, "it won't do to hurt her. All she'll do is cry to her dad anyway, and then he'll go talk to your dad, and you'll both be in trouble. Let her go, and it will be just you two and me."

"What do you think, Fred?"

"Sounds okay to me, but 'e better not try and run if I let 'er go."

"Right, then, just us, and she goes 'ome. And listen, you," Dewey said to Gwyneth, "if you try and go for 'elp, it'll be worth our gettin' in trouble with our dad to get you later. You get me?"

"I get you," Gwyneth said.

Her eyes blazed with anger, and Robin found he could easily hear what she was thinking. She was going to stomp Fred's foot when he let her go. And then Fred released her and she stamped down as hard as she could on his left instep. Fred's howling could be heard for blocks. Robin would have laughed at the sight, but he was too busy dodging Dewey's ham-sized fists.

"Come on, Fred!" Dewey shouted, "Quit your gripin' and help me get 'im!"

"Ow! Ow! Ow! She broke my foot! She broke it! She broke it! Ow! Ow! Ow!"

"Run!" Robin yelled.

Robin jumped the neighbor's picket fence, and Dewey pursued him through the yard. Robin's legs were too short to outrun him over a long distance, and Dewey closed in sooner than Robin could outmaneuver him. Dewey leaped at him, flying in the air until his body made contact.

Robin felt the collision from behind and reached his hands out in front of him to break his fall. The force propelled them both into the flower garden next to the wall of the house. Daffodils, hyacinths, and dandelions flew in every direction, and some of the pieces went into Robin's mouth, along with a good amount of dirt.

He heard a noise, a loud bang, like a gun had been fired. He heard Gwyneth screaming, and Fred saying, "Uh-oh!" Then he felt a pressure begin to build in his head, a fuzzy pressure, as if he had entered a dark, thick, numbing cloud.

He floated in nothing. He felt nothing. He heard nothing, and then he was cold, terribly cold. He began to tingle all over, and it felt like when his leg went to sleep, but it was all over his body. He tried to move and couldn't. He tried to open his eyes and couldn't. He tried to calm himself and couldn't. Panic crept in like a worm in the cold, damp earth, slowly making progress, never retreating.

What had happened to him? Where was Gwyneth and where were Dewey and Fred? Were they going to attack him again? Would they attack Gwyneth while he lay there, unable to move?

Kat-sidhe. He needed Kat-sidhe! Maybe she could help somehow. Robin focused on the fairy princess's name, calling to her in his mind.

"I'm here!" Kat-sidhe called. "What's happened?"

"I don't know," Robin said. "I...I don't feel so good. Gwyneth..." Blackness fell.

⌘ ⌘ ⌘

Gwyneth screamed, and Fred looked on in horror at the scene before them. Robin lay in a crumpled heap, with Dewey on top of him. Dewey tried to get up, but some of the rose bush thorns clung to his clothes. Dewey put his hand down to push himself up and felt dampness beneath it. He looked down to see blood on the ground all around Robin's head.

Dewey yelled out in panic and ripped his shirt and pants on the rose thorns while trying to rush away from the bloody scene before him. Fred stood in one position, stuttering.

"Dew-Dew-Dew!"

Gwyneth came to her senses first and shouted, "Help! Somebody, please! Help!"

Dewey realized that somebody could indeed come to help. That would put him in more trouble than he had ever been in his entire life, and Dewey had been in a lot of trouble. He looked up at the stuttering Fred and hollered one word.

"*Run!*"

Fred realized the predicament last but was the first to run. Dewey was close behind, and Gwyneth was left all alone with the unconscious Robin.

Kat-sidhe transformed into a sparrow, flew in through an open window, and landed on the shoulder of the old man napping in his easy chair. Unfortunately for Kat-sidhe, the house cat had also been napping on the man's lap and was utterly annoyed by the intrusion. Annoyance gave way to the cat's hunting instinct when it thought it saw a sparrow. The cat sprang with its claws extended and ferociously pursued its prey. It batted its paws in the air, hoping to catch some part of the bird with one of its claws. Kat-sidhe flew back out the window, leaving behind a small explosion of golden dust particles that sparkled in the sunlight filtering into the room.

The old man, wide awake now, angrily berated the cat for upsetting his perfectly good nap. That's when he heard Gwyneth's shouts for help. He looked out his window and saw Gwyneth in the yard next to his house, screaming for help. He ran to the back of the house and phoned the ambulance and police.

"It's all right now, miss," the man said as he dashed out of the house. "The EMTs are on their way. Whatever in the world has happened here, and who were those two boys I saw running away?"

Gwyneth rocked back and forth, weeping. "Don't die, Robin. Oh, please don't die."

"No one's going to die, miss," the man said. "He is going to be all right as soon as the EMTs get here."

They could hear the wail of the siren off in the distance. The wait wasn't long, but to Gwyneth it seemed like hours.

Chapter 3
THE MIRROR

Robin had the sensation of floating. It was like flying but without purpose. He looked down, but all he saw were dark clouds that enveloped him. Then he heard a familiar fluttering noise, the sound of wings furiously beating to keep a tiny fairy aloft.

"Is that you, Kat-sidhe?"

"Yes, I'm coming as fast as I can. Call out to me again so I can find you. This fog is impossible for me to clear."

"You can't make the fog disappear with magic?"

"I can, but this isn't ordinary fog. It's your fog; you created it to protect yourself, and you made it so well that it is impenetrable. Ouch!"

"That could leave a mark," Robin said. Kat-sidhe had just run into his knee, and Robin caught her before she bounced back out of sight.

"Where were you, anyway? I was calling for you, you know," Robin said. He held Kat-sidhe in his hands as she rubbed her forehead.

"But I did come, and straight away, too," she said. "I took the form of a small bird and flew in the window of the house to wake the owner. His cat tried to eat me and this is all the thanks I get? You should have called me sooner so I could have prevented all this."

"Ah, that's not fair. How was I to know Fred and Dewey were waiting for us? Besides, I wanted to make sure Gwyneth got clean away."

"But that's my job! I can do that perfectly well by myself, thank you! You've caused yourself serious trouble, Robin Gilman, and now I'm not sure if I can help at all! I am taking you to Yggdrasil now!"

"I didn't mean to do anything wrong, you know," Robin said. "I wish you would laugh like you did the first time I met you."

"Robin! This is serious! I laugh when I am happy, not like now. Make this fog go away!"

"Me? But I'm not magic like you. Am I?"

"Please, just concentrate like you did when you called me, and it will go away. I'll explain how it works later."

"All right, all right!" Robin said.

Robin calmed himself and concentrated on clear blue skies. He wished for the same skies he flew in those times he dreamt of flying. The fog lifted, and Robin saw Yggdrasil.

"There it is," Kat-sidhe said. "Yggdrasil. Mother Lilith! Mother Lilith! We need you."

Robin landed on the ground beneath Yggdrasil, and Kat-sidhe hovered in front of the tree without speaking as other fairies began to arrive. The beautiful voice of Lilith filled the air. Once again, he trembled in the presence of her flawless beauty, and once again he saw all around Lilith and through her. All the fairies who had arrived for her appearance were silent.

"Welcome, my children. Welcome. And how are you, Robin?"

"I...I...I'm fine, thank you."

"Are you aware of what has happened to you?"

"Nothing's happened to me. I don't think anything has happened to me." He stared at Lilith and then asked, "What has happened? Why am I here? Wasn't I just on the way home from Dinas Bran? I mean, I don't remember falling asleep, and usually I'm asleep when I dream of flying."

"You are not asleep, Robin, though I wish that were the case. I'm afraid you are going to be here a while, and I'm afraid you will need to make some very serious decisions about your life while you are here. Do you remember the two boys who were bullying you and Gwyneth?"

"Dewey and Fred, but what have they got to do with this?"

"Nothing and everything. They are teachers, you see. They agreed to teach you some valuable lessons about life. A contract was made, but unfortunately the contract has been altered by an enemy. Dewey and Fred are not at fault, for they were deceived."

Lilith touched the left side of Robin's chest, where his heart would be. "Do you know what dwells inside this body of yours? It is called your soul, and it is the very essence of what you are, not this three-dimensional body. Only your soul is real; your body is temporary and will fade. Your soul is eternal. Do you understand?"

Robin looked at his chest where Lilith touched him. Even though he could see through her arm and hand, he could sense her touch, and it unnerved him.

He looked at her and said, "I think so."

"Your religions—most of them on your plane of existence, at least— teach you that when the body dies, you achieve release and eternal life. I tell you your life is eternal before you incarnate."

"And what does it mean to incarnate?" Robin asked.

"To incarnate means to go within a physical body and exist within it until it reaches an exit point. Most souls choose to incarnate many times, because they wish to learn as much as they can." She leaned closer to Robin, "It means to be born, to grow up into adulthood, to live your life, and to find your way closer to the source of your creation before your body wears out."

"Then that means my true self, my soul, lives in my body. It can't get out until it is time. Does that mean that when it is time to leave, that would be called death?"

"Yes, that is most accurate."

"Is that what happened to my mother?"

"Again, the answer you seek is yes."

"Will I see my mother again when it is my time?"

"Yes, beloved child. You will see her again. Know that she is with you all the time and is your spirit guide until that time. Know also that you will experience at least five different exit points, and you will be given the opportunity to choose to go or stay until you reach the final exit point. This final exit point is predestined and cannot be avoided. What you are experiencing now is the first of your five possible exit points. Do you understand?"

"You mean I could die?"

"I mean you could choose to die or to continue to live. Kat-sidhe opened your third eye the night when first we met. It is the eye that looks within and sees the invisible. Close your eyes and imagine a third eye opening in the center of your forehead. The more often you practice this, the easier it will be, and it will help you to learn about yourself. Use it now to see."

Robin saw nothing unusual at first, but as he concentrated, a silver rope appeared. It stretched out as far as he could see, disappearing into the clouds. He looked down and saw it was attached to his navel. He could feel its tug.

"What is it?" he asked.

"It connects you to your physical body. It can be cut, and if it is, you will be permanently outside your body."

"So, right now, I'm outside my body but not dead. But I could be if this silver rope thing is cut?"

"Yes, but you are the only one who can cut it. If that is what you want, it will be so."

"I could die? I don't like this. I want to go back."

"It is too soon. I must tell you now that severe damage has been done to you, and the consequences could prove to be your undoing."

"I'm not damaged!" Robin declared. "There's nothing wrong with me at all! Why did—"

"Robin, in this universe the damage will not be present. Should you return to your own universe, however, you will discover how serious the damage is. Do you understand why I said you are not asleep and why I said this is not a dream?"

"No, I don't. I don't understand at all."

"On your original plane of existence, you are unconscious. You have received a cruel blow to your head. Your soul instinctively left your body in order to seek assistance in repairing the damage. It is not something you consciously think of doing; it just occurs. I caution now against returning to your universe until your chance of survival without permanent damage to your mind is much improved. Do you understand?"

"But I have no memory of being hurt. How can this be?"

"You have very powerful guardian angels. They have assisted you in exiting your body without your bodily functions ceasing so that you could come here for help. You are very important in the overall scheme of things. It has been foretold."

"What? What's been foretold?"

"You are a link to a certain parallel universe. These two universes must merge so that they will both continue to exist. The problem is it was not meant to happen this way."

"I'm not sure I like where this might be going." Robin said. "Maybe there's been some sort of mistake. You said I was a king once and now...I mean, I can't be the only...what did you call me? Oh, yes...I can't be the only link, can I?"

"Of course you can. You fly, don't you? You are traveling when you fly, not dreaming. It is called astral travel, and it will take you from one universe to another. It has taken you here, in fact, to Yggdrasil, the gateway to all the universes."

"How long will I be here, then?"

"As long as it takes. I think a journey to your parallel universe is in order. There you will learn what you must do. Kat-sidhe will escort you to Peter's world."

"Wait!" Robin said, "I've got more questions, please!"

"I allow you one more question," Lilith said, "and then you must proceed."

Robin knew what he must ask. "Who was that man in the house? I never saw his face."

"He is the one who would usurp the Creator's throne, and this enemy wants you to return to your body immediately for his own evil purpose."

"Enemy? But even if he was kind of creepy, he gave my dad what for. Why would an enemy do that?"

"It was not for your sake he did this. Now you must go with Kat-sidhe. You will have assistance, and I will be watching over you. Until we meet again, my child, fare thee well." She was gone before Robin could blink, and Kat-sidhe was in front of his nose, waiting.

"What am I going to do now, Kat-sidhe?" he asked.

"You are going to go with me."

"But what if I decide I don't want to do this?"

"Then you will be returned to your body. What will you choose?" Kat-sidhe said.

"But Lilith said my mind would be disabled if I did that."

"It is your choice, Robin. Even the Creator will not violate your free will. You must choose now, however."

"Why does it have to be complicated like this? Why can't things be the way they once were?"

"Because once an event has occurred, it cannot be changed, no matter how much we might wish it to be. It is why one cannot go back in time. The future is nothing more than possibilities, and what those possibilities are depend on what you choose. Please, Robin, the time to choose is now. No more wasting time."

"All right, then," Robin said, "I will go with you, though I don't know what it will bring."

"You will find out what you should do soon," she said. "And remember, I will always come when you call."

Robin was already flying again, and Kat-sidhe flew backward without watching ahead, just like the first time he met her. Now that she wasn't so serious, his heart felt lighter.

Soon, they flew over Dinas Bran. A thick mist enveloped the hill. Above the mist, Robin could see crows circling the ancient fortress below. They called out to each other in their raspy voices, and Robin thought he understood them in his mind, though not with his ears. *Safe by the east wind, safe by the north, safe by the south, and safe by the west* they seemed to say. Robin and Kat-sidhe landed near the southern wall of the crumbling ruin.

"Do you know what some people call Dinas Bran?" Kat-sidhe asked Robin.

"Yeah, I do know. It's called Crow's Nest."

"Did you know it is a place of great history and, more important, great magic?"

"Magic? I like magic. Gwyneth told me about something else…oh, yeah…the Holy Grail is here. The crows watch over it. What kind of magic is here, then, Kat-sidhe?" Robin could hardly contain himself. Maybe Kat-sidhe knew where to find the magic he needed to find the Holy Grail.

"There are many different types of magic. You will learn them all." Kat-sidhe flitted back and forth as she spoke, but then she stopped and looked Robin directly in the eye. "I must leave you here, now."

Fear crept in, and Robin only thought of how much he didn't want to be alone. "But...but...why? Can't you stay just a bit longer? Please don't leave me now."

"You will be alone but for a few minutes and, as long as you stay put, there will be no danger. The crows will guard you. Watch them now, with me. See how they circle? They stay aloft to see far, far away. When danger approaches, they land on the ground to warn you. If that happens, you must hide. If they remain circling in the air, you are perfectly safe. I will see you again, you know."

"But who will be here? I mean...well, you did say I shan't be alone but for a few minutes. Who will it be then?"

"You will know him when you see him, and he will know you, though you have never met. When he arrives, do not be afraid. No harm will be allowed to either of you. After the first one arrives, a teacher will come."

"Kat-sidhe, please don't leave me. Can't you be here until at least the first person arrives?"

"Please don't be distressed, Robin. This is something you must face on your own. Watch the crows and be patient. You won't have long to wait, I promise."

Robin blinked, and she was gone. The only sounds he could hear were the crows and the wind on the hill. He looked out in the direction of Llangollen but saw only the thick fog that had enveloped the small town. It would have been a nice way to pass the time, he thought, if he could have played at identifying landmarks in the town like he and Gwyneth had done.

That had happened just that afternoon, but it seemed so long ago. The crows continued to call out to each other but remained in the sky. Then, one of the crows changed the way it was calling out to the others. As its voice changed, so did the direction in which it was flying.

To Robin's horror, it flew directly at him and then landed on the ground. He searched in panic for a place to hide and saw an outcropping of the castle wall that formed a small hollow concealed behind a giant oak tree. He dove for the hollow and made sure he could see from behind the oak tree but not be seen. The crow strutted toward his hiding place.

The crow spied him and rapidly hopped over to where it could see him unobstructed. It turned its head to one side and peered unblinking at him.

~ *Gilman's Parallel: The French King* ~

Then it performed a curious act that Robin had never seen a bird do before. It pointed with one wing to the south and down the hill. As if it were a human, it spoke.

"Peter...Peter...Peter!"

"Shut up!" Robin hissed under his breath. "You'll give me away!"

The crow regarded him with the same curious look. Then it hopped even closer and its voice rang out even louder than before, "Peter...Peter...Peter!"

Desperate to keep himself concealed from any possible danger, Robin tried to make the crow fly away by waving his hands at it. "Go away! You're going to give me away! Shoo! Shoo!"

"Robin...Robin...Robin...shoo...shoo...shoo!"

The crow's hysterics alarmed him. He could only imagine how much danger he might be in, and the crow wasn't helping by pointing him out to whoever was approaching. Robin heard footsteps getting louder as they crunched the gravel on the walkway.

"Powys Fadog, you old loud bird, what is it you've found? Something good to eat?" a new voice said.

The sound of the voice petrified Robin. Sweat began to trickle down his back, over his brow, and into his eyes. He didn't dare breathe or try to move. Silence was his only hope. The new boy's voice rang out again, and this time, Robin knew he had heard the voice before.

"Powys Fadog, why aren't you up flying with your brothers? You're always too curious for your own good. Tell me what you've found." The boy was close now, too close.

Suddenly it struck Robin like a thunderbolt. This was the same boy in his dreams, the one who had shouted at him to go away. Robin wished he could run away. At least if it came to it, they were the same size, and if he was lucky, Robin thought he could surprise him and get away in the confusion. But how to do it?

Robin could see the back of the boy as he bent down to let the crow hop onto his wrist. The crow preened itself while perched on the boy's arm and allowed the boy to scratch the top of its head. The crow rubbed its head against the hand that scratched it, and Robin realized it was tame and quite affectionate toward the boy.

The boy wore a tunic and patched-up light khaki pants that had seen better days. His pant legs were tucked into black boots laced up to just below his knees. Around the tunic was a belt that held a sword unlike any sword Robin had seen before.

Swords had always fascinated Robin, and he had several books about them that he had received for his last birthday. He had often spent hours of his free time, and just as much when he should have been doing his schoolwork, absorbed in learning about how many different kinds of swords there were. But this sword was different than any of the ones in his books.

The scabbard concealed its true shape, but it was the scabbard and the hilt of the sword that gave Robin reason to be so curious. The hilt had been patterned after the head of a bear, and the scabbard had the design of a dragon and a bear fighting carved into its wooden surface.

Robin tried to lean closer for a better look and put his hand on a ledge to push himself up, when it gave way. The boy spun around, feinted to his left, then dodged to his right and took the sword out of its scabbard all in one motion. It was like watching a ballet, but with obvious deadly intent.

"What the...!" the other boy exclaimed.

The crow was already in the air, cawing out its alarm to the other crows. Immediately, all the crows descended and were on the ground between Robin and the boy with the strange-looking sword.

"Hey! Put that thing away before you hurt someone!" Robin shouted.

Just as Robin looked at him, the boy kicked dirt into his face. It got in his eyes and mouth, and Robin sputtered, trying to see through his blurred vision. The boy grabbed Robin's arm and brought it up behind his back as high as he could. Robin felt the ice cold steel of the sword against his throat.

"Why are you spying on me?" the boy asked.

"I wasn't spying on you. I was told to wait here for someone."

"Why were you hiding?"

"Well, I couldn't be too sure how friendly the locals would be, now could I? Besides, I was told to hide if the crows landed."

"What are you talking about? Only one crow landed, and it was just Powys. He wouldn't harm anyone."

"I didn't say the crows were dangerous! I said...will you let me go so we can talk properly? And put that sword away; it makes me nervous!"

"Promise you won't try anything?"

"You're the one with the sword, and you want me to make a promise?"

"Er...right...well, okay then. But don't try anything funny."

He let Robin go with a shove in order to make some distance between them. Robin stumbled forward but caught himself from falling flat on his face.

"Hey!" Robin said. "What was that for? Why does everyone I meet have to try and beat me up in the first place? What did I ever do to you? Hang on! I know who you are! You were trying to make me go away and... whoa! You look just like me!"

The boy stared at Robin in silence with his mouth wide open, not moving a single muscle. He slowly backed away, his terror unmistakable.

"This is a joke, isn't it?" they both said at the same time.

"Someone put you up to this, didn't they?" Again they spoke as one.

"Put me up to what?" Together again.

"I...I know you, too! You're the boy I saw flying! Myrddin told me about you. You can't be here. You've broken the rules. Go away!"

But Robin had no intention of going away. This boy had his face. He had his hands, his hair, and his feet. His eyes were greener but not far from the same. There was also a mole on his right cheek, just below his eye. It was like looking into a mirror, except Robin had the sensation that he was the image in the mirror and the boy was the reality looking in. They stared at each other in dumbfounded silence.

"What's your name, anyway?" Robin asked.

"Oh, sorry, it's Peter, Peter Robyn Gilman."

"Whoa!" Robin said in a whispered tone. "I'm a Gilman, too, but my name is Robin Peter Gilman. This really is too weird."

"What are you doing here?" Peter asked.

"Well," Robin began, "there was this fairy, and her queen, Mother Lilith, said she should bring me here to meet someone. I wonder if she meant you?"

"No, Myrddin said it would be against the rules," Peter said. "This isn't supposed to be happening."

"But it is happening, and neither one of us has been hurt," said Robin. "So I don't see why you're so afraid to have me around. I'm confused, though. Mother Lilith said it would be safe, but you just said Myrddin told you it was against the rules. What did you mean, and who's Myrddin?"

"I'm homeschooled, and Myrddin's my tutor."

"So he's not some druid wizard?"

"How did you know that? I mean it is true, he is a wizard. He's teaching me magic, too. Look, maybe I misunderstood, but Myrddin told me that if you met yourself from a parallel world, you couldn't occupy the same space or there would be some sort of violent end to it all."

"Just keep that sword put away and there won't be any violence at all," said Robin.

"Oh, this old thing? It's called a Kampilan sword. It came from my dad's collection of swords. Dad teaches me martial arts, and I'm learning how to use it."

"He's teaching you to use a sword? I wish I knew how."

"It's more of a ceremonial sword than anything else. I...er...I sort of borrowed it."

"What's that hook on the point for?" Robin asked.

"It was used in a time of war on the Philippine Islands," Peter explained. "The hook was used by the warrior headhunters. They would tie their victims' heads to it by the hair so they could carry them back to their villages and display them."

"Whoa, it sounds like it's a valuable sword," said Robin. "Don't you think your dad will be mad at you when he finds out you took it?"

"Well, as long as he doesn't find out, he can't be mad at me, can he? The trick is not to let him find out at all, you see. But I had to nick it. I can't be out here in these times without some sort of protection now, can I?"

"What do you mean, 'these times'? And what did you mean when you said something about meeting yourself? I mean...well, I suppose we are nothing more than each other's doubles. That is right, isn't it? We are not each other, are we?"

Peter stared at him with his bulldog jaw jutting out just like Robin's did when he pondered a serious situation. "It's possible we are more than just each other's doubles, you know."

Chapter 4
MYRDDIN

"I'm you!" they said at the same time. "No, you're me. This isn't right."

"We're the same," Peter said.

"This is nuts. We've already touched once and nothing happened," Robin said.

"Well," Peter began, "the sun is still shining, and the fog is even starting to lift. I suppose that means we can be close to each other for a while. I was wondering, what did you mean when you said a fairy brought you here on orders from Mother Lilith?"

"What he means is Kat-sidhe escorted him here for assistance."

Startled, they both cried out at the new voice. The owner of the voice chuckled under his long white beard at the sight of their faces. He stood next to the giant oak, holding an oaken staff mounted with a bright, shining crystal. For all his apparent age, he was as spry as either of the two boys. He wore a green druidic robe clasped at the neck by a golden triskelion. Embroidered golden pentagrams and sickle-shaped silver moons shimmered on the robe with a light of their own.

"Myrddin," Peter said, "I thought I'd never see you again." Peter ran to the ancient man and embraced him.

"Careful, now," Myrddin said, "you'll bowl me over, and I'm not as young as I used to be. So, you two have finally met and found out that you can be on the same plane of existence without permanent damage."

"I'm going mad, aren't I?" Robin said.

"No, young lad, you are not mad. You have ridden the dragon is all, and the dragon has brought you here for an education. I am one of those you were supposed to meet. Both of you are supposed to be here, and both of you are in need of my assistance. My name is Myrddin, and I am at your service."

Then he leaned over and, inches from Robin's face, said, "I am the one who helped Uther Pendragon and his heir, Arthur, rule over what you know as Camelot. I am the druidic wizard commissioned to protect the Holy Grail that lies here, hidden in the ruins of Castell Dinas Bran. I am the one who travels between all planes of existence to keep magic alive!"

Robin swallowed and, in a small voice, said, "I thought that was just a legend."

"*Just a legend? Just* a legend? No wonder you have the least amount of magic I have ever witnessed in any universe! Do you know why you never see fairies, gnomes, leprechauns, unicorns—my favorite creature you know—dragons, elves, and all other kinds of magical creatures and folk in your universe? I'll tell you why, lad! Because you...stopped...believing... in...them! And now, *now*, you think we are all just...what did you call me? Oh, yes, a *legend*!"

Again Myrddin leaned close to Robin's face and said, "Do I look real to you, boy? Hmm? Well, I can tell you I am real, and your first lesson is to start believing again! Go on, tell me what you think. There will be an exam on this subject, I'm afraid, and I'm glad I'm not the one who has to take it."

"I...I'm sorry. I apologize. Please, I never meant to offend you. I'm just curious is all. I promise I won't call you a legend again. You are quite real. I see that now."

"Apology accepted. Now, both of you listen. This is the most important thing I can tell you at this moment. You are not doubles. You are actually the same. Your bodies are the mirror image of one another but they share the same soul."

"But I thought you said we couldn't be near each other or even touch lest we both die," Peter said. "I mean, how can we be the same if there are two of us, anyway?"

"What I said was that if you merged and united your physical bodies on a permanent basis *before* the time was right, there would be damage. Not only to yourself, but to everyone and everything that exists in your two worlds."

"What do you mean, before it's time?" Robin and Peter asked as one.

"The worlds you live in are parallel. These two worlds must merge and become one. That means everyone and everything that has a double in each of the two parallel worlds will physically merge and only one will remain. Only then will it be time for Robin and Peter to merge. Did I confuse you?"

"Yeah, you think?" the boys said at the same time.

"But, of course, I did," Myrddin chuckled. "Your soul is eternal and not bound by the laws of the physical universe. Therefore, it may divide itself and coexist within two different bodies at the same time. That way, the soul can lead two or more parallel lives at the same moment so that it can experience more than one life at the same time. Your soul is leading two parallel lives, and before me at this moment, in your personal history, I see two bodies standing before me in which resides this very same soul."

"Does everybody have a double?" Robin asked.

"No, it is a rare occurrence. Having a parallel life is difficult for the soul but allowed if the benefit is sufficient to outweigh the detriment."

"What detriment?" Peter asked.

"When the merging occurs, the two parts of the soul will wrestle for a time until harmony is achieved. Both parts of the soul will have learned about life from two entirely different points of view but, nevertheless, they are the same."

"We're the same?" they asked at the same time.

"Quit interrupting!" Peter said.

"I didn't interrupt," Robin shot back, "you did!"

"Enough, gentlemen," Myrddin said. "You are both the same soul; it is your respective environments that are different. Environment changes a person's character, but it is the person who allows the change for good or ill."

"You're talking about..." Robin began.

"Personal choices," Peter finished.

"But I might not make the same choice Peter would make."

"And I wouldn't be such a scaredy-cat like Robin." Robin glared at Peter.

"Perhaps not," Myrddin said, "but I dare say Robin would be more diplomatic. Now, both of you listen. Here, on Dinas Bran, you have met each other. In one life, the boy is athletic and confident. He is able to achieve his goals with ease. He has both parents, and they love him very much. The other has been beaten down by his environment and has had to endure many trials. He is not so athletic, not so confident, and nothing has come easy in his life. His mother has been taken from him, and his father is abusive. Both of you, think! You know which is which, and you both knew the moment you met that you were more than just physical doubles.

"One thing is the same, though. You are both in line to inherit a throne that has no country. That much is the same in each world. How you achieve this will be different depending on your personal choices. There is something you must do first, however."

"Which one?" Peter asked.

"No, not just one," Robin said.

"Both of us, together!" they said. "What happens now?"

"Ah, you have both caught on admirably. Now I will tell you what must happen before I commission you with the task that lies ahead." Myrddin indicated that they should both sit down.

"Ouch! Watch where you are going!" The boys had run into each other as they sought to sit down on the same rock beneath the oak tree. They stared in fascination at each other.

"I foresee a problem," Myrddin said. "What it is, is, you are both within the same universe and, in the event immediate action would be required, considering you are both thinking alike, it is possible you might get in each other's way. There is also the possibility you would disagree on the proper course of action. It would not be a major problem, unless the situation became dangerous. It will be rather good practice, actually. First I must summon the Dragon's Breath so that we can make it happen."

"Make what happen?" Robin and Peter asked.

"The sharing, of course. In this particular case it is you, Robin, who must merge with Peter. That is because you have assumed an ethereal substance in order for us in this universe to perceive you. Your real body is back in your own universe and is about to be repaired by some bumbling idiot who calls himself a physician. Questions?"

"What did...shut it, you...it's my turn!" Robin and Peter said. They glared at each other.

"Maybe we should let Robin ask his question first, shall we, Peter?"

"What did you mean when you said my real body was about to be repaired?" Robin asked. "And who did you call an idiot?"

"I called him a *bumbling* idiot, and he is some fool physician who actually believes he can heal with his limited knowledge. He is about to perform what is called surgery in your universe and what I call an invasion of your person. Do not worry, however; your guardian angels are there helping his angels to guide his hands. If the outcome is as predicted, you will be called back to your universe in no time at all. Until then, both of you must merge. The soul is the same, though the life experiences are different, and it will assist you well while you are on your quest."

"You said we couldn't merge without damage," Peter said. "Not permanently, anyway. Robin will go back to his world, won't he?"

"Not to worry, Peter. This will not be a physical merging. I need both of you to stand here, beneath this oak tree."

"Wait," Peter and Robin said, "what's the hurry?"

"This will last only for a few days, and during that time, you have a lot to do."

"Do what?"

"Find the Holy Grail, of course. Then, Robin must return it to his universe."

Both boys stood in trepidation, silently waiting for Myrddin to make the next move. Myrddin closed his eyes in meditation and then began to intone after a brief silence.

"Anail nathrock, uthvass bethudd, dochiel dienve! Cum saxum saxorum in duersum montum oparum da, in aetibulum in quinatum...draconis!"

Myrddin chanted the phrase three times and then pointed his oaken staff at the two boys. There was a loud roaring, and a bright white light surrounded them. Robin immediately felt warm, happy, and contented. Peter disappeared!

This was not what Robin had expected. He was the one who was supposed to disappear, not Peter. He looked at his feet and saw boots instead of his usual sneakers. He next looked at his shirt and discovered it was a tunic that had seen better days. He felt his face and looked up at Myrddin, who seemed to be very old and tired at that particular moment.

"The merging has been successful. Now you occupy one body and experience one life. It is you, Robin, who will be in complete control of Peter's body. Peter's consciousness will remain in the background, but you will be able to converse with him and he with you. You each have life experiences that will contribute to the success of your quest. You have until you are called back to your own body to complete the task that lies ahead. Do you understand?"

"I think you mean that if I am called back, I will be living in my parallel life again and Peter will be all alone to finish what we start together. But how can my experiences help Peter? I mean, most of my experiences have been rather humiliating...you know, everyone trying to beat me up and all. Shouldn't he be the one in control?"

"Peter can be somewhat arrogant. For this reason, his personality will remain in the background as an observer only. It is your humility he needs more than anything else. That is what will balance him. His athletic ability and confidence will balance you, and you will take the infused memory of it back with you once you return. Peter will retain the infused memory of humility when once you have left."

"You lost me. What do you mean by *infused* memory? Hang on, when did he agree to let me be in control?"

"Peter and I had a conversation as you merged—not with words but one soul to another. It is difficult for him to make this concession, but he sees the greater good that will come of it, and now it is so. He has been trained in the martial arts and weaponry since the age of four and is an expert in these things. Because of the merging, you will know how to use a sword and you will know the martial arts. What Peter knows, you know, and what you know, Peter now knows."

"But I don't know anything special like he does."

"Yes, actually, you do. You have a better sense of right and wrong, and this will temper Peter's use of the weapons he knows about. You know restraint. Unknown to Peter's father, he would use that sword without restraint, endangering himself and others. You, on the other hand, would consider the consequences. You are both being given power, and power without restraint can become most evil. What you both receive from each other will stay with you even when you return to your original state.

"Now I must explain your task. The mist has lifted now. Look out toward your home."

Robin looked, and instead of the town of Llangollen, he saw a great expanse of water dotted with several small islands. There were houses and roads that led to the water's edge, and where he was near enough to see, there were rooftops of houses that peeked above the water, giving evidence that at one time they were above water. He shivered.

Chapter 5
EARTH CHANGES

"Was there a flood?" Robin asked in a hushed tone.

"If you mean from a rainstorm, then the answer is no. What you are seeing is the Irish Sea."

"No, that can't be. That isn't Colwyn Bay. Is this going to happen in my world? What else has happened here?"

"Are you afraid, Robin?"

"I'm scared out of my wits!"

"There is nothing wrong with being afraid. What you do despite your fear is what will define you. Earth changes are taking place here. Earth, in this universe, has entered the fourth dimension. Earth, in your universe, is still in the third dimension. Once your universe enters the fourth dimension, then the two universes will merge and become one."

"What do you mean by earth changes?"

"The world's temperature has risen due to global warming, and the polar ice caps have melted. What you see before you now is the result of that melting. There have also been earthquakes and violent storms. The world's geography has changed quite suddenly and, I'm sorry to say, many have lost their lives."

"And this, all of this, will happen in my...my world?"

"Yes, it will be so in your world."

"What about me and Peter? I mean, what if I die when this happens in my world?"

"You will survive even as Peter has survived the earth changes here."

"Is there any place that I could go where it would be safe?"

"Some areas of the Earth will escape severe damage, and they will be safe. There is one event, however, that is most unpredictable. Damage will occur, but it's not known where. This event will be the reversal of the poles and the realigning of the Earth's axis."

"Reversal of the poles...the axis? What are you saying?"

"The Earth will literally turn upside down, and the axis will no longer be tilted. This will cause the planet to rotate faster than ever before, and time will no longer be the same. It is not known how many humans will survive. All that is known is that this event is about to occur in your world."

"Does that mean it's happened here?"

"Yes, and for a moment, the laws of gravity were suspended. There were earthquakes and violent storms. There is also a rip in the fabric of time, but even I do not properly understand the consequence of that. I must study this particular event further, as it is something I have never witnessed before."

"I'm not supposed to do something about all this, am I?"

"You must become king. To do that, you must obtain the Holy Grail, hidden here in this universe, and transfer it to your universe. Once you do this, I will explain the rest."

"Look," Robin began, "I'm almost thirteen years old, but I'm not sure I can do all that even if I am in Peter's body. You couldn't get anyone else, then?"

"I am positive you are the right person for the job, young Robin."

"Yeah, sure, that's what everyone else has been telling me. Will I have your help if I say yes?"

Myrddin smiled, and his smile seemed to bring light from all around. "Yes," he said, "you will have my help, Kat-sidhe's help, Mother Lilith's help, and help from your guardian angel. But, and this is most important, you should know the reason for the merging of these two particular universes. The magical creatures that exist here once existed in your universe, and by the merging, they will exist in your universe again. Therefore, you must prepare the people in your universe by educating them about the magical ones that exist so that they will believe in them once more. To do this, you must demonstrate your magical talents."

"Talents? What talents? And who's my guardian angel?"

"You will meet Michael, your guardian angel, soon. As for your magical talents, you can already hear the thoughts of others, can't you? You can also move objects without touching them. You can manifest from nothing, walk through walls, levitate, and make the unexplainable happen."

"Since when?"

"Since always. You have but to learn how to manifest these talents. I can help with that."

A puzzling thought occurred to Robin, and he frowned.

"I believe you have a question."

"I think so. But it's difficult, too. Peter has a mother and father here, doesn't he? They wouldn't be close by, would they?"

"Oh dear, I was afraid you would ask that question."

"Was it wrong to ask?"

"No, of course not. You were correct, you see. It is most difficult. This will be the temptation, to stay here before it is time, and you must resist at all costs. Do you know what wisdom is and how it is different from knowledge?"

"I suppose you could call it experience, couldn't you?"

"Yes, and no. Wisdom comes from learning from our mistakes, and our mistakes occur before we have the knowledge necessary to make the decision not to commit the mistake. Wisdom, therefore, is the acquisition of knowledge after the fact."

"So, why would the knowledge that Peter has parents be...is his mom...is she my..." Robin's voice caught before he could finish.

"Your mother and your father have parallel lives in this universe just like you do. Peter is your parallel life. Your father has a parallel life also, and your mother as well."

"Is...is she...alive?"

"Yes, but, Robin, please, you must..."

"I want to see her. Now, please."

"You don't understand, Robin."

"What's to understand? Here, she's not dead! Here, I can hear her voice again..."

"All you say is so. But she is Peter's mother here. Not yours."

"She is, too! If Peter is me, then his mom is my mom!"

"Yes, but not from her point of view. She will not understand if she notices your personality and not Peter's. She will think Peter has been possessed by a doppelganger. This is an evil omen in this world. It is a forecast of death and disaster. You must be careful not to reveal who you really are."

"As long as I'm careful, I can see her?"

"Yes, I never meant you could not. I only meant for you to understand the importance of caution."

"How do I make sure I act the way Peter would?"

"Peter will be able to help you there. Allow him to speak to you and guide you. You must do as he says in this regard, or your experience here will be more than you can bear."

"All right, I'll be cautious. I'll be wise before a mistake is made, if that's what you want." Robin turned to look out over the flooded land below through his watery eyes.

"Very well then, you will meet Peter's parents. I must go now, but I will return soon."

"Myrddin," Robin began in a hushed voice. But when Robin turned to look at Myrddin, the wizard was nowhere to be found. "Myrddin!" he called, "Myrddin! Where are you?"

Alone once more, Robin walked over to one of the crumbling castle windows and looked for a way down from the hill, but all he saw was the vast sea dotted with stranded islands of land. But where were Llangollen and the house? *Peter would know*, he thought. *But if I'm supposed to have his abilities, why not his memory?*

He looked into the sky and saw the crows flying overhead. He decided he was safe for the moment. He continued to peer out of every available window and viewing point, trying to discover a way down and a way to get home. Then it occurred to him that maybe home didn't exist anymore. Maybe his home was under water like everything else.

His body gave an involuntary shudder as he considered his last thought. As he looked near the edge of the water that surrounded the hill of Dinas Bran, he saw two boats. Who could they belong to? he wondered. Just then, he heard the sound of running footsteps and the silence was shattered by the crows as they screamed out their alarm.

The crows landed all around Robin, an unmistakable sign of approaching danger. Then Robin saw a girl running pell-mell while looking over her shoulder. When she turned her head back to see the path ahead of her, Robin was shocked to see it was Gwyneth...but not Gwyneth. Her hair was a dark shade of brown rather than the blond of the Gwyneth he remembered, and it was curlier. Even at his distance from her, he could tell she was in a panic.

"Help, Peter, help!" she yelled when she spied Robin. Before he could react, she clung to him and desperately tried to catch her breath. "Fred and Dewey!"

"Oh, no! They're here, too?"

The sound of their footsteps revealed the awful truth, and Robin steeled himself. *This isn't going to be good*, Robin thought. The two boys lumbered into view and shouted in triumph at the discovery of their quarry in the arms of their enemy.

Robin hesitated for a brief moment. Suddenly, Peter's thoughts were his and he understood. He struck out with his outstretched arms as if to take them both down. At the last moment, he struck out first at Dewey on his right and caught him with a backhand fist flush on his nose and mouth. Spinning around, he hit Fred next, but Fred moved away so that the blow merely glanced off his cheek. Robin drew the sword out of its scabbard.

"Leave her alone, both of you!" he shouted.

Dewey picked himself up off the ground where he had fallen, wiping away the blood pouring from his nose and mouth. He collapsed and fell back to the ground, groaning, while Fred looked on in helpless disbelief.

"You broke 'is nose," shouted Fred.

"You should feel lucky I didn't break yours! Stick around and I may break it for you anyway!"

"All right, all right! We'll leave. But this isn't over yet!"

"Yeah!" Dewey said through the hand that was holding his bleeding mouth and nose, "Thid idn'd ober yed!"

"Fine," Robin said in disgust, "let's finish it here and now then, shall we!"

"No, no, we're leavin'," said Fred as he helped Dewey regain his feet. Robin breathed a sigh of relief when they disappeared beyond sight and the crows once again took to the sky above. The danger had passed.

Gwyneth held onto Robin and sobbed away her panic into his tunic. Robin noted that she was also dressed in the same manner as he was, in a tunic and pants, though it seemed her clothes were in better repair than his. He put down the sword and hugged her back.

"All right?" he asked her.

"N-no. I mean, yes. Oh, Peter, I'm so sorry! I didn't see them until they were halfway across. I know you said I should wait by the boat until you returned but I couldn't face them alone. I'm ever so glad I found you."

"It's all right now," Robin said as he held her. "You're safe."

"We'd better get home for dinner."

"Oh! Well, yes, actually I am rather hungry now you mention it. But how do we get back?"

"We brought the boat. But you knew that. I mean, you did know, didn't you?"

Robin shrugged his shoulders and then indicated by a wave of his hand that they should start down the hill toward the boat. She glanced at Robin curiously and then turned around toward the beach where the boat was.

"When did all this water happen, anyway?" Robin asked.

"Are you sure you're okay, Peter?" she asked in alarm. "You don't seem to be quite yourself."

"Oh, I'm myself all right."

"You know," she thoughtfully said, "you might have bumped your head or something when you fought Dewey and Fred and might have been stunned. But I think it was awfully brave of you, so thanks for that."

Grinning at her, Robin said, "You are welcome, my lady, and I count myself fortunate I was able to defend you so successfully." That said, Robin bowed at the waist and doffed an imaginary hat. He was pleased to see a smile begin to appear on her face.

"Don't make fun of me. You know I don't like it. Come on, we better hurry before the tide goes out."

Robin halted abruptly and stared at her. "That's right. This isn't a flood. It's the sea come in, isn't it?"

"Why are you asking questions you already know the answers to?" she asked, increasingly alarmed. "You saw it all happen, same as everyone else.

You saw the news when polar ice caps began to melt and the panic when the axis shifted. Are you sure Dewey and Fred didn't get to you back there?"

Robin quickly recovered and replied, "Er...yeah, maybe they did and I just didn't notice. You know, in the heat of the battle and all that."

"Well," she finally said, "we better hurry back home for dinner. We don't want to make Mum mad at us."

They made their way down the rest of the way to the boat. Robin pushed it out into the water and climbed in once it was free of the beach. Gwyneth easily started the motor and expertly turned the small craft toward one of the stranded islands. On the way back, Robin considered that his relationship with Gwyneth was somehow different, but he wasn't quite able to decide what exactly it was that had changed, not that it was a bad change.

Gwyneth glided the boat into a small marina that appeared to have been constructed in haste. Several other boats were tied up at the dock, and Gwyneth maneuvered the boat into a slip between two of them. Robin hopped out as they drew alongside the dock and tied the boat to a cleat as if he had been doing it all of his life.

He held his hand out to her as she climbed out of the boat. He let her take the lead and followed close behind. This way, he could find out where he was since everything seemed so changed and upside down to him. He noticed how hot the sun had become and thought it must be the middle of summer.

"When did it last rain?" he suddenly asked her.

"A month or two, maybe late January or February."

"Hang on!" Robin said as he stopped walking. "That would make this March or April then, would it?"

"Whatever in the world is wrong with you, Peter Gilman?" There was no hiding her alarm now. Every question Robin asked only confirmed her suspicion that he had been injured in the brief fight with the Wilkins brothers.

"Nothing is wrong with me!" Robin replied indignantly. "I'm just trying to figure some things out, is all."

"It's early April, if you must know, and the Irish Sea has flooded everywhere. It's hardly rained in the last nine months, and the news reports say the water will cover all of Great Britain in about one to two years from now if the polar ice caps keep melting at their present rate. Why can't you remember these things for yourself, anyway, Peter? You were there, same as I, and you saw it all happen, same as I."

"Yeah...but how long ago did this happen?"

"After the Seattle earthquake last summer, just before we came over to Llangollen!" Gwyneth snapped. "Peter, we were in Seattle that day. The whole ground shook forever. Most of the Pacific Coast disappeared. The news reports said it was a 9.5. We saw bod...bod...bodies...bodies all over."

"Don't cry," Robin said as he held her. "I...er...forgot how it affected you." He tenderly wiped her eyes with his tunic and smiled at her.

"We better get up to the house. Mum will miss us. You better explain yourself, though. Your not remembering is more than a knock from Dewey and Fred."

"Sorry, it's just, well, it is rather hard to explain, you know. I'll explain after dinner when we get the chance."

They reached the house, and Robin walked toward the front door. He sensed that Gwyneth had not kept up with him. He turned around and discovered she was at his house, impatiently waiting for him.

"Oh, sorry," he said. "I went to the wrong house then, did I? So is your mom done fixing dinner, then?"

"You better have a very good explanation for this, Peter. And in case you're wondering, yes I'm sure *our* mum has dinner waiting in here, since she rarely fixes it over at the Reynolds' house unless the oven's gone missing or there's no wood to be found!"

Robin felt like he had been hit in the stomach. She had said *our* mum. None of this was right. But then why should it be? he wondered. It was an alternate universe and maybe it was supposed to be upside down.

Gwyneth opened the kitchen door that accessed the carport and walked into the kitchen, followed closely by Robin. Robin's heart stopped for a moment as he stood in stunned silence at who was cooking dinner in the kitchen. He desperately tried to gather his wits. His own mother stood with her back to him, removing meat pies from the wood stove and placing them on the cooling rack.

"Come on, you two," she called out as they walked in, "set the table. You both should have been home ages ago. Peter Gilman, how did you get so filthy? Wash up before you touch anything and hurry up; your father is starving. The twins are back, William."

"Yes'm," Robin mumbled, not trusting his voice to say much more.

He ran to the bathroom, thinking this was probably the cruelest joke anyone had ever played on him. His mother was dead in his universe, but here she was very much alive. Not only that, his mom had said *twins*. He and Gwyneth were brother and sister. Oh, how he had longed to see his mother one more time. Now she was here before him as if she had never gone away. Myrddin had warned him about how hard it would be.

He resisted the temptation to run to his mother and tried to appear calm. Gwyneth set the silverware and napkins about as he walked over to the china closet and took out four dinner plates.

"Honestly, Peter, not those ones!" Gwyneth exclaimed. "Those are for guests. Put those away and get the others."

"Oh...er...right. You couldn't tell me where they are then, could you?"

She looked at him uneasily and then said, "You better get a hold of yourself. Look on the lower shelf, next to the linens."

"Oh, right then. How could I be so thick? And there is nothing wrong with me. It's just...well, we need to talk after dinner." Robin kept his voice low so only she would hear him. It proved to be a good decision since his mother walked in just then and his father came in from the den.

His father affectionately messed his hair up as he passed, and Robin barely succeeded at keeping his true emotions in check. The last time his dad had touched him, he'd left a nasty bruise on his cheek and an invisible scar on his heart. Robin's anger at his father welled up inside him.

They all sat down at the table, said grace, and in no time they were eating the best meal Robin had had in a long time. William Gilman smiled, making Robin uncomfortable.

"What did you do today, Peter?" asked William.

"Went exploring," Robin mumbled.

"You didn't take the boat out, did you?"

"No, sir."

"Well, someone did."

Robin felt trapped. His own father had never shown any interest in his whereabouts before, but Peter's father wanted to know everything. Robin wondered if he would get so mad that he would start yelling, or worse, hit him like his own father had.

"By the way, Peter, the Kampilan sword's gone missing. That's not your doing is it?" Robin flinched at the mention of the sword and tried to remember where he had left it. Then he remembered. He had set it down after he fought Dewey and Fred. It was at Dinas Bran.

"I...I...er..."

"It was me took the boat out, Dad," Gwyneth lied. "Peter just came along for the ride."

"Oh, so you both went exploring. I'd like the sword put back, though. I didn't forget about it, you know, even if your sister did try to change the subject. It's an antique, son, and not like the sword you and I practice with."

Robin fearfully waited for the shouting to start, but William calmly finished his meal without another word. Maybe this father was different in this universe, he thought, and didn't go about hitting his children. Then he wondered if his mother was different here. His mother got up and began clearing the table, but Robin stopped her.

"I'll clear the table for you and do the dishes."

"Well, I certainly won't stop you from that. Thank you, dear."

Then his mother reached out and hugged him. Robin thought for certain he would lose it in front of everyone. He put his arms around her, holding her tight in quiet desperation.

"Peter, are you all right, dear?" she asked.

"Yes, I'm all right," Robin managed to reply, using all the inner strength he could muster. "I just thought I'd give you a hug."

He grabbed some of the dirty dishes and took them to the kitchen before anyone could see the tears still in his eyes. Gwyneth got up to help with the dishes.

While William and Cerridwen Gilman relaxed in the den, out of earshot, the two children cleaned up. Gwyneth kept looking at Robin apprehensively, but Robin was silent, not trusting his own voice.

"I think you better tell me what's happening now," said Gwyneth.

"I don't think you are going to believe me," he said.

"After what I just saw? You must be mad. Who else are you going to talk to anyway if not your twin sister? Besides, what were you crying for, anyway?"

"Not so loud," Robin hissed at her under his breath. "I don't want Mom and Dad to know! You might understand, but I'm pretty sure they won't."

"You've got to talk to someone. And since when did you start calling her mom? We're Welsh, not American. We say Mum, not *Mom*!"

"Look, thanks for covering for me about the boat and all. I'll try and explain later, when Mo...Mum and Dad can't overhear. Just keep an open mind, all right?"

"I covered for you because you're not a very good liar, you know," said Gwyneth. "And I'll understand a lot more than you think I will. You sure you wouldn't like a go at it now?"

"What did you say?"

"I said, are you sure you wouldn't..."

"All right, all right, Gwyneth, I'll tell you. Boy, you're pushy!"

"Gwyneth indeed!"

Gwyneth stomped out of the room without as much as a backward glance. Robin didn't close his gaping mouth until after he heard her slam her upstairs bedroom door. He unenthusiastically turned back to the dishes, and try as he might, the dishes took much longer than he would have preferred.

When he was finished, he ran upstairs. Once upstairs, however, he realized he didn't know which door was his. It could be the same door as it was in his universe, but what if it wasn't? He heard a door open behind him as he stood in the hallway and saw Gwyneth staring at him.

"I bet you don't know which door is yours," she said in a matter-of-fact tone.

"Do, too!" Robin said in irritation.

"All right then, go on in if you want."

"All right, I will."

Robin knew he was being stubborn, but his mood wasn't helped when he observed Gwyneth conceal her laughter with her hands. He quickly grabbed the door knob to the room that was his in another universe and began to turn it.

"No, no, not that one! That's the guest room. Yours is down the hall."

"It's not funny!" Robin said. Then he walked to the end of the hall and stopped when he realized that this bedroom door had been his dad's in his universe. "What are you playing at? You're not trying to get me in trouble, are you?"

"Who, me? Not on your life. I'm just trying to find out which one you are."

"All right, then. I'll play your game! Which am I?"

"Well," Gwyneth said, "you are certainly not Peter."

"And you are not my Gwyneth!"

"You're right. I'm not Gwyneth. I'm Brigid," she said. "What did you do with Peter?"

Robin stared. Her name was Brigid! She wasn't Gwyneth! But that still didn't explain how she could possibly know anything about what had happened unless someone had told her!

"I...I...I didn't do anything with Peter. It just happened. What exactly do you know about this?"

"Who are you? Are you Peter's double like Myrddin said?"

"Myrddin told you about this? What did he tell you, and when?"

"Shush! Not now! Mum and Dad are on their way up to bed. Quick, duck into my room!"

Once he was in, she shut her door and then faced him. "Myrddin has been teaching us for some time now. He told me that Peter and I had parallel lives in another universe and that one of our lives would be visiting for a short time. He also said that it would change us forever. Peter didn't much like the idea, really. I suppose that you must be Peter's parallel life, then?"

Robin felt a great sense of relief when she explained herself to him. At least, he thought, she knew what was going on and that might make it easier to deal with the situation.

"But you're not my sister where I come from. You're Gwyneth, and we're friends. Dewey and Fred are the same, though: no brains and no pain."

"Like I said, my name is Brigid, not Gwyneth. Why don't you tell me what's happened, but keep your voice down so Mum and Dad don't hear."

Robin told Brigid about his universe, how it was different and how it was the same. He also told her what his mother had been like, how she had died from cancer, and how his father hit him. Sometimes she was rapt with attention and eager to hear more, and other times she was reluctant to hear any more at all, especially when he told her about his mother's death. Brigid stretched and yawned when he stopped speaking.

"Will you go back to your universe soon? Not that I want you to, mind you; it's just, I was wondering if my brother is still there inside, or has he gone somewhere else?"

Robin stared at the floor for a moment before answering. "I think he's here…inside I mean. That's what Myrddin told me. In my universe, I could have never bested Fred and Dewey like I did today. I can only guess that it was Peter who did that. I suppose that means we are both here inside; it's just that I'm the one speaking now."

"Peter's the one bullying them here. They always go after me to get to Peter. I guess it's the opposite in your universe."

"I wish it wasn't. I wish…no, there has to be some reason why it happened the way it did in my universe. I wonder if it has something to do with becoming king?"

"What…king? But Peter's supposed to be king here, too. If that much is the same…but no, it doesn't make sense."

"Nothing makes sense. It's all upside down. Maybe in a way that does make sense, being upside down and all."

"You said you had some sort of accident. Would that have something to do with it?"

"Yeah, I suppose." Then very seriously, he explained, "I was told there was a chance I might not survive the accident I had, you know. I was told I would have to go back when it was time and when my body was properly repaired. I think that means Peter will be the only one inside and I will be just a memory. But I like it here a lot, especially knowing you're my twin sister."

"But you will go when it's time, right? Robin?" Brigid was hard pressed not to show her uneasiness at what he could possibly answer next.

"Of course, I'll go. Even if I like it here better. It's not like I'll have much of a choice. And even if I did, this isn't my universe. I don't belong here."

Chapter 6
THE HOLY GRAIL

Robin got up early before the others. He hadn't slept well the night before, worrying about how his father might react if he didn't return the sword. If only he could get to Dinas Bran and get the sword before he was missed and return it to its proper...but where did his father keep it? Brigid would know. He ran to her bedroom door. He quietly urged her to wake up while she mumbled irritably about rude people who never knocked before they entered a room and something about never having any proper privacy.

"Come on, Brigid," he implored, "Dad's going to be up soon. I just need you to tell me where to put the sword."

"You woke me up for that old thing?"

"Well, yeah, I did. Peter told me it was really old and Dad would be upset if it went missing. The least I can do for your brother is not get him in any trouble, you know."

"This is really weird. You're talking about Peter as if he were someone else. You feel as much a brother to me as he is."

"Look, just tell me where Dad keeps the sword. I've got to get going."

"Off somewhere?"

"I've got to get to Dinas Bran."

"I'm going, too!" she said as she sprang out of bed.

"No, we'll both get in trouble."

"So what?" she said. Then her eyes narrowed. "You left the sword at Dinas Bran, didn't you? That means you're in trouble already, and besides, I'm awake. I'm going!"

"Well, hurry up, then!"

The morning brought hot, hazy sunlight. This was just like the weather in August, Robin thought. But it was early spring, Robin thought, not late summer. If this was the temperature of early spring, he wondered what the heat of summer would be like.

Soon they dragged the boat onto the beach at Dinas Bran. By the time they reached the summit, they were both sweating from the exertion and the muggy heat of the day. There on a ledge, beneath one of the crumbling window sills, lay the Kampilan sword.

"Now I've found the sword, we better get back," said Robin. "We're going to be missed and maybe even be in trouble for being gone as long as we've been."

"Right, then, we better go. Mum and Dad have been awfully stressed, really. They worry about where we are going to get enough food and water to last us until we make the move."

"What do you mean, move?"

"Well, we can't stay around here very much longer, now can we?"

"Because of the water?"

"Listen, even Dinas Bran could go under water before the year is out. It's because of all the Earth changes."

"Let me get this straight...you said there were earthquakes?" asked Robin.

"Yes, there were several horrible earthquakes at first, in the Pacific Northwest. The volcanoes erupted, too."

"Mount Rainier, I bet."

"Yes, that was one and...I remember Mount Baker, too. There were tsunamis and loads of people died. California, too. But you know what was most amazing? The earth shifted!"

"How did it shift?"

"Well, that's just it. I really don't know how, but where we are, here in Llangollen, we're farther south than we were before. We're just north of the equator now. That's why it's so hot. The North and South Pole icecaps are breaking up and melting. That's why there's all this flooding. And not just here; it's flooding all over the world."

"What else happened?"

"It hasn't rained here for a long time. It's odd, really. There's water everywhere, but you can't drink any of it. All of England and Wales has become a desert. Scotland and Ireland, too. And deserts are getting all the rain. Places like Japan and Hawaii are gone. North America is split in two, but our house in Redmond, Washington, is still there. That's where we're going, just as soon as we can."

"But the project at the Penddol site, Dad has to finish, doesn't he?"

"That was in Clwyd County, Robin. There is no Clwyd County now."

"Oh, wow. This all sounds so...horrible."

"That's just it. And there's more. The earth is spinning faster and faster, and no one knows how fast it will eventually go. We can't even set our clocks proper because it changes every day. And the Grand Canyon in Arizona...it's all underwater!"

"No way! But how?"

"Because of the big earthquakes in California. Everyone said it would fall into the ocean. Well, it did. The ocean came in and flooded all the way to the Grand Canyon."

"You mean up the Colorado River?"

"Yes, that's the one. Mum and Dad say we have to leave by the end of the week. At least our house in Redmond survived. It doesn't feel so good having to leave Llangollen, though."

"I like it here, too, but Redmond is where we're from."

"Maybe it's where you're from, but Peter and I are from Llangollen. We're not Americans, Robin. It's why you have to say *mum* all the time or you'll be found out."

"Oh, wow, everything's so different. But Mother Lilith said what happens here will happen in my universe. I wonder if it will be the same...or different?"

"When you go back, just stay away from the coast. Stay on high ground, Robin. Only the people on high ground survived here. Come on, we better go."

They climbed back down and piloted the boat back to the makeshift marina. Just as they walked into the house, Robin was startled by his father's voice.

"So, you left it at Dinas Bran, then?" he asked Robin. "Haven't I told you before that it's very old and not for playing? Give it here then, son!"

Robin's heart was in his mouth. Would his father hit him for his carelessness? He silently handed the sword back to his father and waited for the blow to land. His father reached out his hand and, frozen in horror, Robin saw the hand descend on top of his head. But when it landed, it was soft and affectionate, and it messed up his hair.

"Use the practice sword next time. Your mother's got breakfast on, and after, we have to start packing for the move. So in you two get, and be quick. We've a lot to do today."

During the day, Robin thought about the way his father in Peter's universe had treated him. Why was Peter so lucky to have a father like this? Why couldn't his father be this kind? He liked this father a lot.

The busy day was soon over. Exhausted, Robin went to sleep as soon as his head hit his pillow. He wasn't sure how long he'd been asleep when he woke with a start. He was sure there was someone in his room. He held his breath and peered into the darkness.

"Robin," a voice whispered in the night, "are you awake?"

"Who's there?" Robin whispered back.

"It's all right. It's just me, Peter," the voice answered.

"No way! You're supposed to be in here, inside my body. Would you mind if I turn the light on? It's awfully hard to see you."

"You'll find I'm easier to see in the dark," Peter said just as Robin reached for the light. "I'm not sure why; and it's my body, too, you know."

"Right, I know that. How did you get over there without my knowing it, anyway?"

"Myrddin helped me with it."

"Is Myrddin here now? Where is he?"

"He's on his way with Kat-sidhe. He asked me to wake you and tell you that."

"Oh, right, was there something we were to talk about?" Robin asked as he sat back down in his bed.

"Nothing special. But I was wondering, why you didn't take Fred and Dewey's heads off when you had the chance?"

"But I did. Did you see me break Dewey's nose? I never could've done that before."

"Yeah, but they'll be back."

"Nah, we're moving anyway."

"So are they."

"Not...not to Redmond!"

"Afraid so. They were only here in Llangollen because their dad works for my...our dad."

"Ah no, but why Redmond? I mean, why not somewhere else?"

"Why wouldn't they go there? It's where they come from. Their house is near our place, in fact. I thought you knew all this."

"No, see, in my universe it's the other way round. I'm from Redmond, and they're from Llangollen. This isn't good."

"It's what I just said. If you'd used the sword properly, no more Dewey and Fred."

"Oh, come on! You're not serious, are you, Peter?"

"I told you before, it's a Kampilan sword. It was made to take heads off."

"I could never!"

"They wouldn't be around anymore to pick on my sister if you had!"

"No! That's just wrong! You can't just take someone's life like that, unless you have to save your own life or someone you love!"

"Oh, I see. Then Brigid doesn't mean all that much to you, does she? Maybe the Fred and Dewey in your universe aren't all that bad, but here they are bent on one purpose, and their target is always Brigid. You better react faster and harder next time or I'm taking over!"

"Don't talk to me that way!" Robin shot back. "And don't you dare say I don't love Brigid!"

The door swung open, and a shaft of light pierced the night, making the ghostly image of Peter disappear until the door was shut again.

"Will you be quiet?" Brigid whispered harshly into the room. "You'll wake Mum and Dad! We should all be asleep in bed. Whatever in the world are you two thinking?"

"Hullo, Brigid," Peter mumbled into the darkened room. "You're right, of course. Myrddin's going to be mad now, too."

"What are you talking about?" Brigid asked. "Why would he be mad?"

"Because you weren't supposed to be awake for this," Myrddin said. He had suddenly appeared out of the shadow of night. Kat-sidhe appeared next, followed by two more fairies.

"Why not? This isn't the keep-everything-from-Brigid club, you know."

"Forgive me, my lady," Myrddin said as he bowed before her. "It was for your own safety."

"Is he ready to go, Myrddin?" Kat-sidhe interrupted.

"In a moment. I must explain the situation to him first so he doesn't have to go in uninformed. Do you know of the legend of the Holy Grail, Robin?"

"He won't even use a sword properly! How do you expect him to get the Grail if he won't even do that much?" Peter's words stung like no other person's could have. Robin wasn't very sure that Peter was far from wrong.

"That is enough out of both of you!" Myrddin scolded. "How can I instruct you if you continually deny your abilities, Robin? All you have to do is pick up the sword, and Peter's cellular memories will take over.

"And you," Myrddin said as he rounded on Peter, "Robin is correct. Just because you don't like Fred and Dewey is no reason to maim or kill them. Brigid was not in mortal danger, and Robin showed great restraint when he stopped them. This is the balance you need. Robin needs to be more aggressive and confident when it is called for, and you, Peter, need to show more restraint. You are so hot blooded when it comes to the protection of your sister. How can you help her if by murdering someone you will only be pursued in order to be brought to justice? Who shall protect this lady if you are sentenced by the Department of Corrections? You have as much to learn from Robin as he does from you!"

"You heard us?" Robin and Peter both asked.

"Yes, I did. While you two are like this, I can hear if I want to. It's not automatic, but I must do it by intention."

"I'll remember that," Peter mumbled to himself.

"I heard that, as well."

"Excuse me a minute," Robin broke in. "What's the Department of Corrections?"

"It's our justice system here," Brigid said. "The corrections officers know when a crime is committed and hunt you down. They catch you and then they sentence you. Nobody escapes, and whenever they hunt for anybody, there is never a question about the guilt of the person they look for."

"What, there's no trial? What about one's day in court?"

"This isn't your universe, Robin," Myrddin interrupted, "and things are different here. When a person commits an act of violence, they leave an imprint that is recorded in what is known as the Akashic Records. The corrections officers can access those records, and the proof of the crime is there. You would call their abilities magic in your universe, but here it is all perfectly normal. Justice is meted out under what we call the eye for an eye laws."

"You mean, if I had taken Dewey's head off, then..."

"The Department of Corrections would have hunted you down, caught you, and sentenced you to death by beheading. The only way out is if your actions are ruled as justified."

"What would justify killing?"

"If, as you had pointed out to Peter, you had killed to protect your own life or the life of another, then the corrections officers would know that from the Akashic Records and would not pursue you."

"How do you know if they're pursuing you?"

"If they had, you would have been sentenced by now. The Department of Corrections acts very quickly."

"Killing them would have been justified!" Peter said. "Why should I wait for them to hurt her? Just because they were corrected later on wouldn't change the fact that she would still be hurt, would it?"

"I don't know, Peter, but maybe it's good I didn't take Dewey's head off. I'm not sure I like your universe. You're lucky, though. You've got Mo... Mum, and your dad loves you."

Peter started to say something but thought better of it. Then Myrddin gently put his hand on Robin's shoulder. Robin decided to change the subject back to the Holy Grail.

"According to what I've been taught, it was the cup Jesus drank from at the last supper. I think the Knights of the Round Table went on quests to find it."

"Quite correct, actually." Myrddin's praise made Robin cheer up a little. "The legend tells us it was found and then hidden at Castell Dinas Bran. Like all magical objects and mystical things, it transferred to this universe when your universe stopped believing in magic. I might add that it is a lot more than a cup for drinking. It holds the records of certain blood lines, which can be used to determine certain rights of inheritance.

"There is one in particular who with this information could find out who the future king is and use that information to gain power over that person. It could ultimately lead to having the power to rule the world. Therefore, it is the future king who needs to know this information so that he can protect himself from the other."

"So the future king needs to find these records to become the king."

"Yes, that is most correct. If the other finds it first, he will plunge your world into a most desperate tribulation. It is you who must retrieve the Holy Grail from its resting place and return it to your universe. You must keep it safe from the other."

"Me? Then what I heard…that man who called my dad a king…is he my enemy?"

"*Ouch! Get away from me!*" Brigid waved her arms at a fairy who was pulling her hair while a second one braided it so fast, its tiny hands were blurred. They flew away out of reach, but as soon as Brigid stopped shooing them, they returned to continue their work, giggling the whole time. Brigid was not amused at their antics.

"Kat-sidhe, make them stop, please," Brigid pleaded.

"I don't know, Brigid," Peter said. "I rather like it, actually. You should wear a braid in your hair more often."

"Oh! Just shut it, will you?" Brigid said as she took her braided strand of hair in her own hands to see what the fairies had done to her. "This isn't funny!" The fairies exploded with laughter at her outburst, which only put her in a fouler mood.

Still trying to undo the braids, Brigid said, "Myrddin, I'd like to help find the Holy Grail, too, please?"

"No, Brigid, the road Robin travels is much too dangerous for you. I cannot allow it. Dangerous enough for Robin to take a sword, in fact." Myrddin manifested a sword and handed it to Robin. It was a long sword, double bladed, and its haft was inlaid with gold. Two angels were positioned at the end of the grip so that their wings formed a circle while they knelt in prayer facing each other.

"Whoa," Peter exclaimed, "that's a Templar sword! I want one for my birthday!"

"But, Myrddin," Robin began, "what sort of danger do I need a sword for?"

"The other person who seeks the Grail is afoot and will stop at nothing to obtain it. Kat-sidhe and her fairy guard will escort you for protection, but I give you this magical sword to be used only if you need it. It will stay in this universe once you return and become Peter's sword." Peter grinned at this.

"The Holy Grail must be moved tonight," Myrddin continued. "Before you go, however, I must warn you not to trust any stranger offering help you see along the way. Do you understand, Robin?"

Kat-sidhe flew in front of Robin. Robin's heart raced with excitement at the prospect of flying. And then, before he had time to think much more about it, he was flying with Kat-sidhe in the lead.

"Where's Peter, Kat-sidhe?"

"I am looking at him!" she replied.

"No, no, not me. I mean Peter. You know, my other self."

"I am looking at him!"

"Oh, come on, Kat-sidhe, I'm trying to be serious here. Peter was in the room and then he wasn't. What happened to him?"

She stopped so quickly that Robin bumped into her. With her hands on her hips, she sternly looked him in the eye.

"I'm looking at him!"

"You mean he's here," Robin asked while pointing at his chest, "inside me?"

"Dinas Bran is below us."

The crumbling walls of Dinas Bran were bathed in silver moon glow, and the giant oak's massive form loomed before him. Then he saw a creature slink away into the shadows and hide from sight. A chill passed through him as he turned to ask Kat-sidhe if she had seen it.

Kat-sidhe put her hand to her mouth to silently warn Robin. As they landed near the oak, fairies flew from the branches of the tree and surrounded them. But as soon as the fairies appeared, the furtive creature reemerged and ran straight at them. All the fairies but Kat-sidhe fled.

Its painful shrieking pierced the night air. Robin drew his sword and took a broad stance, ready for the creature's assault. He smelled its foul stench as it began to run around in circles, shrieking the entire time.

"Stop where you are, orc!" Kat-sidhe shouted. "Your kind is not welcome here!"

Astonished at her sudden daring, Robin lowered the sword ever so slightly, but it was enough for the orc to notice an advantage. It charged, and Robin lashed out with the sword but Kat-sidhe had already magically repelled the creature, making its back strike the giant oak with a dull, sickening thud. Still wielding the sword, Robin cautiously approached the downed orc.

"Careful," Kat-sidhe cautioned, "orcs never travel alone."

Robin stopped and stared at the tiny fairy that had just demonstrated more power than he could have imagined. "You've gone awfully serious."

"Let me make sure it is safe. Besides, the orc may only be stunned. They are quite resilient, you know," Kat-sidhe said, and then called, "Come out, my little ones, and find the other orcs. Leave no stone unturned." The oak exploded with fairy activity, and sparks of their fairy dust descended about Robin like burning embers as they began their search with furious intent.

"I've never seen you this angry," Robin began, "maybe this wasn't such a good idea."

"The consequences of not retrieving the Holy Grail would be worse. Have patience; we will clear the area of all unfriendly creatures."

Robin stared at the orc lying crumpled against the trunk of the oak and guardedly poked at it with the sword. Black blood oozed from its ears and mouth. The head was bald except for a few strands of greasy hair. Its mouth, twisted in a grimace of death, revealed shadow-colored teeth with razor sharp points. Its green and sickly looking skin stretched over a distended belly.

Except for a filthy loincloth, the orc wore no clothing and its stench was more than Robin could stomach. A retching sound came from behind them, and Robin spun around to seek the source. Brigid knelt on the ground behind them wiping her mouth.

"All right, Brigid?" Robin asked.

Coughing and sputtering, Brigid managed to say, "What is that awful stench?"

"It is the putrid body of an orc," Kat-sidhe answered, "and, if it's making you sick, it's your own fault for not following Myrddin's wish that you not be here! What are you doing here, anyway?"

A very distraught fairy flew in front of Robin and spoke to Kat-sidhe so fast that even if he knew how to speak their language, he wouldn't have been able to distinguish the words. Then, as abruptly as she had arrived, the fairy flew away.

"Both of you, *now*," shouted Kat-sidhe, "stand with your backs to the oak tree!"

Quickly, Robin grabbed Brigid and helped her up. Brigid gagged again, since they were directly beside the rapidly decaying body of the fallen orc. Robin couldn't help but notice how swift the decay was and wondered how anything could rot so fast.

"What's happened, Kat-sidhe?" he asked.

"That was the captain of my personal guard. She tells me there are about a dozen orcs on their way. We are about to be attacked by them! Stand ready now, and at all costs, you must protect your sister!"

The orcs appeared out of the shadows, shrieking as they came. Round and round, they ran about the three standing in front of the mighty oak, closing in on them. Then one of the orcs broke away from the pack and ran straight at Robin. Another orc broke away on the heels of the first. Electricity surged through Robin.

Kat-sidhe dispatched the first one. The second one was close behind, and Robin struck it across its forehead. Black blood flew in every direction but mostly all over Robin. Three more orcs broke away and began their attack before Robin had time to breathe.

Robin swung his sword again and for a moment closed his eyes to keep out the sweat and orc blood. One of the orcs had survived both Robin's sword and Kat-sidhe's powerful magic, and seeing that Robin's eyes were closed, seized the advantage. It grabbed Brigid, who screamed in a high pitch that matched the shrieking of the orcs.

Robin opened his eyes again and swung the sword down on the arms of the orc, slicing bone and sinew. The surprised orc stared at the stumps where its arms used to be, and Robin dealt it a second deadly blow. The two disembodied hands still clutched Brigid in their death grip. Wide-eyed with terror, Brigid pulled them off and threw them on the ground in disgust.

Kat-sidhe slew two more, and then only five remained, but they were the largest. The orcs ceased their shrieking and running in circles, standing before them as if trying to decide if it was worth the effort or not.

The largest of the orcs spoke in a hissing drool, "Orcs more we are. The Grall we want. Live you shall if Grall you give. More come. Wait for more we shall."

"Then you shall face us all!" Kat-sidhe declared. As soon as she spoke these words, her fairy guard flitted in from all directions. The orcs watched and then the largest orc spoke once more.

"Give Grall now," it said. "Take Grall to our Lord we must. Die we shall by hand of Lord if Grall not bring. We die now; we die later. Die no matter so now we die. Give Grall so no die."

"Keep one can we for eating?" one of the other orcs asked.

"Give Grall and small one for eating. No die if give."

"You are not in a position to bargain, orc," Kat-sidhe said. "But if you leave now, we shall let you live. My fairy guard is many, and you know full well that the last time the fairies faced the orc hordes we were outnumbered a thousand-to-one and still the victory was ours."

"Die by Dark Lord hand we shall. Must have Grall, food for eat. Give now. No talk. Give now."

Brigid groaned when she heard the discussion concerning her invitation to be part of an orc dinner. To the waiting orcs, the sound of Brigid's groan was like that of an injured animal. They were no longer able to contain their excitement, and much like wolves about to take their prey down, they rapidly advanced.

Robin never had a chance to bring his sword to bear. Kat-sidhe's fairy guard reacted in a swift blur. Four orcs died and one lay at Robin's feet, gasping in a horrible death rattle. He looked at Robin, and the venom in his gaze made Robin take a step backwards.

Robin caught himself and demanded, "Tell me about your Dark Lord!"

"Send for Grall he did. Say no Grall, no live. More come. Grall will take. Find you they shall. No hide, no run, no hope."

"Robin, leave him," Kat-sidhe ordered. "We must take what we came for and leave or we will have to fight again, and sooner or later one of us could be seriously injured or worse."

"Right, then," said Robin, "but how do we get the Holy Grail? Where is it, anyway?" The orc shrieked at Robin's words and began cackling.

"Not know where Grall. Not know where Grall. *Not know where grall!* Not have Grall." It clutched at Robin's legs. "Trick me you did. Think I you are the one. But not know where Grall…" With a last rattling gasp, the orc died while grasping at Robin's legs, and his stench rose in the air as soon as he passed.

Robin stood in silent disgust while staring at the dead orc. Brigid let out a low moan, slowly sat up, and surveyed the scene before her.

"What did you follow me here for?" Robin asked. "What if you had been hurt, or worse? Hang on. How did you get here to begin with and… your hair…it's all braided."

Her hair indeed was entirely braided. Robin chuckled at the sight. One or two braids were pretty, but all of her hair braided was actually quite funny.

"Shut…up!" Brigid snarled. "The two fairies that braided my hair, remember them? I let them braid all of my hair in return for their escorting me here."

"Robin, we must do what we came here for," Kat-sidhe said. "We can deal with Brigid's situation afterwards. I will deal with the two who brought her here personally. Please accept my apologies for their indiscretion."

"Er, Kat-sidhe, it's not your fault. I know you would never have let them if you had known. Besides, she wasn't hurt or anything, and I'm sure we can protect her until we get back."

"Your words are kind, Robin, but the danger is great, greater than any of us imagined."

"I never meant to do any harm, Kat-sidhe," Brigid spoke up. "Please; I would never intentionally put anyone in danger."

Kat-sidhe flitted to her and said, "You are more important to us than you realize, my lady. I know you meant no harm, and hopefully no harm will come to you or anyone else as a result. I am embarrassed to think the two who brought you here disobeyed my orders to protect you. I must find out why that is, but in the meantime, please stay close and do not defy any command I give you. Can you do this?"

"Yes, I will," Brigid said in a small voice.

"Robin, you must take the Holy Grail now," said Kat-sidhe.

"But where is it? I wasn't kidding when I said I didn't know."

"Use your invisible eye, the one I opened for you when first we met. Close your eyes and concentrate on the Holy Grail and it will be revealed to you," Kat-sidhe replied.

Robin closed his eyes and began to think what the Holy Grail must look like. It appeared before him, hidden inside the oak in a hollow he hadn't noticed before. Robin confidently walked to the opening and reached inside. He felt a hard object and grasped it tightly. A magical presence filled him with joy and overwhelmed him with emotion. As strange as it was, he felt familiar with it.

In his hands was a golden goblet wrapped in a cloth that appeared to be woven of silver thread. Inside the goblet was a scroll with the strangest writing he had ever seen. He quickly put it inside his tunic.

Suddenly, an arrow struck him squarely in the chest, blinding him with searing pain. He couldn't breathe and desperately tried to catch his breath while fighting away the panic that threatened to overwhelm him. Just before he lost consciousness screams and shrieks filled the blackness of the night.

Chapter 7
THE SIKORSKY SEA KING

The slamming door woke William Gilman from his alcohol sleep. His head pounded from the sudden jolt as the sunlight glared into his already inflamed eyes. He stood on his unsteady feet and winced from the increased pounding.

"Robin," he yelled, "can you possibly slam that door any louder?" The intensity of the pounding in his head redoubled when he yelled, and he rued his own loud voice.

"You are mistaken," a soft, fey, male voice said. "It is I, the servant of His Eminence."

Dressed in a woolen suit, a man casually entered the room, pulling latex gloves on. The gray skin on his face was stretched almost to the point of bursting, as if it was meant for a child's head. Where his eyes should have been were eyelids grown together over empty sockets. Nevertheless, he approached as if sight was his while William gaped at his hideous face.

"Is he here?" William asked.

"Just outside, darling. He has business first and then he will enter."

"Why are you here?"

"Your aura is filthy. Like this room, it is in need of a good cleaning. I must carry out your sentence."

"My what?"

"I must correct your aura. It is the law."

The man with no eyes snapped William's neck before he could move and he lay dead on the floor in front of the eyeless man.

"Are you ready to go, Agas Astō Vidātu?" a new voice called from the kitchen.

"I've just finished, Your Eminence."

"Bring his body, then, before the neighbors see us."

"Not to worry. I've confounded them."

"Good, but sooner the better. This is risky enough."

"Where shall I put him, my Lord? With the woman?"

"No, we'll put him in the boot of his own car."

"Yes, my Lord." He easily lifted William's body over his shoulder and began carrying it out of the room. "Did you call the news people, my Lord?"

"They are on their way as we speak."

"I still don't understand the reason."

"To fulfill biblical prophecy. As it is written, he must receive a deadly head wound and it shall be healed. The whole world must see the boy's wounded head and witness his miraculous recovery. Then will the world wonder how this can be, and I will show them their messiah. Then will I turn him into the beast."

"You know best, my Lord."

"Hurry up."

⌘ ⌘ ⌘

Gwyneth left Robin with the old man and ran home. She banged through her kitchen door, yelling for her stepmother and father.

"What's this all about, then?" her stepfather said as he came downstairs.

"Dad, you've got to come quick! It's Robin next door; he's in trouble! Please, Dad, please!"

"What are you on about? He's not in trouble with his dad, is he?"

"No, but his dad hit him this morning, and I think he's hurt really bad, and...."

"Hit him? Darla, better come quick! The neighbor boy's been hurt!"

"He's hurt?" Darla asked. "Did someone call the EMTs?"

"Yes, but...oh, Mum..." Gwyneth's voice caught in her throat as she sobbed into her apron.

"All right, darling, your father and I will go over straight away and see that he's all right. Tom, you better find his father."

"Oh, I'll get him all right. That prat better stop his drinking. I knew something like this would happen. I should've..." Tom ranted on as he went out the kitchen door, speaking to no one in particular and not realizing he had come to the wrong conclusion.

Gwyneth led Darla back to Robin, and they arrived just as the EMT crew did. Two EMTs surrounded Robin, taking his vital signs and performing their triage. The old man who had called the EMTs stood nearby, wringing his hands. Darla was stunned when she saw them bandaging Robin's limp, bloody head.

"You, miss, how long has he been out?" the first EMT demanded from Gwyneth when he noticed her.

"I...it just happened...I don...don't know."

"Can't have been more than ten minutes," the old man said. "It had just happened when I called you lot."

"Tell Cardiff General yes to the air lift," the EMT commanded. "I'll get the backboard and collar. I don't want to take any chances even if a neck injury isn't indicated."

The third EMT, at the ambulance, radioed for the air lift and informed the others it was on its way.

"All right, gentlemen," he called out, "Cardiff General has just informed me that they are sending a Sikorsky Sea King with an ETA of thirty-four minutes. That means we have to move to a large field for the transfer."

"Right, then, let's get him to the Penddol site."

"I'm going too!" Gwyneth declared as the EMTs finished strapping Robin to the backboard.

"You'll do no such thing!" Darla said.

The EMTs lifted Robin and belted his backboard to a rolling stretcher. Gwyneth quickly seized Robin's hand.

"Robin, please wake up. Don't leave me, Robin. Wake up." Then she gasped out loud.

"What's happened?" asked the first EMT.

"He...he...squeezed my hand just now," she managed to say.

"Brilliant, miss; talk to him. He probably won't answer, but he will hear you and it might help him come out of it."

"Come on, Robin, wake up. Please, wake up."

His voice groggy and hoarse, Robin finally answered her, "What did you follow me for? Don't you know how much danger we're in?"

"Oh, Robin, we're safe now," Gwyneth said, her voice squeaky and breathless. "There's no danger for me anymore, only for you. You have to stay awake."

"You are not making sense, sis. I found the Holy Grail, did I tell you? I had it in my hands, but someone knocked me down and I couldn't breathe, but I'm okay now. And did you see me fight the orcs? Kat-sidhe helped, and she was brilliant, but I did my part and I'm awfully glad you're all right. I was scared for you."

Gwyneth's eyes flooded with tears, and Robin heard the sound of her crying. He slowly opened his eyes and looked at her curiously.

"Who's making you cry now, sis? You're safe, you know. The orcs are all gone. We just got to get back to the house and find out what to do with the Holy Grail. Wait a minute...this isn't Dinas Bran. Where are we? Who tied me up? What are all these tubes doing in my arms? Brigid, quit crying and tell me what's going on?"

"You're going to the hospital. You've been hurt pretty bad, Robin. But you have to stay awake, all right? Don't go back to sleep."

"We're not on Dinas Bran? Quick, tell me if the Irish Sea has flooded all around."

"Robin, you're talking crazy and it's scaring me. We are in Llangollen, and there is no flood."

"Oh no! I can't be here. I have to go back. Peter can't do this by himself. It's another world, Gwyneth; you've got to come with me. I can't explain now, but you've got to come with me."

"No, Robin. No! You can't go away again! You might not be able to get back! Stay awake, stay awake!"

"I have to see it to the end," Robin said as his voice began to trail off. "You've got to see what I've seen. When you sleep tonight, dream about flying and call for Mother Lilith. She will find me for you and we'll be together. Don't worry; it's perfectly safe, and I do mean to come back."

"Robin, no! You just simply can't go back to sleep! Not now!"

"Remember, when you sleep, fly. Fly, Gwyneth, fly."

Robin's eyes closed, and his breathing became regular. But Gwyneth was comforted by the way he was holding her hand. His grip was firm as he clung to her. Robin lay unmoving and lost in another world, completely unaware that he was in the ambulance. Robin was flying.

"We've got to take him now, miss," the EMT said.

The rear ambulance door shut and the van pulled away heading off in the direction of the Penddol site. Tom brought their car around, and Gwyneth and Darla got in. A tall, thin, impeccably dressed bald man also got in his car and followed them to the Penddol site. The man's car remained at a distance and went unnoticed.

"Did you find Will Gilman?" Darla asked Tom along the way.

"I couldn't find the sot anywhere," Tom replied. "It's like he disappeared. I even went into the house and almost got arrested when I came out."

"Not really?"

"Yes, really. The police are looking into the murder of a prost...lady of the evening. There's a detective wants to ask Gwyn some questions, too. None of it makes sense, though. I thought Gwyn said Will hit Robin and I thought that was how he got hurt."

"Oh, Tom! That's horrible! We should have done more."

"Done what? Look, I know it's horrible and all, but how were we to know it had gone that far? Besides, it wasn't Will that did that to the boy."

"What do you mean, not Will?"

"It's what the police told me. Apparently this was no accident. They're looking for two boys, and I think they meant that they're the ones who did this."

"He was attacked? My Gwyneth, too?"

"I'm not sure, but Gwyn was there when it happened. There's more."

"Oh my!"

"They were searching Will's car, the boot specifically. They wouldn't let me see, but...Will's been murdered."

"Tom...Gwyneth!" Darla warned. Too late, Gwyneth had heard from the back seat and trembled at the news. She knew she had to find out more; the question was how to do it?

"What's going to become of him?"

"Will's boy? I don't know, but it doesn't look good."

They drove the rest of the way in silence. The ambulance arrived at the Penddol site with its lights flashing, alerting the neighboring populace of its desperate mission, followed close by Tom and Darla. The television crews came next, making such a scene that all hope for privacy was gone, but the EMTs were used to this sort of situation and ignored the pleading news anchors waiting outside for an interview that would never be. The bald man's car arrived last, keeping its distance to avoid being seen.

"Everything is proceeding as I have planned," the bald man said to his eyeless servant.

"But, Your Eminence, why must I wait here when so many down there need correcting?"

"Agas, my friend, you must remember this universe is out of your jurisdiction. You were only able to correct William Gilman and that disgusting woman because they both have parallel lives in your universe. Without that connection, your powers over them here are nonexistent."

"I understand, my Lord."

"You are a good and faithful servant, Agas. Now I must give you another task."

"Command me as you will, my Lord."

"You must return to your universe and watch Peter Gilman. If he commits a crime, you must not correct him. Will you do this for me, my good and faithful servant?"

"It is against my mandate, Your Eminence. But because you have asked it, I shall see to it. None shall correct him unless you say."

"I am pleased you would compromise your principles for me in order that I may achieve my ends. I know it is a sacrifice and it will not go unrewarded."

"If I had eyes, I would weep for joy, Your Eminence. Until we meet again, I wish you God's grace."

"Thank you for the sentiment, Agas, but my position assures God's grace. Go now and do my bidding."

Agas Astō Vidātu sat in the car momentarily silent. He opened the door and a bright light shone all around him as he stepped out. In the time it took to open a door and enter a room, he was gone. The bald man leaned back in his car seat, closed his eyes, folded his hands in his lap, and smiled. Agas Astō Vidātu had slipped away and entered Peter's universe.

The noise of the Sikorsky Sea King's rotor blades and turbine engines was deafening when it landed. Robin was strapped in and the air lift was soon on its way to Cardiff General Hospital.

⌘ ⌘ ⌘

Gwyneth and Darla sat in the hospital waiting room while Tom checked with the receptionist. It wasn't long before he returned with news about Robin.

"I checked with the receptionist," Tom said. "He's in surgery now."

"Oh, Dad!" was all Gwyneth could manage to say as she hugged him.

"It's all right, princess," Tom comforted. "Robin's going to be all right. No more tears now. Hey, I know…what do you say to a good meal and maybe a nice hotel room? We can be back here early tomorrow to check up on Robin. Besides, the doctors won't know anything for certain until morning."

⌘ ⌘ ⌘

That night, Gwyneth dreamed about wonderful glorious flying. Below her, she saw the vast expanse of the Irish Sea. Off in the distance, she noticed a series of tiny islands that appeared to have homes and roads that seemingly lead to nowhere. The closer she flew, however, the more she saw that the roads didn't stop at the water's edge but disappeared beneath the Irish Sea, continuing on to some unknown destination deep under the water.

Crows were flying in circles above one of the islands. A giant oak tree stood at the very apex and amid the crumbling ruins of an old castle. She flew lower and saw the ruins were Castell Dinas Bran. What she saw next made her gasp out loud. Fairies were everywhere.

Chapter 8
GENETIC ENGINEERING

Robin desperately gasped in all of the air he could. It seemed an eternity had passed since he had taken his last breath. It felt wonderful to be able to breathe again, even if his ribs hurt with every effort. He groaned and tried to sit up, but someone pushed him back down.

"Hey, let me sit up!" he wheezed.

"Not until I've taken the arrow out, you won't!" Myrddin said.

"What arrow? This one stuck in my shirt?" Robin easily plucked the orc arrow out. As he did, the Holy Grail fell out of his tunic, where he had secretly put it. Robin marveled that the silver cloth that wrapped the Holy Grail and the ancient scroll was undamaged.

"It looks as if your lineage is your salvation," Myrddin observed. "That arrow could have just as easily pierced your heart."

Shaking off the cobwebs in his head, Robin looked at Myrddin and slowly realized he was back in Peter's room.

"Where's Brigid, is she all right?"

"Do not fret about your sister, dear boy," Myrddin said. "She is perfectly well and sitting next to you."

Robin turned and saw her. He grinned at her, not just because he was happy to see her, but the sight of her braided hair still made him laugh. He reached out and tenderly took her hand in his. Kat-sidhe flitted in, distracting Robin. Brigid slyly took the scroll and, while the others talked, read it.

"Myrddin," Kat-sidhe said, "it is as we feared. We have been betrayed, and I must confess that it is I who am at fault!"

"How could you have known they were seeking instruction from another?"

"But I should have read the signs. Even Powys Fadog and his Morrigan Badbh would land on the ground whenever they were present at Dinas Bran. I should have seen that *they* were the danger and not anyone else."

"Even I would have thought the same as you. Besides, we have two children before us who are perfectly safe and the Holy Grail is recovered."

"Kat-sidhe, it's not your fault," Brigid confessed. "It's mine. I let them braid my hair and they said they would help me go with Robin, even if Myrddin said not to."

Robin gaped at Brigid. This meant the two innocent-looking fairies who had braided her hair, giggling the whole time, had carried out the wicked plans of a most malevolent enemy. Someone had placed her in harm's way, and this someone wanted the two of them together when the orcs attacked.

"But you can't blame them entirely, either, Kat-sidhe," Robin interrupted. "They couldn't have done it on their own. Maybe they were fooled or enchanted by someone."

"You humans are all alike!" Kat-sidhe spat. "You think just because we giggle and are tiny that we must be innocent fools! Look at me, Robin! Where is the weapon I used to kill the orcs that lay at your feet? Tell me how some giggling fool of a fairy is capable of that? Why did the orcs stop their attack? Because of you? Those two are not brainless! They are well aware of what they've done! They made a decision of their own free will and entered into a contract that has bound them to the side of the great shadow!"

Kat-sidhe stared at Robin in a violent mood. He shivered, and the hair rose up on the back of his neck. For a moment, he thought she might take her rage out on him. Brigid continued to study the scroll.

"They have each been given new names," Kat-sidhe continued more calmly, "and have been excommunicated from our ranks. They are now called Bleak and Gloom. Their new names will forever mark them for having chosen the shadow path."

"I see that you still have a question, Robin," Myrddin said. "You may as well ask now, since I don't believe Kat-sidhe could get any angrier than she is already."

"Maybe I'll ask later, if you don't mind."

"No, ask me now," Kat-sidhe said. She hovered in front of Robin's face, and the look in her eyes demanded he ask his question.

"Well, if you don't mind, then," he started, "Myrddin mentioned the two fairies received instructions. Who gave them those instructions?"

"He is the enemy Mother Lilith warned you about."

"Does he have a name?"

"Lucifer."

"What? My enemy is the...the devil? This is nuts! I'm not fighting him!"

"All is lost, Myrddin," Kat-sidhe said.

"No, all Robin needs is knowledge. Knowledge is power, if you know how to use it. This will be the power he needs to fight this evil."

"What knowledge?" Robin exclaimed. "Everyone already knows who the devil is. What more could I know that would help me against the devil?"

"The truth will set you free, Robin," Myrddin said. "You must first know that Lucifer is real, but the idea of the devil is the legend invented by the fearful mind of man. Lucifer uses this legend to exist and has done so since its first inception. He knows that if a lie is allowed to exist long enough, it will become the truth of the ignorant mind, and the belief in the lie allows him power over all mankind."

"How does that work?"

"The belief that he is an all-powerful ruler of the underworld strikes fear in the heart of mankind. It works because the fearful allow the one they fear to have this power over them. Please understand that he has no power except that which we allow."

"But I thought he had power beyond that?"

"He knows magic and that is true, but even this power will not be enough if you believe. Believe he has no power and it will be so."

"Just like that? But it's not what I've been taught."

"Ah, yes, what you've been taught. Let me tell you what I know to be true. It is Lucifer who caused the two worlds to split against the will of the Creator. He works by illusion, shadow is his trademark, deception is his instrument of choice, and true power his greatest ambition. This is why uniting the two parallel universes is so important. Once they are united, the Creator's will shall be done in heaven even as it is done on earth."

"If I *allowed* him to have power over me, what could he do to me? Come to think of it, why me? I mean, who am I that I could stand against one so evil?"

"He could do to you whatever you believe he could. Fear creates ethereal electricity. Lucifer can use this ethereal electricity and charge himself much like a battery. This power exists only as long as he is feared. That means without someone who is afraid of him, he will lose his power the same as a battery would when it loses its charge."

"But if we don't believe he has power in my universe, then wouldn't that be enough?"

"He would still have Peter's universe. He knows if he can keep the two universes from merging, he will still have this universe, the magic one, to rule. If the two universes merge, then you will be the first of mankind to be both a man and a magical being. This will strip Lucifer of his power over all magic."

"I'll be...magic? But I thought magic left my world because we stopped believing."

"Magical creatures left your world because you stopped believing in us," Kat-sidhe said. "We were unloved, but magic remained. It is why I can go between the two parallel universes. If you believe in magic and your ability to use it, others will see this and start believing again."

"Magic is a universal principle," Myrddin continued. "You and Peter have magical abilities now. When everything merges, then it is you and Peter, merged together, who will have the power and authority over magic that Lucifer has now. Lucifer will then lose everything, and he will stop at nothing to prevent this merging. It is why you have a parallel life. That way it will happen as predicted."

"Predicted...like in a prophecy?"

"A prophecy says," Myrddin said, "that a king of French descent and German background will inherit a throne with no kingdom. This king will be known as the king of kings, and he will rule over all that is magic. This king will take his throne, and the two universes will merge, but not before a time of terrible war and terrible changes in the earth.

"The leader of your country has begun a war he will not finish by himself," Myrddin concluded. "He believes he is doing the will of the Creator, and his supporters reinforce his belief by their consent. But I fear a world war has begun, and the time approaches for the French king to assume his throne. Only then will the merging begin, for it is the French king who will reintroduce the Fairy Kingdom, and when this happens, this universe will be embraced by the universe you come from."

"But who is this king that comes from France?" Robin asked. Brigid sputtered and coughed when he said this, and Robin gave her a curious glance.

"He is the king of the quatrain. He is the king that David Poreaus predicted in the seventeenth century. He is the king of the lilies and he is the one the prophet Nostradamus spoke of. Michel was actually quite a good student of mine, I might add."

"But it doesn't make sense. Everyone says I'm king, but I'm not French. I'm Welsh."

"Robin," Brigid said, "don't you know? Your ancestors came over from France during the French Revolution. They were Huguenots and moved to Wales with the help of a Protestant minister. Some of them changed their names to escape detection, and others married into Welsh and English families. After they arrived in Wales, most of them immigrated to the Americas and started colonies there. Many of their original names are in this scroll you found—names that belong to you and me!"

"All of that is in the scroll? The thing is, I'm not from your world, and who I'm related to might be different in mine. That's right, isn't it, Myrddin?"

"You and your twin sister in this universe are indeed related to the bloodlines recorded in that scroll. In your universe, you are related to the bloodlines in a slightly different way. The outcome is the same, however.

Where you are in the ascendancy order to the throne is unclear both in this universe and in the other. Where you are in the overall plan is clearer, even though some of what you must do is still hidden in clouds. You and your sister are both intricate parts to the scheme of things. Was that a better answer?"

"Myrddin," he slowly began, "how can there be a throne that doesn't exist?"

"What a profound question. The throne you refer to is a magical throne and it has dominion over all that is magic. It even has dominion over the most powerful magic there is: love. You are the king in your universe, and Peter is the king in this universe. That does not make you better than any other, just different than most.

"What Lucifer wants is to control you and rule each universe through you in yours and through Peter in his. What you are inside is your greatest attribute and possibly your very salvation. It's in your blood, you know. It is your inheritance, or rather your lineage, for lack of better words. Your ancestors have given you what you need by the DNA that came down through the ages and runs through your bloodlines. Look in that scroll Brigid reads and there you will find your family tree, and there you will trace your family back to Uther Pendragon, or perhaps beyond."

Brigid, still reading the scroll, suddenly looked at Robin. "I found it," she said. "It's all here, near the end of the scroll. Joseph and Mary of Nazareth..."

"What?" Robin exclaimed. "No way!"

"See for yourself."

Robin quickly plopped down beside Brigid, and they both looked at the pages before them. Jesus was the son of Joseph and Mary, and Robin was astonished when the scroll followed the lineage through his daughters, but not the sons, for seven generations. Then it continued on as it followed the line through the sons until he came to the name Uther Pendragon of Avalon. He shivered and gave Myrddin a questioning glance.

"This is what you meant by my...DNA?" Robin asked.

"Yes," Myrddin replied, "it's in your blood."

"But the church says Jesus never married. He never had children. He rose from..."

"The church is well aware of this. It is kept secret in order to keep the masses in line. It would never do to have the masses lose their faith."

"Oh, yeah? Did you consider I might lose my faith?"

"In your ancestor or God?"

"But he was the son of..."

"And Jesus also said, 'Know ye not ye are the sons of God?' We are all God's children, Robin, but *you* are directly related to the bloodline of Jesus. That means you've inherited the same abilities Jesus had."

"But I can't do miracles."

"It's interesting— what Jesus did was called miraculous. When done by another, it's called magic. He also fought Lucifer and now, by the DNA passed on to you, you have the tools necessary to make that same fight."

"But he was crucified! Is that what's going to happen to me? And I really do need an answer, 'cause I think sometimes I might be going mad. I mean this whole business, it's all gone a bit round the bend, if you'll pardon my saying so."

"Not if I can help it. And not if you resist Lucifer's influence. Besides, you will have the help of Michael, the Archangel."

"Oh, great, I'll have the help of an angel that nobody has ever seen. My head's going to explode. What have you gotten me into?"

"Not just you," Brigid said. "Peter, as well. And you certainly don't want orcs in your universe."

"All right, what if I do unite the universes somehow, and the orcs cross over. Wouldn't that be bad for everyone? I mean, I can see most of the good reasons, but in my universe, there are no orcs that try to kill you or even eat you. What kind of evil will I release when it happens?"

"Evil, you say?" Myrddin asked, raising his eyebrows at Robin's question. "What about the evil in your universe?"

"But, I live with that evil all the time and I know how to deal with it. I'm asking about the orcs and other things."

"Very well, I will tell you what I know about orcs and the other things, as you put it. It all began many thousands of years ago," said Myrddin, "and here you must know that another wizard of old told this to me. And this ancient wizard repeated a legend handed down to him by another. It is difficult to tell, you see, what has come or gone or passed our way from what men say. But this is the story as it was told to me. Do you know what a centaur is?"

"Half man and half horse!" Brigid said.

"Legend tells us that Zeus, the father of the gods, was married to Hera," Myrddin continued. "She had children by human men. Zeus became jealous and cursed the offspring of her unholy unions and made them half man and half horse, calling them centaurs.

"Zeus and Hera were actually genetic engineers that lived on ancient Atlantis. Their knowledge of genetics was unprecedented and the humans of that time thought, however mistaken, that they were gods. Their creations were abominations in the sight of the Creator, and so Atlantis was destroyed. These creatures were magical, and those that survived the destruction of Atlantis exist in Peter and Brigid's universe to this day.

"The truth is the centaurs were made by mixing human and equine DNA in a bottle in order to make a docile slave, capable of performing hard labor and freeing the humans to pursue more civilized interests."

"They were slaves?" Robin asked.

"Yes, they were slaves."

"That's horrible. No one should be a slave!"

"Civilization, of course, is in the eye of the beholder. Now, look out this window and tell me what you see."

Robin and Brigid both looked out the bedroom window together. Little grotesque men were dancing around a campfire while some of them beat on drums. Round and round they danced until they all came to an abrupt halt just as the drums ceased. They all shouted and passed around tankards full of foaming froth as each drank his fill. Then the drums began again, and the grotesque little men began their frenzied dance once more.

"Are they drunk?" Robin asked.

"Hmmm, I'm afraid so," Myrddin said. "They celebrate your victory over the orcs. They do not often appear to us, but tonight, well, they're quite drunk. They're gnomes, and they guard all underground treasure. Excuse me for a moment." Myrddin leaned out the window. "Cob. Cob, a word, if you please?"

One of the gnomes vanished before Robin and Brigid's eyes. He reappeared beside them with a loud pop. Robin jumped, and Brigid let out a yell. The gnome gulped down the contents of a large tankard.

"Aym Emperor Cob!" the gnome said in a loud voice. "An' yer the king! Ye av the olly gral! Phat would ye do I wander, mak us slavs?"

"Er...I think you want to know if I would make you slaves," said Robin. "Slavery is wrong. If there are slaves when I'm king, I will free them all."

"Aercs ayr slavs! Would ye frey tham?"

"Orcs are slaves? Myrddin, I don't understand! If orcs are slaves, then who do they belong to?"

"They belong to Lucifer," Myrddin explained. "There are two things that gnomes hate: slavery and orcs. The gnomes have good reason for this, too. In Mu and Atlantis, the gnomes were slaves of the Nephilim. They were experimented with."

"Nephaylim mak mansters! Nephaylim use craestals and gnome blod and ayp blod and mak mansters! Aercs ayr mansters!"

"That's horrible!" Robin cried.

"It's an abomination," Myrddin said, "but the Nephilim called it *genetic engineering*. They taught the humans of that time to be genetic engineers as well. Genetic engineering produces monsters, and that is for sure, but the Nephilim knew one more secret that has yet to be rediscovered by mankind. They knew how to genetically engineer creatures that could reproduce."

"You talk like the Nephilim aren't human."

"They are an alien race from beyond our solar system. Their aim is to assimilate us by mixing their DNA with ours. The legend of Zeus and Hera is truer than you realize, for they were Nephilim. Nephilim DNA, mixed with ours, produces giants that are dark by nature, and the survivors of this mixing are in league with Lucifer."

"Are humans a genetic experiment? Am I..."

"Some human races are a result of their breeding with us, but you are related to a line of kings that was kept pure by the Creator to bring balance to all of creation. The orcs and many other magical creatures and some of the human races were experimented with and the results exist in Peter and Brigid's universe."

"But why in this universe and not mine?"

"I will answer that," said Kat-sidhe, "Many thousands of years ago, the continents of Atlantis and Mu sank beneath the sea in a great earthquake. War broke out, and Lucifer led the orcs against the magical kingdom. Most of the humans joined him and very few supported us. We were outnumbered a thousand to one. Many of us died, and we thought all was lost, but Mother Lilith persuaded the Creator to aid us with angelic hosts. That is when Lucifer divided the two universes.

"By dividing the universe in two, Lucifer spread the forces of good too thin to be totally defeated by them. The Creator wants the two universes merged in order to reconcile all differences between Himself and Lucifer."

"So you were all here and not in my universe when it happened?"

"No, we chose to be in this universe."

"But the orcs are here! Why would you go where your enemies are?"

"Because the humans in your universe stopped believing in us. It became against their religious beliefs. We held a conclave and unanimously decided it was better to go where we were believed in than to stay. Besides, orcs can reach adulthood in three years and reproduce like the vermin they are. If we had not chosen this universe, only the orcs would be here now."

"Aercs ware kilt bae faeries," Cob suddenly shouted. "We halpt tham! Aym sak!"

Cob crossed the room to the window, weaving and crashing into furniture and the occupants. There was a loud pop, and Robin saw him reappear by the campfire, bending over and emptying the contents of his stomach on the ground. The other gnomes paid him no attention and continued their frenzied celebration.

"Myrddin," Robin asked, "how did Cob know I was king? Why did he think I would make them slaves?"

"I think Cob was being suspicious of you. The magical creatures of this universe have their own prophecies concerning the king, and some believe the king will be a pawn of Lucifer. Also, since the magical creatures are fourth dimensional, they can travel between the two universes and remain unnoticed."

"So this is why I've never seen unicorns," Robin said. "This is why I've never seen elves or other magic creatures. But we know about them. Some of us believe. I believe."

"That is easy for you to say since you have seen what your world only thinks may exist. There is a matter more pressing, however. Kat-sidhe and I must find out why the orcs are suddenly so well organized. If it means what I think it does, then the one who controls them wants war. We will discuss plans next evening. So, if you are ready, Kat-sidhe, we will go and let these two sleep."

Myrddin and Kat-sidhe silently disappeared, and Brigid was soon asleep in the chair beside Robin's bed. Robin lay back against his pillow, wincing from the pain that still persisted in his bruised chest, and stared up at the ceiling. Too many thoughts danced in his head, crowding out any hope for peaceful sleep. His life had gone from tragic to decidedly insane.

When he finally fell asleep, he dreamed he saw Gwyneth flying overhead. Then she flew down to Dinas Bran. Robin tried to catch her and warn her about the orcs. She landed beneath the oak tree, and as Robin drew near, he heard his mother call him down for breakfast.

"Not just yet, Mum," he cried. "I have to warn Gwyneth about the orcs."

"Peter Robyn Gilman, get down here for breakfast or I shan't save you any at all! And see if you can wake your sister; she's not answering me."

His mother sounded really impatient this time, and Robin quickly sat up in bed, crying out in pain because of his injured ribs. Brigid was still asleep in the chair beside his bed.

"Wake up, Brigid. Mum just called us down for breakfast and she sounds a bit tense." Robin gingerly got out of bed as Brigid ran to her room.

Everyone packed for the second day in a row. Robin helped carry the heavier items down to the water's edge to a large staging area. From there, the gear would cross the Atlantic on a large transport.

The long task of packing for their move was finished by sunset, and Robin was exhausted. Robin fell asleep as soon as his head hit the pillow, but this time he didn't dream about flying. Instead, he dreamed of vast orc armies in mortal combat and people suffering from the horrors of war. He tried to wake up but continued to dream as if what unfolded before him had a hidden message.

The orcs advanced on Paris, setting fire to everything that had stood for centuries. They took no prisoners, and the light resistance was easily overrun. All the men, women, and children in their path died.

His dream took him to the Vatican in Rome, where the offices of the papacy burned and the orcs celebrated their easy victory in the streets. The pope shook hands with the orc general and laughed. Some of the troops engaged in an effort to bring down the walls of the buildings. Then he saw seven cardinals with their hands tied behind their backs and kneeling before a large orc wielding a broadax. "These are the unfaithful," cried a voice. He woke up, yelling when he saw the ax strike the first cardinal on the back of the neck.

"All right, Robin?" asked Peter, sitting in the chair beside his bed.

"Not really. What about you?" Robin replied.

"Well, I'm a little scared about the invasion, if that's what you mean."

"Could you see my dream, too, then?"

"Yeah, but I'm not sure how I got in the chair. Maybe it's because of the dream. Hey, you did okay at Dinas Bran—with the orcs and all, I mean."

"I'm not that good in my universe."

"No...no, you did brilliant! Too bad about that one arrow, though."

"You know, if Kat-sidhe hadn't been there, we would be dead now. She took care of more of them than I did and saved my life at least a couple of times in that fight. I was terrified."

"Ah, come on, there was nothing to be scared of. Besides, you know how to use that sword fairly well now, and you can take care of yourself in any situation I can think of."

"I think maybe you are a little overconfident. I also think you were scared I was going to muck it all up. Go on, then, admit it. You were just as scared as I was."

"Promise you won't tell anyone?" Peter sheepishly asked. "The truth is, I was scared because I wasn't the one in control. You were. Well, what I mean is, I would have rushed into the fight, but you held back, sizing up the attacking orcs. That was smarter, and it paid off. I'm sure that if you had rushed at them, they all would have attacked you at once, not two or three at a time. That's what gave you the advantage, and that's what gave Kat-sidhe enough time to deal with them before they could get to you or

Brigid. By the way, she always follows me wherever I go, so get used to it. It's a bit annoying, really."

"She's different from Gwyneth in my universe. They mostly look the same, but Gwyneth isn't so afraid of her shadow. But I like Brigid a lot, and I'm not trying to run her down or anything, it's just...well, she's the same and she's as different from Gwyneth, just as you and I are."

"She's used to depending on me," Peter said after careful consideration. "What I mean is, she thinks I have the inner strength she doesn't have and always looks to me for that strength. The truth is, she's just as strong, but she's never been forced to use her own inner strength. Maybe what she needs is some practice at it?"

"I don't know," Robin said. "Maybe you're right. But I'm not sure I could just sit by and see her get hurt if she failed to find her own inner strength in time. I mean, what if something went wrong? It seemed to me that at Dinas Bran she was trying to find that strength inside, and if I hadn't been there to protect her, who knows what would have happened?"

"You saved her life there, you know. You gave no thought for yourself and saved her, and that says a lot about you."

"Are you talking about the orcs, or Fred and Dewey?"

"Both, actually. Fred and Dewey would act violently toward her if they should ever catch her alone. That must never happen."

The sound they heard next silenced them both. They listened intently into the night and heard the sound a second time. It was laughter and two whispering voices coming from Brigid's room.

Robin quietly opened his bedroom door. With Peter behind him, like a shadow, he crossed the hallway and knocked softly on Brigid's door. He could hear his own heart hammering in his chest as he anxiously awaited a response.

The door swung open. Brigid sat on her bed, holding her knees close to her chest. Gwyneth sat on the foot of the bed, grinning at Robin. Unable to contain herself anymore, she knocked him over trying to hug him. Peter stared at her with his mouth open, and Brigid had to remind him to close his mouth since, she explained, it was impolite to stare at someone to begin with and even ruder if you did so with your mouth open.

"How did you get here?" Robin asked her.

"Just like you told me. I dreamed about flying," Gwyneth answered.

Chapter 9
CROSSING OVER

"You know, sis, I rather like you as a blonde," Peter said.

"Who's there?" Gwyneth cried out at the sound of Peter's disembodied voice.

"Shush," Robin quickly whispered. "Mum and Dad will hear. It's all right, Gwyn. It's just Peter. He's a bit hard to see, though, really."

"Oh, sorry," Peter said. "Is this better?" He moved out of the dark corner.

"Are you Robin's double, then?" she asked. She reached out to touch him. His image shimmered and blew away like smoke in the wind. When she withdrew her hand, the wisps collected back together, and Peter's image reemerged in the shadows.

"This is spooky," Brigid said. "Myrddin said you'd be hard to see, but I never imagined..."

"I don't know," Peter grinned, "I think it's rather cool, actually. You'd be surprised what you can do and see when you're invisible."

"Peter Robyn," Brigid scolded, "you're not supposed to take advantage of this like that!"

"And you're surprised that he did?" a new voice said. All four yelled before they realized it was Myrddin who had quietly entered the room.

"She's right, you know," Myrddin said. "This is meant to be a learning experience so you and Robin will know what to expect when you merge permanently. It is not for spying on the neighbor's daughter."

"Hey," Peter said, "how did you know?"

"Your body is ethereal at this time, Peter. You are invisible to those who don't know you but easily detected by those to whom you are close. That is all right with you, isn't it?"

"Oh, yeah, right. It's just brilliant!"

"Good! Now I must tell you what is to happen next. Robin must go back to his universe tomorrow. You, of course, will go back with him, Gwyneth."

"Go? What do you mean? It's too soon!" Robin's stomach knotted up.

"Surgery was performed and, thanks to some very powerful angels that watch over you, the surgeon made no errors. This means you will wake from the anesthesia by tomorrow. The choice is ultimately yours, of course. It's my opinion that you should return. But I perceive that you wish to ask a question. So, please, ask now, for the time grows short and you must make the choice."

"Look," Robin began, "it's not that I won't choose to go back, because I do know that is what I will do. It's just, well, I've only been here a short while and I've grown fond of everyone. I want more time." Myrddin reached out and put his hand on Robin's shoulder.

"Your mother will always be with you wherever you go. Eventually these two universes will merge and you will be physically with her once more. This is the temptation to stay here that has worried me the most. You will have to let her go, and in time you will be glad you did. I know it is hard, and I am so sorry that you must make this choice; nevertheless, it is your choice to make."

"All right, then, I will go back," Robin said, fighting back tears. "But I was wondering if I could at least see my mum one more time before I go?"

"Yes, there is time for that, and even if there wasn't, I would make the time. Your mother must not see Gwyneth, however. She will not understand. So you must stay out of sight until then, dear girl. You do understand, of course?"

"I...I...er...yes," Gwyneth managed to stammer. "But I don't understand. Why is Robin here? Will he be all right when he returns? He's been horribly hurt and...oh, Robin, I didn't know your mum was here! It's so cruel!" Gwyneth frowned and then asked, "Does that mean my stepparents have parallel lives, too? Are they next door?"

"Ah, yes, right then, it's this way, you see. Your mother and father do not have parallel lives in this universe. They rather thought they would be having enough to be getting on with raising you and helping Robin when first they agreed to be your parents."

"But what will become of them when the merging happens?"

"Good question, that," Robin murmured.

"Unfortunately, I've never experienced a merging before and, therefore, can't tell you for certain. I do know that the merging will do them no harm."

"So," Gwyneth said, "they'll survive it?"

"I don't see why they wouldn't. Now, as to Robin's injury. He may have residual headaches for a time and trouble remembering certain events, but his headaches will go away and he will remember most clearly those events that had previously escaped him.

"I must leave, but I will return on the morrow. Both you and Robin must be ready to go then. You should discuss amongst yourselves what each of you knows so it is clear what events have taken place. All the knowledge you discuss will be shared by all of you in each of your own worlds, and each of you will play a major role in what is to take place in the near future. Now I must go; Kat-sidhe awaits."

One moment Myrddin was before them, and the next he was simply gone. They began whispering excitedly about their individual adventures, all about the orcs and how Robin had kept Fred and Dewey at bay. They told Gwyneth about the earth changes, the Holy Grail, and the scroll that contained the list of the royal generations, proving a succession to a throne that didn't exist.

Then it was Gwyneth's turn to fill the others in on what had been happening in Robin's universe. She explained how Fred and Dewey had ambushed them and the horrible accident that had nearly cost Robin his life. Then she told them the most wonderful story about her arrival into their universe.

When Gwyneth arrived, there were so many fairies, she could scarcely see the grounds of Dinas Bran. They flew all around her, calling her name out as if they had known it forever. Kat-sidhe was there and helped her land gently beneath the giant oak. Then she was taken to Yggdrasil, and beneath the giant ash, Mother Lilith spoke to her. Gwyneth described how beautiful she was, trembling as she spoke, with the memory of the meeting still fresh in her mind.

"Mother Lilith told me what Robin and I must be about in our universe," she stated. The others leaned forward, hoping to elicit an explanation from her, but Gwyneth was suddenly lost in deep thought.

"Go on, then," Robin blurted out after a long pause. "You just can't keep us hanging, you know. What did she say? Does it have anything to do with the Holy Grail?"

"What...what did you say?" Gwyneth said.

"I said, does it have anything to do with the Holy Grail? But if it's difficult, you can take your time. I mean, if you would rather..."

"No, it's not that it's difficult, it's just, I'm not to say until you actually return to our universe."

For a moment, Robin paused while he tried to formulate the words he needed. "Doesn't Mother Lilith trust me to do the right thing? Or is it because you can't say in front of Peter and Brigid?" He looked up at Gwyneth and peered into her blue eyes, looking for an answer they could all understand.

"Hang on! You mean to say, we don't get to know?" Peter sprang up from where he sat on the floor, and the expression on his face betrayed his fury. "That's just not right! We've got just as much right to know what you lot are doing as you have to know what we are about!"

"Shut it, will you?" Robin chided. "Mum and Dad will hear us. Besides, I think this is pretty serious, what she knows, and if she was told not to say, then maybe we better not pry."

"Oh, I see. So you'll get to know when you get back, and Brigid and I will just have to hope you're doing the proper thing? I'm not sure I like the idea of trusting you when I don't even know what it is you're up to!"

"You don't trust me? Now look! I handled Fred and Dewey and saved Brigid's life! You even said I did all right a bit ago! Just exactly what is it you want from me?" Gwyneth and Brigid grew alarmed at Robin's anger and loud voice.

Peter's jaw jutted out and he glared at Robin. "You shouldn't have taken two blows to kill that orc, you know, when one should have finished him."

"You killed an orc?" Gwyneth asked. "To save Brigid's life?"

"Well, yeah I did," Robin shrugged. "I guess I must have left that part out when I told you about them. Of course, some people don't think my efforts were good enough." He glared at Peter, who stood with clenched, fists glaring back.

"You know, maybe you two should go back to your universe and just not come back!" Peter cried. "And don't bother to say good-bye on your way out, either, 'cause I don't really care anymore what you do!"

"That's awful two-faced of you!"

"You know," Brigid began, "this has got to be the weirdest scene I have ever seen. I've heard it's all right to talk to yourself, but it's a sign of insanity when you answer your own questions and argue with yourself out loud." Gwyneth silently nodded in agreement.

Both boys glared at each other. Robin secretly wondered why they had argued at all. What would happen if they disagreed when it came time to merge permanently? What would happen if Peter wanted to do something Robin didn't?

"Look," Peter said with a sudden tone of regret, "I'm sorry. I just don't want anything happening to Brigid."

"Peter, do you think we'll still be aware of each other when I leave?" Robin asked.

"What do you mean by that? I'll know you are there, and you'll know I'm here, but I don't see...hang on! You want to know if you'll still be able to handle a weapon like at Dinas Bran? And maybe I'll learn to not be such a stuffed shirt and become more cautious. You think?"

"Yeah, maybe we are going to have enough of each other inside of us so Gwyneth won't have to tell you anything at all about what we are supposed to do for you to know what we will be doing. You'll just know."

"There is something else Mother Lilith told me," Gwyneth said.

"*What?*" the others said all at the same time.

"She said we all have to learn magic."

"But I thought Peter and Brigid already knew magic," Robin pondered.

"I wish we did," Brigid said. "The truth is, though we believe it's possible, we've never allowed for it in our own lives because there is so much of it all around. I guess we're a bit lazy, actually."

"That is just too weird," Robin said. "So much magic and so much to learn and you've never bothered. What I wouldn't give to be here and learn. And your...our dad...what I wouldn't give to have him in my universe. You guys are really lucky."

"What's Dad like in your universe?" Peter ventured.

"He hits me."

Chapter 10
GOOD-BYES

"Peter," Cerridwen called, "out of bed now!" Then she muttered to her husband, "How can your son have so much energy all day long and then not have enough to get up when he is called?"

"He's your son, too, dear," William answered. "Besides, we had an awful lot to do yesterday, and I don't much feel like it myself."

"Maybe you can wake him."

"Peter Robyn, time to go, son. Your mum's got to leave, and I need your help carrying her bags!"

William opened his door, and light invaded Robin's dreams. He opened the drapes and reached down to mess Robin's hair up. It didn't much matter, though, since his hair was sticking out in all directions after his restless night.

"What time is it?" Robin asked in a voice drowsy and thick with sleep.

"It's five thirty and time to help. I'll get us breakfast later, but for now we have to get your mum down to the ferry right away."

Robin filled with sudden dread. "Mum's leaving? Now? Why?" Robin sprang out of bed and was about to bolt for the door when his dad caught him.

"Whoa, whoa, son, what's the matter? She's just going on ahead to Paris to get us a flight out of Orly and then we'll meet up with her there and fly back to Seattle together. It's only for just a few days."

"But I thought we had more time."

"Paris is safe for now, but we have to make our move before the orcs take over. Hey, come on, Peter, it's not as if it's the end of the world." Despite the reassurance, Robin couldn't help thinking that it was the end of his world. He was losing his mother again.

Telling his father that he would leave soon for another universe where his mother was dead was totally out of the question. He pulled away and looked into the eyes of a man who truly loved him and treated him the way he wanted to treat his own children when the time came. In this universe his father was gentle and kind, yet handled him with a firm, caring hand that guided him without forcing him.

"Where are the bags, then?" Robin managed.

"In our room, and, Peter, it will be all right. She's going to be fine, and there'll be plenty of time. You'll see."

"No, there won't!" Robin made a hasty exit and ran to his parents' bedroom.

Robin knocked on his parents' door and, not hearing a response, he opened it. The suitcases were too heavy to carry both at the same time, so he picked up the nearest one, not seeing his mother enter the room.

"There you are, sleepy head," she chided. "Why didn't you wake when I called you?"

Startled, he dropped the suitcase. It burst open, spilling its contents on the floor.

"Ah, no!"

"Peter Robyn Gilman!" Cerridwen said in exasperation. "Just take the other and come back for this one! I really don't have time for this!"

"I'm sorry, Mum! I didn't mean to!"

"Just get the other bag downstairs then, will you?" Her sharpness cut Robin like a knife.

Robin knew he was close to losing control. He picked up the other suitcase, avoiding his mother's glare so his blurry eyes would not betray him. A voice in his head interrupted his misery.

Tell her you love her. Just tell her. Tell her. Tell her you love her now. Over and over again the voice repeated the same words until he thought his head would break open.

"Mum?" he called just before he walked out the door.

"What?" Cerridwen replied in a brusque tone. She didn't bother to look up, concentrating on repacking the clothes that had fallen on the floor.

"I love you!" Robin blurted out. "I'm going to miss you!" He bolted for the hallway and down the stairs, lugging the suitcase and trying to get away somewhere, anywhere, to be alone if only for a few minutes.

His mother called him back, but Robin knew he couldn't possibly explain himself. The voice in his head spoke to him again. *I didn't know it hurt this much. Is this really what it feels like? I hate it, I really, really hate it, and it's not fair that she's gone in your universe.*

Is that you, Peter?

Yes. How can you stand it? This really hurts.

I know. But in my universe, it can't be undone, and now it's like losing her all over again.

Maybe when the two worlds merge, it will be undone.

Even though his heart ached beyond anything he had ever experienced, it seemed as if a light had suddenly illuminated all of the dark corners of his life. "That's it!" he cried aloud. "Peter, you're brilliant! That's it exactly! It's got to be the reason for all of this! I just know it is!"

You're mad, you're starkers, you're a loon! Keep it down or the whole house will hear you. Peter was almost visible to him now, even in the morning sunlight.

"Yeah, okay, but don't you get it? If we are the same person, we'll merge completely when the worlds merge. And my mum, your mum, will be with me, with both of us again!"

"Peter, what's taking you so long?" his mother called. "Quit talking to your sister and come up the...OH!"

Robin hastily wiped his eyes on his sleeves and ran back upstairs. Brigid was on the landing with a look of amusement on her face while their mother leaned against the railing.

"Who were you talking to downstairs?" Cerridwen managed to gasp as she tried to catch her breath.

"No one, Mum," Robin said in his best innocent voice.

"You two are impossible!" she declared as she gathered them both together in her arms, holding them close to her heart. "Impossible not to love," she whispered to them.

Robin desperately clung to her. This was a moment that mustn't end, he thought. His heart felt as if it would burst from all the longing he had inside. His mother released him, but he held her tight, refusing to let go. He hoped his eyes would have enough time to dry if he could only hold her for a few seconds more.

"Peter, are you all right?" she softly asked him.

"No, Mum, no...not until I see you again."

"Hey! No hugs for your dad, then? Well that's just perfect, isn't it?" his dad said with a twinkle in his eye. "Come on, then, it's time to go."

Cerridwen was on the ferry too soon for Robin's liking. He watched it sail away, and the smaller the ferry became, the larger the hole in his heart became, but it was hope that kept him from losing what self-control he had left. *After this*, he thought, *everything else is going to be easy.*

On the way back, his father explained that a cargo ship would take their larger belongings back to Seattle. They would join their mother in Paris in one week, since London's Heathrow Airport was under water. They would fly back home out of Orly.

"Should we fix breakfast for you, Dad?" Brigid suddenly interrupted.

"Well, actually, that would be rather nice," William Gilman said, delighted with the idea.

Robin knew, however, that she meant to prepare enough for four. When they returned, he helped his sister while trying not to think about his mother and how much he missed her. Robin took breakfast up to Gwyneth before their father could see.

He knocked softly on the door, and Gwyneth cautiously opened it up to let him in just as his father went down for his breakfast. Once they were sure he was downstairs, they risked whispering to each other, and Robin filled her in on how it had all unfolded, including his conversation with Peter.

"You know, Robin," Gwyneth thoughtfully said, "it sounds as if you and Peter are sharing each other's experiences. Just like me and Brigid here in this universe. You did figure that out, didn't you?"

"Er...well, yeah, I did," Robin replied. "But I was wondering why we are not in the same family in our universe. We are brother and sister here, and I rather like that, but not there."

"It explains why we get along so well, knowing we are related this way. I'm not sure it's necessary to be actual brother and sister to care for each other the way we do."

Feeling uncomfortable, Robin pondered what she had just said and decided to keep his thoughts to himself and change the subject. "What do you suppose is happening to Fred and Dewey now?"

"I should tell you what the police asked Fred and Dewey. It was rather curious, 'cause they wanted to know if they had acted on their own or if someone had put them up to ambushing us."

"That's ridiculous. Why would anyone hire those two dopes to rough us up for in the first place, especially considering they seem to enjoy doing it for free?"

"That's just it, Robin. That's what makes the question so odd. Why would the police think something like that, and why would they even suspect that someone was so interested in you and me that they would go to such lengths to get at us?"

"I don't know, but it makes you think, doesn't it?"

"Dad's in his chair, asleep," Brigid announced as she entered the room.

They heard a loud popping noise, and Myrddin and Kat-sidhe appeared in the room, surrounded by more fairies than they could count.

"It is time," Myrddin somberly stated. "Your father has been made to sleep until we return, and will not awaken before then. Don't forget the Holy Grail and the scroll, Robin."

Robin retrieved it from under the bed where he had hidden it for safekeeping. He wrapped it carefully in his tunic. Without a word, the fairies surrounded the children, and they were soon all flying. Robin didn't want it to end, but all too soon, they saw Yggdrasil. Mother Lilith appeared in a mist and spoke to Robin.

"Have you chosen to return to your universe, my son?" she asked.

Robin nodded his head rather than trust his voice. He glanced over at Brigid and Gwyneth to see them wiping the mist from their eyes, which persisted despite their best efforts to keep it away.

"And did you make this decision of your own free will?"

"It's my decision," he managed to say.

"Then it is time for you and Peter to divide and return to your own vessels once more. Are you ready now or shall I allow time to say your good-byes?"

"Er, time would be good, if it's allowed." Mother Lilith smiled and drew back. Robin turned around and walked over to Brigid and embraced her. Then he turned back to Mother Lilith and asked, "Will I see Brigid and my mother again when the two universes merge?"

"Yes."

"But what about Brigid, and Gwyneth in my universe? In my universe I don't have a sister. How can something like that be explained?" Then he softly expressed an even more distressing thought. "How can I explain my mother if she is dead in my universe. I mean, won't people ask questions?"

"I tell you that the problem of Gwyneth being your sister is being solved at this very moment. As to your mother, is it not enough to know she will be physically with you once more at the merging? I cannot explain any further, but Gwyneth will explain your destiny once you have returned. And, Robin, it is not so much an obligation but rather a destiny that you must fulfill. Nevertheless, you do have free choice in all matters of importance. It is time, so say your good-byes now and remember that you will all soon be together again."

Then Myrddin approached, his cowl still drawn over his head. He asked Robin to stand beneath the giant mountain ash, Yggdrasil. Myrddin conjured the dragon's breath using the chant as he did before. It felt to Robin as if a cord attached to his heart pulled him gently and firmly forward.

Robin looked at Peter lying beneath Yggdrasil, his eyes closed in apparent peaceful sleep. Peter opened his eyes, gasped for breath, and sat up. Myrddin immediately helped him stand. Robin could see a silver cord attached to Peter where his heart would be and saw the same cord attached to his own heart. The cord disappeared, but the sensation of being attached to each other remained.

"All right, Peter?" Robin asked.

"All right," Peter sputtered. "And you?"

"I think so. Thanks for everything."

"I'll give Mum a hug for you when I see her next. And you know, maybe I should be the one thanking you. I never would have known how much Mum meant to me if I hadn't felt how it would be to lose her."

Robin and Gwyneth began to float in the air. They could see Peter and Brigid standing beside Myrddin and Mother Lilith, holding each other as they rose slowly upward.

"I have unpleasant news to tell you," Kat-sidhe said with an apologetic tone. "There is the possibility that a tear in the fabric of the two universes has occurred and magical creatures can cross over without restriction, including those with evil intent. This tear will increase in size over time, but it is not known how rapidly this will happen. You both must be vigilant. The good is that I will be able to cross over more easily as well, and will continually be on guard."

Robin and Gwyneth nodded to indicate they heard and understood rather than speak the fear they both felt. This meant things had become more dangerous. As they flew, Robin pondered all that had happened, trying to make sense of it.

Soon they were flying among the crows that circled above Castell Dinas Bran, where it was still surrounded by the Irish Sea. Powys Fadog flew in front of them, rasping out their names as if to say good-bye to them.

And then the scene changed, and Dinas Bran was no longer an island surrounded by a great flood, and Robin knew they had entered his universe. He was both melancholy and elated. But more than this, he was apprehensive since with every passing moment he was drawing nearer his own wonderful and terrifying destiny. It was a destiny that Gwyneth would help him find.

Chapter 11
PRINCES DU SANG

The frosty morning invaded the hotel room through the open window, stealing the warmth from its exhausted occupants. Gwyneth sat in her bed, rubbing the sleep out of her eyes, and wondered if everything she had dreamed were true. She got up and shut the window. She saw her face in the window's reflection. It was covered with glittering fairy dust, and as she looked, the sound of giggling startled her.

"Who's there?" she cried out.

Silence was her only answer. Her parents stirred in their beds.

"Mum, Dad," she called out, "come on. We've got to go see if Robin's awake, right away. Please?"

"Give us a moment, dear, and get under the covers. It's frightfully cold, and your feet are bare," Darla scolded.

Tom's mobile rang, and he answered it with a groan as Gwyneth slid beneath the down comforter.

"That was Robin's grandmother," he announced. "She arrives at Cardiff International tomorrow morning."

"How is that possible?" Darla asked.

"She apparently got word somehow and, by unhappy coincidence, she had a trip planned anyway. She also informs me that she is upset about the way things were handled. She seems to be a bit of…let's see, how do I put it? A bit of a battleaxe. We should get a move on if we're going to see Robin."

"Right then," Darla replied.

When they arrived, they were surprised by the buzz of activity in the hospital. The news reporters being filmed by their camera crews spoke excitedly about the miracle boy of royal descent who survived a near fatal accident. Gwyneth could scarcely believe what she heard, thinking they surely mustn't be talking about Robin.

Gwyneth held her mother's hand but released it suddenly when they were near Robin's room and ran the rest of the way. She stopped when she entered the room. Doctors and nurses surrounded his bed, speaking in excited tones. The room went silent when the others heard Gwyneth gasp, and they all turned to stare at her, making her most uncomfortable.

"Hi, Gwyneth!" Robin beamed. "Have you had breakfast, then? It's not very good here, but you're welcome if you're hungry."

She threw her arms around him, burying her face as she sobbed uncontrollably. Darla and Tom entered just in time to witness the event and held back to give them a moment.

"Hey, I didn't mean it was that bad," Robin said with an impish grin. "No need to lose control over a bad breakfast."

Although his head was bandaged, Gwyneth could still see that it had been shaved. His eyes had dark circles under them, betraying that the ordeal had taken away most of his usual energy. Tom and Darla spoke with the surgeon while several interns stood off to the side, discussing his medical condition in mumbled undertones.

"When did you wake up?" Gwyneth eagerly asked.

"Early this morning. I've still got a bit of a headache, but the doctor seems to think that will go away with time. Oh yeah, I almost forgot! Somehow my inner ear is affected and I'm kind of wobbly when I try to walk—dizziness, you know. It's a bit like being carsick, really, but no car."

"Well, that can't be good, can it? Will it get better?"

"Oh, yeah, but it won't be right away," Robin said. "What are we supposed to do about the Grail, anyway? I'm dying to know!"

"Don't say that!" Gwyneth's misty eyes returned for a moment. Then Gwyneth became still, looked at her hands in her lap, and wrestled with how she would tell Robin the information that Mother Lilith had entrusted her with.

"I've got to tell you something," she whispered. "It's dead serious, too. Do you remember the scroll that was with the Holy Grail? Well it's proof of my lineage, too."

"Your lineage?"

"Yes, but there's something else..."

"Hang on a minute. What about my dad?" Robin immediately realized Gwyneth thought he was talking to her. He didn't feel like explaining he had just overheard Tom and Darla talking about his father.

"What, you heard us?" Tom asked.

"Yes, sir, 'fraid so."

"This might not be the best time," Darla kindly began, "but...we've some rather bad news, Robin. Your father is...." Her voice caught in her throat.

"Dad's all right, isn't he?"

"I'm sorry, Robin. The police are looking into it, but your father...he..."

"He's dead, isn't he?" Robin knew before anyone could reply.

None of this was right, Robin thought. Darla moved near him and gathered him in her arms to hold him against the storm that raged in his heart. But Robin felt anger mixed with his unexpressed grief for his mother and pulled away. Everything had become so confusing.

Again Darla pulled him close, and this time he gave in as he sobbed uncontrollably.

"What's all this!" one of the doctors said.

"The boy's father is dead, and we've only just told him," Tom stated.

The doctor took Tom by the arm and steered him into the hallway for a private word. Darla continued to hold Robin and noticed Gwyneth was crying, too. Darla reached out and gathered her in her arms, as well.

"What is it, doctor?" Tom asked, out in the hall.

"This isn't good for the lad. I know he had to be told, but I would have wished it later than sooner. Are you close to him and his family?"

"Closer than anyone else in Wales, I suppose. Why do you ask?"

"Your wife seems to know what he needs just now. He needs a family around him, you see."

"Oh, well, I suppose we are here by providence then. We do plan on remaining until his grandmother arrives. That's the least we can do."

"Thank you for that. I'd like him to get some rest now, however. You can return tomorrow if you like. I'll see to it that you are allowed family visits with him."

"Thank you, doctor. I'll try and get my wife and daughter out as quickly as possible. Perhaps you know of a back door we could use, to avoid the press."

"You're right to avoid that lot. Did you know his grandmother and his father were royals? Some obscure line of kings is what I heard. It's why the press is so interested in him."

"Royals, you say," Tom said. "That explains the circus. They'll be after us next if they find out we've been to visit Robin."

"Tell you what, I'll send a nurse around with something to help the boy sleep. It's what he needs most now. Then we'll help you slip out the back."

⌘ ⌘ ⌘

The next morning was filled with tension. Robin was anxious at the prospect of seeing his grandmother. He thought it was odd that his grandmother should be so commanding yet he had never seen the same in his father. His father could be a tyrant, but Robin had often seen his mother defy him. No one dared to defy grandmother, however. It was as if she were the queen and the world her kingdom.

Robin knew she missed nothing and forgot nothing and often kept him from getting away with things that other boys would. She wore reading glasses that made her dark eyes shine. It was her presence that was most amazing, despite her being no more than five feet tall. She would always smile when she entered a room, and the occupants would hush and turn to look at her as if she had been announced. She was gracefully beautiful and silently terrible all at the same time.

Robin heard the cane she used for walking before he saw her. She smiled as she entered the room until she saw the desired effect. The surgeon took no notice of her as Tom and Darla listened to him explain Robin's condition and prognosis. Now she used the cane as a device to gain the surgeon's attention.

"Madam, please refrain from using that cane as a weapon. Can't you see I am talking to his guardians?" the surgeon cried.

"You most certainly are not, young man. I am Morgana Victoria Gilman, the boy's grandmother and only legal guardian. I demand he come home at once!"

The smile she used when she entered the room was gone now, and her face was set like some massive bulldog about to seize its prey. Robin thought he could see her jowls quiver with anticipation. One thing was for certain: as long as he wasn't the target, it was great entertainment to watch his grandmother in action.

"Madam, I must protest. I will certainly answer any questions you have if you are indeed the boy's grandmother, but not unless you stop poking that cane at me!"

"Tea, fetch it now. I have business to discuss with these people." She stared at Tom and Darla and cocked her head slightly like a raptor eyeing its next meal.

The surgeon, muttering under his breath, stomped out of the room and could be heard explaining why Food Services should send up tea immediately. Tom and Darla, cautious in their demeanor, silently placed three chairs in a small circle.

"It seems my grandson has not fared too well under your care," she said as she looked over her reading glasses and regarded them with a calculating smile.

"First of all, let me correct the misconception that Robin has been or ever was in our care," Tom calmly replied. "It was our daughter who told us he was injured, and we did what was best in our opinion. Not even the wisest among us here could have foreseen Saturday's unfortunate incident. Besides, he is alive and well fed by the looks of what's left of his breakfast. I would have thought one would have been more grateful." Darla's effort to kick her husband was utterly in vain.

"Forgive my intrusion, my lady, but perhaps I should have a physician examine the boy and then we can determine how well he has been cared for."

The man who spoke had entered the room unnoticed until his ancient, rasping voice chilled them, though it was barely above a whisper.

He walked out of the shadow and revealed himself to be an impeccable dresser. Despite his sycophantic bearing, there was the unmistakable hint of power behind his words. He was a tall man with a tanned complexion and was clean shaven, including his head. His smile made Robin uncomfortable.

"That is an excellent idea, Lleus. I would be forever in your debt if you were to see to it right away."

"Excuse me a minute," Tom interrupted, "but I don't believe we've been introduced. I am Tom Reynolds, and this is my wife, Darla. My daughter Gwyneth is over there by young Robin." Tom extended his hand.

"Lleus DeVyla Zeifer at your service. I am in the employ of the Lady Morgana Gilman. Now perhaps you should tell me what vested interest you have in her grandson?" Lleus did not offer a hand in return.

"Well, my wife and I," Tom began, somewhat taken aback, "are his neighbors. We have been acting on young Robin's behalf until his disposition is settled."

"Consider it settled, then. We leave as soon as he is medically fit to travel."

"Hang on," Tom bristled. "You just can't come in here and..."

"But we have, and I'm afraid your protests are for naught. Now if you will excuse me, I must see to retaining a doctor that is knowledgeable enough to ensure that young master Robin will be fit to travel."

Lleus Zeifer was out of the room before anyone could stop him. It was almost as if a spell had been put on everyone in the room, fogging their minds and befuddling their speech.

"Grandma, you're taking me back? Why? Can't I at least stay for the Eisteddfod Festival?" Robin could feel panic creep in, and he desperately wanted it to go away. Once more, his life had suddenly gone completely out of control.

"The Eisteddfod is months away, and we must get you back in time to finish the school year out at Overlook School."

"But, Grandma, what if I don't want to go?"

"That is enough, Robin. I know what is best for you, and my decision is final. You'll understand more when you're older."

"Yes, ma'am," Robin mumbled.

The last thing Robin wanted to hear was that he should wait until he was older. But arguing with his grandmother had never turned out in his favor. He knew he had to appear to submit to the idea. Secretly, however, he was making plans to run away. He knew he had to stay near Gwyneth if he was ever going to figure out the secret of the Holy Grail and the ancient scroll, and leaving now could be an insurmountable disadvantage.

Morgana scowled at the nearest nurse and crossly asked the unfortunate woman, "Where is my tea?"

"I will see to it straight away, madam." She hastily walked out of the door and nearly ran into Lleus and one of the resident doctors, who was carrying a tray with a silver tea service and several cups of the finest china available on such short notice.

"Dr. Dahliwal, whom I have engaged to be the personal physician to the Gilmans, will pour tea," Lleus announced.

Lleus stood beside the door, watching the nurse retreat to her work station, his nostrils flaring and his feral eyes seeking out her every move. Dr. Dahliwal set the tray down and proceeded to ceremonially pour tea, serving Morgana Gilman first. He stood by the tea service, unmoving. The aroma from the silver tea pot warmed the room as Morgana took a sip. She smiled and looked up at the others.

"You may all join me if you like, and I'm sure the good doctor won't mind pouring for you."

Lleus bent down to whisper in Morgana's ear. She smiled at his words, and Robin wondered what this man was up to. He didn't know why, but he was both curious about Lleus and repelled by his presence. Lleus looked at Robin for a brief moment, but during that moment, Robin saw his head become like a dragon's, and his eyes turned blood red. Then the vision, as brief as the glance that Lleus had given him, was gone. Robin trembled.

"Dr. Dahliwal," Morgana began, "when you are finished with that, would you be so kind as to examine my grandson and tell me if he will be fit for travel by tomorrow?"

"Oh yes," Dr. Dahliwal replied. "It will be most pleasing to do so, my lady."

He poured the last cup of tea, emptying the pot. The others, seemingly in a trance, walked over to the tea service and helped themselves. Darla brought over two cups of tea for Robin and Gwyneth, who exchanged alarmed glances at each other. Robin and Gwyneth were not affected in the same manner as the others. There was no fog in their minds, and they knew they were resisting a most unfriendly enchantment.

Robin felt as if a numbingly chilly wind waited outside his mind, looking for a way to enter. Robin and Gwyneth discovered they knew each other's thoughts without speaking.

Robin looked at Gwyneth with a meaningful glance and thought, *So, it's true, is it? You can read my thoughts and I can read yours, just like a real conversation?* At first, there was only silence. Just as he gave up on the idea, he heard Gwyneth's thoughts in his head as if she had spoken the words aloud.

Yes, it is true! But I think it's rather scary. I don't want you to read all of my thoughts, you know. I mean, there are some things that should remain private, don't you think?

Wow, this is so cool! Yeah, you're right, some thoughts should be private. But I don't think we can read that deep into each other's minds. I think this is just for having a private conversation between ourselves. They both grinned at each other.

You don't suppose someone else could hear our thinking conversation, do you? A worried look came over Gwyneth's countenance.

I...I don't know. I hadn't considered that. I tell you what, though. If anyone here could do that, it would have to be that Lleus character. I don't trust him.

That's me, too, Gwyneth thought. *Oh, oh, here comes the slimy Dr. Dahliwal!*

Robin spluttered his tea at her description of the doctor and began coughing and laughing at the same time while the tea came back out his nose. He looked up at Gwyneth and saw that he had sprayed her.

"Sorry, I couldn't help it. It went down the wrong way, you know."

"Please, young lady, if you would be allowing us a moment of privacy?" the doctor said in a monotone as he drew the curtains around Robin's bed.

Gwyneth silently got up and took a chair beside Darla. She wondered if she could contact Robin telepathically from across the room. She concentrated on a question that had formed in her mind.

Did you hide the Holy Grail somewhere special, then? she thought.

Ow! That hurt! Yeah, under the mattress. But not now, Gwyneth, I'm right in the middle of the evil alien doctor's probe. Robin cried out in pain next, but swore under his breath at the doctor's rough handling.

I heard that, Gwyneth thought. *What's he doing, anyway?*

He's unwrapping my...OW!...bandage to look at the...OW!...incisions... "OW!" Robin swore again, only this time out loud.

"Dr. Dahliwal! What are you doing with my patient! You have no right to examine him without my say so!" The surgeon had returned, having been tipped off by the nurse who had earlier escaped the room.

"It is quite all right, sir. He is doing just fine, and I am only trying to reassure the boy's grandmother by her request." Dr. Dahliwal finished his examination and busily rewrapped Robin's head.

The furious surgeon jerked back the curtain and shook in anger with his subordinate, and Dr. Dahliwal blankly considered his superior as if in a stupor.

"And tell me, good Dr. Dahliwal, what are your findings?" the surgeon said through gritted teeth barely above a whisper.

Lleus grabbed the surgeon by the elbow and pulled him away. "Perhaps you need the situation explained to you so that you may better understand your position. I will be most happy to oblige in that regard."

"But he is my patient and Dr. Dahliwal's expertise is not in the same area as mine," the surgeon protested. "But I suppose it couldn't hurt to hear you out." The surgeon's attitude changed abruptly as Lleus waved his hand before his eyes as if he was drawing a curtain across a window.

"Your services have been most welcome but they are no longer necessary," Lleus explained with a smile. "Your surgery was completed satisfactorily enough, and I have retained Dr. Dahliwal as the Lady Morgana Gilman's personal physician. Dr. Dahliwal, therefore, is no longer an employee at this facility and, as a result, will answer only to myself or the Lady Gilman, through me."

"I will leave you to your privacy then," the surgeon said.

He walked out of the room without any further protest. Darla, startled by the ease at which Lleus had persuaded the surgeon to relinquish his charge, fought off the effects of her clouded mind.

"Please don't expect me to sit idly by and do nothing, Mr. Zeifer," Darla said. "Robin has been through a most horrendous ordeal, and to make him travel as soon as you propose would be most unconscionable. What do a few more days matter to you, anyway, I should like to know?"

"Mrs Reynolds," Morgana Gilman interrupted, "there is more at stake here than you realize. I would explain, but it concerns a private family matter and it is my wish that it remain as such."

"Certainly you at least plan on a funeral service before you leave?" Tom asked as he too suddenly came to his senses.

"But, of course, we arranged for the funeral, Mr. Reynolds," Lleus said. "He is to be interred next to the boy's mother here in Wales on the morrow. That is if Dr. Dahliwal thinks the boy will be ready to attend by then." Robin thought he could almost see dust that was as old as the universe itself coming out of his mouth as he spoke.

"Oh, yes, my Lord, he is healthy enough, but if I might suggest that I travel with him just in the event he is having a relapse?"

"Be ready to travel when next the sun rises, then, doctor, and I will be sure to compensate you for your trouble. Now, at this time, the Lady Morgana wishes a private conversation with her grandson. If you would all be so kind as to exit this way, please." Lleus indicated the door and, one by one, the others walked into the hall.

Robin was nervous but determined to face this man who had insinuated himself into his grandmother's life. Whatever else she was, she was still his grandmother, and it seemed to him that this man was taking advantage of her. He looked into the strange man's eyes and thought they looked more reptilian than human; he even blinked lazily like a gecko would while sunning itself in the hot afternoon sun. His tongue flicked out to moisten his lips, and for a moment, his eyes turned blood red and then returned to their original black color. Robin blinked and shook his head, wondering if what he saw was only an illusion.

"Your grandmother sleeps."

Robin silently looked around the man and saw indeed that his grandmother's head had fallen forward, and she sat snoring in a chair, fast asleep. He looked back at Lleus, waiting expectantly to hear what he would say. Then the thought occurred to him that he was all alone with a very dangerous person and there was no one who would know in time to help him if this man became violent.

"Do you know what significance the Holy Grail has, especially where you are concerned?"

Robin decided to play the innocent and said, "I'm sorry, but I'm not sure I understand what it is you're talking about."

"The Holy Grail, my Lord, and the record of the lineage of the royal house. Succession to the throne must be by primogeniture. Do you know what that word means?"

"Er...no...sorry, sir."

"Don't mention it. You see, my Lord, the throne passes down from the king to his first born son. Unfortunately, there have been times when only daughters were born and times when the second born...well, let's just say that the second born showed more ambition than his elder brother."

"Could you not call me 'my Lord,' please?"

"Forgive me, my Lord, but you see, I am fully aware of your station, and protocol demands a certain decorum and servile attitude. I am here to assist you in your quest for knowledge about the Holy Grail and the scroll you found therein, and I am here to ensure that you succeed. By the way, does it still hurt where the orc arrow struck you?"

"Oh, yeah it does a little, but...hang on! You weren't there! How could you possibly know about that?"

Terror crept into the corners of his mind and filled his brain to overflowing, edging out any common sense. Robin got ready to push himself off the bed and run, no matter how much his head hurt, and it was beginning to hurt with blinding pain.

"Relax, dear boy. It was Myrddin that informed me of your plight."

"Myrddin, really? How is he? Did he say what I should do next?" The pain had moved just behind his right eye and across his forehead.

"Myrddin is busy with another task at this time. Because of this, I am here to help you with your education. He is most pleased with your progress so far and wishes only the best for you, which is why I am here."

Robin held his head in his hands now, keeping his eyes closed while the pain increased by leaps and bounds. It nauseated him almost to the point of being beyond what he could control.

"I don't feel so good," he managed to say.

"Let me magically enter your mind, and then I can take the pain away."

"I don't want anyone in mind just now, thank you," Robin said, even though he was sorely tempted.

"It won't be permanent but only enough so you will know I am your friend."

Pain blinded him, and Robin lay back in his bed, trying to keep the contents of his stomach where they belonged. He opened his eyes to look at Lleus once more. "Okay, but just for a little bit."

"As you wish. No harm will befall you and I will leave your mind when the pain goes away as promised. Close your eyes and imagine a soft golden light. The light is your friend. Allow the light to surround you. I will enter your mind now if you are comfortable with that and take the pain away."

"Hurry, it's really hurting bad," Robin pleaded.

The pain rapidly subsided as a presence entered his mind and a feeling of wellbeing cloaked his thoughts. Next he thought how grateful he was that Lleus had taken the pain entirely away. He heard a still small voice in his head.

Can you hear me, my Lord?

Yes, I can Mr. Zeifer. Thank you.

So, do you believe I am your enemy still?

No, I don't. Only a friend would do this.

Then sleep for now, my Lord. I will return at a later time, perhaps this evening, and we will begin your new journey to knowledge."

Robin felt the presence leave. He fell asleep, and just before he gave in to dreams, he thought that the room smelled like Easter eggs gone bad.

Chapter 12
THE NEPHILIM

Robin awoke with a start and tried to sit up. He lay back down when he felt a sharp pain in his head. The light in the room had changed from the brightness of morning sunlight to the shadows of the approaching evening, yet in the failing light, he saw that someone sat next to his bed. He thought he smelled something familiar and then he remembered. It was mothballs, and his grandmother had always smelled that way ever since he could remember.

"Grandma," he softly called, "is that you?"

"What...what...who said that?" his grandmother said. "Oh, you're awake, dear boy. Are you feeling any better?"

"My head still hurts when I move around, so as long as I lay still, I suppose I'm all right. Grandma, how long has that Mr. Zeifer been your assistant?"

"I hired him shortly after your mother and father took you away to work on that Penddol site pavilion. I never should have allowed you to go away last fall. But we can't change what's happened now, can we? We just have to make the best of it."

Robin was taken aback by the gentleness in her tone. It wasn't often she spoke this way to anyone. It seemed to him that she was in a rather wistful mood, too. Perhaps she was thinking about his dad, he thought.

"I'm really feeling badly about Mom and Dad, and I know you must, too. I miss them a lot."

"Your father was a good man, Robin. He wanted only the best for you and your mother. By the way, the funeral is tomorrow and Dr. Dahliwal says you could take a small excursion by then. He will be with us just in case your headaches become too severe for you to cope."

"How long was I asleep?" Robin said. He had changed the subject, wanting to keep his thoughts about his father to himself.

"You were in a state of delirium this afternoon. You kept saying that fairies and orcs were killing each other or some sort of nonsense like that."

Robin pondered her last statement. It could only mean that he had either dreamed and didn't remember the dream, or he had gone back to the other universe. In either case, he decided to take the mention of it seriously. Gwyneth would know for certain, and until he could manage his injuries better, she would have to be his eyes and ears.

"Are Gwyneth and her mom and dad still here? I should like to see them very much, please."

"They have long since returned to Llangollen, and we won't see them until tomorrow, I should dare say. They are not part of our family, you know. You have to be the man about the house now, Robin, and the family is the most important thing in your life at this moment in time. You must associate yourself with only certain people from this moment on. Some people are beneath your station, you understand, and others are more...shall we say...acceptable."

Your grandmother is certainly back to her old self.

A chill went down Robin's spine, and the hair rose up on the back of his neck as soon as he heard Gwyneth's voice in his head. Then his head filled with a piercing, sickening pain. He broke out in a cold sweat.

Not so loud, he thought back to her. *It makes my head pound and it makes me sick.*

It's not supposed to make you sick, Robin! I've been trying to contact you ever since we had to leave your room. I think...no...I'm sure that Mr. Zeifer blocked me out of your head somehow! You've simply got to get away from that man!

No, we were wrong about him, Gwyneth. Myrddin sent him and he knows all about the Holy Grail and the orc arrows and the scroll and everything else. He's on our side, and he said he is going to help me decipher the scroll and understand what it means.

Robin, no! He's not supposed to help. Mother Lilith said you and I were to solve it and no one else. What did he say to you exactly? You've got to tell me!

He said Myrddin was busy elsewhere and he had come to help me with my education is all. What's the big deal, anyway? Myrddin can't be everywhere, and if he needed to take care of something in the other universe, I'm sure he would send only the best to help us.

Robin, haven't you been listening? Mother Lilith said we had to do it on our own!

Well, he's here to help, and I can't see what the big deal is about him, even if he is kind of slimy. Besides, it's not like the orcs are attacking or anything like that.

Oh, Robin, don't you know what has happened? The orcs have attacked! The entire fairy kingdom is at war. Kat-sidhe told me to tell you that she won't be able to come for a while if you call on her. At least not until the orcs are under their control!

Robin wrestled with whether Lleus Zeifer was his enemy or not. When he thought about him being an enemy a pain stabbed at his head just behind his eyes. When he considered him a friend the pain went away. *Mr. Zeifer is here to help, Gwyneth.*

No, Robin, no! You've got to listen to me! Mr. Zeifer is our enemy! He's lying to you! Robin, please... Her voice faded as the pain increased.

Then as suddenly as the pain increased, it went away all together, and Robin opened his eyes to see Lleus Zeifer standing beside his bed. The sun shone from behind him through the window with the last of the day's warm light. Robin thought how beautiful the sunset was and how it seemed as if Lleus Zeifer bore the light of the sun.

"Good evening, my Lord Robin," Lleus said as he bowed before him. "How are you feeling?"

"Better now, I guess."

"Good, then you and I can have a conversation if you are feeling up to it."

"Sure. What will we talk about?"

"Princes du Sang, of course. The holy bloodline of the king and who is in line to inherit the throne by primogeniture. I will show you the legitimist case and prove the proper succession. You are in that scroll somewhere, you know. In fact, that scroll was written long ago just so that on this very day you would be able to discover your destiny. I have a most excellent talent to help others realize their own destinies, you see, and I am most anxious to begin."

The room filled with a golden glow from the last of the sun's rays as it sank below the horizon, and Robin propped himself up on his pillow ready to hear every word that this wonderful, fascinating man could possibly tell him. Robin couldn't remember ever being so excited.

"Have you ever heard the word *Nephilim* and do you know who or what they were?" Lleus asked.

"I've heard some things."

"They were a superior race of people who came to this planet many thousands of years ago."

"You mean from another solar system like space aliens in UFOs?"

"What is so hard to accept about the concept of life on other worlds? Even in your history, colonization was an accepted practice. It is how the Americas came to be so populated and such a powerful force in your world today. And now that you humans have colonized your own world, where else do you think you will go to fulfill your desire for conquest?

"Greek and Roman mythology is full of the stories that tell of their adventures and origins. There is actually more truth to the myths than there is fiction; a person just has to know how to read between the lines."

"I had this picture in my mind of what it must have been like. I've read a lot of mythology, because it fascinates me, and I often wish I could have been there to see it happen."

"Perhaps you were."

"No, that can't be. I mean, I'm here now, and we only get one chance at it, anyway. So I suppose we have to do our best with only one try."

"You have been taught too much dogma. Perhaps that is my fault, but I will try to enlighten you. First of all, a soul is allowed to incarnate as many times as it wishes to. That means you have had many lifetimes before this one, and if you choose to do so, you may have many more. Do you understand so far?"

"But that doesn't make sense to me. I was always taught in church that you could only have one chance so you have to get it right."

"If there are, for instance, a trillion, billion souls in the well of souls, there can't possibly be enough room for them on Earth all at one time, now can there? So one would have to take his turn so the rest could have a go at it.

"Many years ago, many millennia ago, in fact, you humans communicated with the Creator in innocence. The Creator spoke directly with you humans, and His words were recorded by the ones with whom he spoke. Their words became ancient encryptions in the millennia that followed and had to be translated into the myriad of new languages that began to develop. Some of these languages are dead and some are dying. The accuracy of the translation suffered as a result. And that was only the beginning of the problems.

"Another problem was the complacency of man. Man was well fed, comfortable, and in charge, so why should he care about the abstract concepts concerning the Creator? Indeed, it soon came to pass that those who would govern the masses discovered the secret of control by systematically mistranslating the documents until they reflected beliefs that were never intended. These beliefs were false, but for the masses they became their truth, and the lies became their facts until they rabidly defended their so-called holy books to the point of death. The governors made themselves the leaders of their churches, temples, synagogues, and all other places of worship, guiding the masses to believe that to defy the government was sinful no matter how oppressive the governing body was.

"You humans are shameful creatures who commit such acts of violence against each other that it makes the existence of an outside source of evil unnecessary. As to the trillion, billion souls, I tell you that there are a trillion, billion planets in your galaxy alone that are inhabitable, and you would be surprised at how many galaxies there are in this universe alone. Besides, considering how short the average human life span is, one can't possibly learn it all in a single lifetime."

"Oh," Robin said trying to take in all that he had heard. Then he looked up and said, "But you keep saying 'you humans' as if you weren't among us. You are human, too, you know."

"If you say so. Now, consider this, my Lord: the Nephilim were genetic engineers and created many abominations in their time. That was the evil they did, but the good was they were instrumental in mixing the races and producing the wonderful variance we see today.

"Unfortunately, most humans do not like it if one is a different color or has different-shaped eyes or a sloping forehead and high cheekbones. None of those differences matter, you see, since these bodies are only vessels that contain our souls, and if the body has a dark complexion, it doesn't mean that the soul inside is dark. In fact, the soul's beauty is seen through our actions and not our appearance."

"Not all humans care so much about color. I don't care so much."

"It is just my opinion, but I believe it is a realistic one. Now, I need to tell you another important fact. The Nephilim kept one family pure and produced in them an ability that made them different. Not better, just different. This race began with Adam and Eve and has now mixed with all the other races, and the ability in question is latent in all humans from one degree to another. But there is a direct family line in that scroll you found along with the Holy Grail, and it is the written record of the ascendancy to a throne with no country. It also magically updates itself so that it is the only honest record of this line of kings."

"Should we look at it now? If it's that important, maybe I should know right away before we have to leave for the United States. Besides, I should tell Gwyneth all about this, shouldn't I?"

Lleus bit his lower lip before flicking his tongue out to moisten them. "I think it would be wiser to keep what I have told you just between you and me for the time being. Tell Gwyneth nothing, and I will ensure she is properly informed when it is time. Now I am sure you need your rest more than you need to satisfy your curiosity, so why don't you sleep for now, and tomorrow evening we can continue our study into the darkness that keeps you from being enlightened. Of course, if you have it handy, I suppose a quick look wouldn't hurt." Robin thought he saw Lleus salivate in the failing light but dismissed it as his imagination.

Robin reached under the mattress and produced the Holy Grail and the scroll. He suddenly felt dizzy and dropped the scroll. Lleus retrieved it and held the scroll to the light, staring at it in lascivious pleasure.

"Is there enough light for you, sir, or should I turn the reading light on?" Robin asked.

"No, I have never needed light to see into the darkness. Here, put it away and don't let any prying eyes near it." Lleus handed the scroll back. Now Robin was completely satisfied that, although a very strange man with even stranger mannerisms, Lleus Zeifer must surely have been sent by Myrddin.

"Trust no one, Robin. This scroll is dangerous enough to precipitate a world war. You could only imagine what would happen if it fell into the wrong hands. I must go, and you must sleep, my Lord."

"Could I ask one more question before you go?"

"I really do love curiosity in a person, and of all the people I have met in my time, you seem to have an extraordinary amount of it. Proceed with your question, then, but only one more as you need your rest."

"I was wondering how far back I could trace my family in that scroll."

"Sleep on this answer then, dear boy. Your name is there. Trace your name back to Adam."

Chapter 13
THE CLUE

Robin stared at Lleus sitting across from him in the limousine. His grandmother had fallen asleep beside him, and Dr. Dahliwal, though awake, seemed to be in a daze.

"I have hopes that you and your grandmother will be back in Washington State before the week is through."

"Well, that's not what I want. Why can't I stay through the summer like my mom and dad had planned and then go back?"

"I am in the employ of your grandmother, my Lord. Her every wish is my command. I suppose I should also explain that she is now your regent until you should come of age. If she believes that returning to Redmond, Washington, is best for you, then that is what we must do, even if your eventual station is beyond hers."

"Do you mean my being king? How old would I have to be?"

"What a wonderful question. You are advancing far more rapidly than I could have ever hoped for, but it seems your injury has affected your short-term memory. We have spoken of this before. Do you remember I mentioned that your name was on the scroll you found with the Holy Grail?"

Alarmed at his candidness in the presence of the doctor and his grandmother, Robin gasped and said, "Is this the best time to speak of this, sir? I don't mind waiting if I must, you know."

"Do not be concerned with the doctor or your grandmother. I have caused a sleep for your grandmother and have magically closed the doctor's mind temporarily so that we may have this very conversation without interruption or prying minds. They will not remember it occurred even if they understand what is being said. I know you have difficulty staying on task when you study, but I must ask you to study that scroll most closely; examine it as if your very life depended on it.

"What you will find in that scroll is the proof you will need to proceed properly to the next stage of your life. It will legitimately prove your right to the throne. Just imagine what it will be like to be king, Robin. You could have anything you wanted just for the asking."

"Anything?"

"It is your future. You must not reveal the information to anyone until it is the proper time to do so, however. Are we agreed?"

"Agreed!" Robin replied with a smile.

"You will receive the right to certain responsibilities and authority at the age of thirteen. I will explain more at that time, but for now, I will also tell you that there will be a lengthy educational process with which I will be most honored to assist you. When you are eighteen and your education is complete, you will receive the full responsibilities and authority of your future position. I must warn you that there are certain events that, if they occur in your life, will change this protocol and your life forever."

"What events? How will they change things?"

"The age of thirteen is chosen as the time at which you shall learn to master yourself, and it is too late to reverse that particular aspect at this time. The age of eighteen, though selected as proper protocol, can be changed should these following events occur. The passing of your grandmother or any other immediate relative who could act as regent on your behalf. Certain acts of war could change the time line chosen, but you mustn't worry so much about war and let me meddle about with that particular aspect. All will be revealed if you study that scroll most intensely, and the sooner the better."

"I...I'm a king, then?"

"No, that would be incorrect. You are in line for the throne. Your right to succession is governed by the factors we discussed just a moment ago, and your place within the order of the succession is in the scroll. It is that which you must prove."

"I guess it would be more correct to say I'm a prince then, wouldn't it?"

"Yes, my Lord, you are indeed a prince, and the throne is within your grasp if you would but seize the opportunity before you."

Visions of what it meant to be a king popped into his head, and he imagined himself with power, wealth, finery, and indulgence. This was better than flying, he thought to himself. This was better than any of his dreams, and it would certainly make up for all he had been through. His reverie took him to a palace where he was waited on by his father and his mother sat beside him looking only at him with adoring eyes. He ate at the finest table laid with silk linen and set with golden service. The masses bowed down before him and trembled in fear in his presence.

He took out the scroll from where he had hidden it and began to gaze at the contents, looking at names that he had never seen or heard before. Unable to make any sense of it, he looked at Lleus with an unasked question in his eyes.

"Do you wish to ask me something?" Lleus asked him.

"I don't understand what it is I am looking for exactly. I mean, there are an awful lot of names here, but I haven't any idea how to connect them to me."

"Go to the most recent entry of the scroll and you will find the name Gilman there. Trace it back through both your father's side and mother's side. You will find your mother's maiden name when you find the record of her marriage to your father. With patience, you should be able to trace your name as far back as Adam."

"I know you said you would explain when I turned thirteen, but it's not that far away, really, and I think I could understand now. In fact, if I had to guess, I would say that...well it is kind of an odd idea really. Maybe I should wait." Robin had suddenly become fearful of speaking aloud the very thing he knew must be true.

"You are ready when you do not fear the truth, my Lord. Besides, it is a truism that once you know the truth, then the truth will know you and it will set you free. That is when you will become sovereign in all aspects of your life. Are you sure you do not yet wish to speak what is in your heart?"

Robin was in turmoil over his desire to know for certain that he was who he thought he must be. He also did not want to speak something aloud that seemed so incredible that at times he often thought it was only a delusion. In the end, his desire to know won out over his fear of knowing.

"Could it really be possible? I mean...this isn't a dream? In Sunday school, I was taught that Jesus could trace his family back to Adam and Eve. So if I can trace my family, in the Holy Grail, back to Adam, then...well... what I want to know is, are you sure you've got the right person?"

His heart was pounding so hard in his chest that he thought it might burst, or at the very least it might wake his grandmother from all the noise it made. Lleus Zeifer chuckled softly as if he knew something Robin didn't know.

"Only one line of kings can trace itself directly back, the line of kings that David and Jesus came from, the line of kings you come from. You just need to prove it. It is in the scroll. I cannot help you there. Consider it a test of who you are, much like the sword Excalibur was a test for Arthur when he pulled it from the stone."

Robin had only just begun when Zeifer announced they were near the Gilman family plot and it was time to put away the scroll. He opened a briefcase and offered its use to Robin. Robin put the scroll into the briefcase. Lleus smiled and locked the briefcase, putting the key away in his pocket.

"I will always carry this key with me, and I will open the briefcase any time you want, as long as it is safe to do so. You can examine the scroll whenever you desire. I do, however, need to make a copy of it so the Princes du Sang may determine its disposition."

Robin gazed out the limousine's window as they pulled into the outer courtyard of the necropolis. He saw Tom and Darla Reynolds and watched them get out of their car, followed closely by Gwyneth. Gwyneth looked as if she hadn't slept all night, and he wondered if she were all right. Of all the things and people he would miss in Llangollen, it was Gwyneth he would miss the most.

The service was brief and to the point. Robin, sitting in his wheelchair, felt strangely disconnected and couldn't help thinking that he should be crying like his grandmother was. He looked all around at the others, and they all appeared to be at the very least misty eyed, but not him.

Why can't I cry? he thought.

I don't know. Maybe it's because you knew your dad. Why wouldn't you answer me, anyway?

What do you mean? You didn't ask me anything.

Oh, no, you don't! I've been talking to you the entire trip, and you've been ignoring me! You've got to listen to me, Robin! Lleus Zeifer is our enemy and he is not to be trusted!

This isn't a good time for me, you know, and you're wrong about that. If that's what you were saying to me then even if I could have heard you, I would have ignored you. Myrddin sent him, and he's a sorcerer. He's helping me with the scroll.

Oh, Robin, Gwyneth replied, and Robin felt despair in her thoughts. *Kat-sidhe was with me on the trip here, and I talked with her while I sat in the back of Mum and Dad's car. Something evil has happened in the other universe, and Myrddin can't be found. The orcs are gathering for an assault on the Kingdom of the Fairies. Bleak and Gloom are commanding the orcs, and Kat-sidhe thinks...*

There was a blinding flash of light behind Robin's eyes, and his head suddenly felt as if it was being split in two. The pain constricted around his skull like an ever-tightening metal band, making his temples throb and his eyes hurt while waves of nausea threatened to overcome him. Dizzy, he put his head in his hands and leaned forward in his wheelchair as Dr. Dahliwal quickly went over to assist him. Then, as quickly as it began, the pain and nausea went away. The only difference was he could no longer hear Gwyneth's thoughts and could only guess what she was trying to tell him as she made clandestine gestures his way. He knew she thought he was ignoring her again, but it couldn't be helped.

Then the strangest thing happened. A calico cat walked into the middle of everyone at the gravesite with a slow, deliberate gait. It sprang into Robin's lap and settled down. Robin gently stroked the cat as it lay purring in his lap and thought to himself how odd it was that he should feel comforted by its presence. He looked at Gwyneth as she gestured at the cat and mouthed a single word at him, but what it was escaped him. He returned to stroking the purring cat. Tears rolled down his cheeks as he finally gave in to his need to cry.

Robin's head began to feel fuzzy inside and it was almost as if he was looking at everyone around him through frosted glass. A moment later, he began to hear the voices of the others around him again and realized he had temporarily lost his hearing. Robin had missed the entire service due to the way he had been feeling. Someone was pushing his wheelchair back to the limousine, but he didn't really care who it was as he continued to stroke the cat.

"Robin," the voice behind him called.

"Who is that?" Robin started as he tried to turn around and see.

"It's me, and keep your voice down! Your grandmum and that Dr. Dahliwal are straight behind us," Gwyneth whispered. "The cat is Kat-sidhe, and she is going to ride with you back to our place, so don't let anyone shoo her away. Kick up a fuss if you have to."

Then a thought occurred to Robin. "Quick, turn me around so I can see my grandma." Gwyneth turned him around just as Dr. Dahliwal prepared to help lift Robin into the limousine.

"Wait, wait, not yet. I want to ask Grandmother something first."

"Hurry up then, Robin, it's about to rain and I do not wish to get caught up in it," his grandmother replied.

"It's just...well, could Gwyneth ride along with us? I'd like it if she could ever so much, please, Grandma?"

"Oh, very well, but that cat must go."

"But we can't leave the cat, Grandma. It belongs to Gwyneth, after all, and she wouldn't want it left way out here since it would never find its way home. Oh, yeah, I almost forgot, it can't go with her mom and dad in their car because her mom would have to hold it and her mom is allergic to cats, you see."

Morgana relented, and they were settled into the car along with the cat that wasn't a cat. Lleus Zeifer had sent word that he would arrive at the Reynolds' by other means of transportation.

Robin, can you hear me?

Yeah, I can. Sorry about before, but my head started hurting and then everything went all fuzzy and numb. Hang on! If this cat is Kat-sidhe, then how come she changed into a cat? I thought she hated cats!

I hate cats that hunt birds! Kat-sidhe's voice exploded in his head. *Particularly birds that I have changed into! Now I have a question for you, Robin. Have you gone mad? What are you doing trusting that vile, evil man? And don't you give me that look, I've got claws this time, you know!*

Robin was at first astonished that Kat-sidhe could communicate the same as he and Gwyneth could and then by her scolding. He couldn't see what the problem was with Mr. Zeifer anyway and was about to say so, but she continued to berate him.

How is it that any person suggesting they are sent by Myrddin can find you to be so gullible? You were not supposed to make up your own rules as you went along! We are at war, and you are about to go over to the side of evil just when we need you most!

How can you say that to me? I'm not doing that! Mr. Zeifer is perfectly all right and he's already showing me about the scroll and what it means. And he does magic, too. He made my grandma and Dr. Dahliwal fall asleep so we could talk about the scroll and not be overheard. If he was so evil, why is he helping me with it, and why hasn't he tried to take the Holy Grail away from me, I'd like to know? And quit digging your claws into me; they hurt!

The cat hissed and arched its back at him, and then it emitted a low growl as it laid its ears back. Robin shivered at Kat-sidhe's glowing, angry cat eyes. The cat slowly relaxed, and Robin thought he was safe from her wrath at the moment.

Where is the scroll now?

It's safe in Mr. Zeifer's brief case. Why?

The cat spit and hissed again. Robin looked over at his grandmother and Dr. Dahliwal for help and discovered that they had fallen asleep, making it apparent that Mr. Zeifer was not the only one who could conveniently put others to sleep. He quickly looked at Gwyneth, and she had a look in her eyes that condemned him for his actions. He felt ashamed that he had disappointed her, though he couldn't understand why it should affect him this way.

Robin, please tell me you didn't just say what I think you said.

It's not like I gave him the Holy Grail itself. It was only the scroll, just until I could study it some more. Kat-sidhe, would you please keep your claws in. You're drawing blood and it really hurts! Hang on, how come you couldn't talk to me by this telepathy thing before now?

In a burst of fairy dust, Kat-sidhe turned into her fairy self. *I have the ability only when I am near enough. You and Gwyneth, however, can be as far apart as the universe is wide and still do it. There are worse things I could do to you than cat claws, by the way, and I've a good mind to do them now! The cup of the Holy Grail is just that, a cup and nothing more. It is not even the original because it doesn't matter! It is the scroll that matters! The scroll is the bloodline and nations have gone to war over its existence! You may be the future king by birth, but you are not a king in your heart and mind. You are an idiot!* With another burst of fairy dust, she disappeared altogether, leaving him and Gwyneth behind as they traveled in the limousine to the Reynolds' house.

Kat-sidhe was certainly right about one thing, Robin thought. There were worse things she could do, and she had just done it. Her disapproval hurt more than her cat claws could have, and it didn't help that Gwyneth felt the same way. But still he couldn't agree with anything else she had said, especially about Mr. Zeifer. He knew the scroll was safe with him, and he knew that this man had the keys to unlock the very mystery that could catapult him to becoming the king of the magic realm. This was something he wanted with all his heart, soul, and mind.

The limo pulled up to the house, and Dr. Dahliwal once again grew alert and helped Robin out of the car as if he had never been asleep. Robin kept silent, and Gwyneth followed suit as she got out of the car. She walked away from him in a huff.

The doctor wheeled him into the front room of the house, and everyone queued up to file past him and his grandmother, expressing condolences and well wishes. Gwyneth, last in line, hugged him despite being so angry with him, and Robin felt even more uncomfortable than he was already.

"Shall I push you into the other room so you can get something to eat, then?" she asked him.

"You're not mad at me anymore?" he asked her.

"Yes, I am. But I think I can talk some sense into you even though Kat-sidhe thinks you're a hopeless git."

"What's that supposed to mean?"

"Take it how you like, Robin."

"Are you questioning whose side I'm on?"

"I guess maybe I am. Mr. Zeifer was not sent by Myrddin, Robin!"

"How do you know? I've already asked him and he said he was. I believe him because he's been awfully good about helping me with understanding the scroll and everything else. He's helping me to do what you said Mother Lilith said we were to do. Isn't that what we are supposed to be about?"

"I wish Myrddin was here to tell you himself," Gwyneth said, valiantly trying to hold back her tears, "but Kat-sidhe hasn't been able to set him free yet. It's why she's so angry. She cares about you deeply and she's worried about you getting help from that Zeifer character. It's like I said before, Robin. We are at war in the other universe and the orcs are coming here next. You're scaring me, Robin. It's almost as if someone has possessed your mind."

"If Myrddin says Mr. Zeifer is evil, then I'll believe that. Otherwise, I have no reason to doubt him, and I intend to let him help me all he will. Besides, Gwyneth, I'm going back home and there's not much I can do about it, so you might as well quit arguing."

Chapter 14
THE DRAGON REVEALED

It was hot and muggy when Robin awoke the morning of July 4. He thought for a moment he heard Gwyneth call to him, but after trying for several minutes to answer, he gave up. He hadn't been able to contact her since his return to Redmond, Washington.

His headaches and nausea had almost disappeared completely and only a scar was left where the surgeon had operated on him. His hair had grown back but it still wasn't long enough to suit him. Dr. Dahliwal attended to him but more often attended to his grandmother. Lleus Zeifer was a fixture in their lives, even going so far as to help with his home schooling. Robin sighed as he thought about the Eisteddfod Festival in far away Llangollen and wistfully wondered what it was like.

The summer season had already been unusually dry and hot, and the fire danger was extreme. Fireworks were out of the question unless you went into Seattle to see the fireworks display at Myrtle Edwards Park. He hoped he could talk his grandmother into letting him go. With that thought in mind, he ran to the kitchen, slamming the door behind him.

"Robin, is that you?" his grandmother called out to him.

"Yes, ma'am," he answered. "I'm in the kitchen."

He heard her cane hitting the oak floor as she hobbled into the kitchen. She was not able to walk as well as she had at his dad's funeral and seemed to forget events more often than she did before. There were days when she stayed in her bed and then days when she seemed to have more energy than most people her age. Now that Robin was thirteen, she allowed him more freedom and didn't inquire as to his whereabouts as often.

"What would you like to do today?" she asked him.

"Well, I was wondering if I could go to the Fourth of July celebration in Seattle tonight?"

"Yes, if Dr. Dahliwal goes with you. I'm afraid I won't be up to it today. I don't like all those loud noises and crowds. Come with me now. There is something I wish to show you."

Robin followed her to the den. It was filled with books on every subject he could imagine and some he had never before considered. On one of the many bookshelves was a large collection of family photographs, and it was there his grandmother paused looking at the topmost shelf.

"I can't reach. Would you be so kind as to retrieve that album there?"

"Which one?"

"The one without any label."

Robin took a small stepstool from the corner and reached for the album. He had to stretch but managed to bring it down. He handed it to his grandmother and for a moment thought he saw her eyes glisten.

"Your baby pictures are in here. You were born in Toulouse, France, you know. It is the Visigoth capital. But you were raised in Germany for the first five years of your life. I wish your parents had never gone there. It was so terrible, what happened."

"What happened? What do you mean?"

"You are a twin, Robin. Here is your first picture, and that one is your sister's."

He stared at the photos. Robin dizzily sat down in one of the soft easy chairs and couldn't think of a thing to say. Then he noticed his grandmother wiping tears from her eyes.

"Tell me about it," he softly asked.

"I blame myself, you see. Just after your parents moved to Berlin, they asked me to move in with them and help with your care. Instead, I sent money to hire an au pair. She was a German student wishing to learn English. She disappeared with your sister and left you in the house alone. By the time your parents returned, after their evening out, to that cold, dark, miserable house, the only sound they heard was your crying in your crib."

"She was kidnapped? What happened? Did they find her? Didn't they look?"

"Of course, they looked. We all did. The au pair was found a few weeks later in Toulouse. She had drowned in the Garonne River. It was later learned she had been seen with a baby the day before, near the Canal du Midi. How she came to be there or where she went and what happened from that point remains a mystery."

"But why hasn't anyone told me before this?"

"It was so difficult for your poor mother, and you were so young when it happened. I know I've meddled in the past, but on this I resolved to allow your parents to choose their own time. Perhaps I should have done before now, but as you are the only male heir, I rather thought now was a good time as any."

"I'm a...a twin? Is my sister alive?"

"I don't know, but I hope she is."

"Who could have done this? Why, Grandma, why?"

"I don't know, Robin. I just don't know."

She buried her face in her hands, and her body shook with her weeping. Robin tenderly put his arms around her, and though it was rare to see any warmth in her, she briefly took him also in her arms.

"I'll find her, Grandma," Robin whispered. "I won't give up till I do."

"Promise me you won't tell anyone you know about this."

"What...why?"

Before she could answer his question, the housekeeper announced breakfast. Robin's head was spinning as he tried to digest what he had been told, and he found he wasn't as hungry as he normally was and nothing seemed to taste right. He desperately wanted to ask his grandmother more questions, but the entire household was up now and it would be difficult.

Robin needed to think after breakfast and went for a walk in the eighty acres of woods that surrounded the estate. He could hear the occasional illegal firework being set off at a neighbor's house. Whistling Petes were one thing, but the neighbors usually made a trip to Tulalip to purchase bottle rockets, and they could start a fire more easily than the fireworks that stayed on the ground. If he hadn't been given permission to go to the fireworks show in Seattle, he would have sat on the back deck and watched the neighbors instead. It wouldn't have been as spectacular as the Seattle show, but it would have been better than nothing. As he walked down one of the many paths, he saw Lleus sitting on a fallen log, facing east with his eyes closed.

"Meditating?" Robin asked.

"Yes," Lleus responded without opening his eyes. "I prefer to sit in the stillness of privacy. You, on the other hand, seem to prefer the tedium of walking. Tell me, what have you learned so far about your lineage?"

"Oh, yeah, you mean from the scroll? Well, it seems that a lot of my ancestors were assassinated. Kind of spooky, really."

"Are you worried that might prove to be your fate?"

"Yeah, I guess so."

"You are under my protection. I will allow nothing of that nature to befall you. Now, what do you say we look at the scroll together and I can satisfy some of your curiosity?"

"Sure, sure. I'd like that."

Soon they were in Robin's room, where Robin retrieved the scroll. Touching it reminded Robin that he and Gwyneth were supposed to have been the ones to study it. He longed to be able to communicate with her and see her again.

"Tell me what you've discovered so far," Lleus said.

"Well, I've traced my father's side of the family and my mother's side all the way back to Dagobert, a Merovingian king."

"Dagobert was excommunicated by the Church about the time of the Church's formation and shortly after the great conclave that had translated the version of the Bible that existed up until the King James Version was printed," Lleus explained. "Even though his realm had been seized by the Church, he continued to hold the title of king. There was also mention of an ornate throne that had physically existed, as well, but was destroyed in a ceremonial fire at the time of the excommunication. He became known as the king without a throne, and the people of that era were plunged into darkness."

"Wow, it sounds like the family was persecuted. Maybe that's why some of the family went to France while others went to Wales. It's amazing, though, that Mom and Dad married 'cause that brought the two sides of the family together."

"Correct, and you are the first male child of this union and the only possible heir to the throne."

"Yeah, maybe, but there was one other part of the family that married into another royal house. Wouldn't they have a claim? And what if they wanted the throne for themselves and had something to do with the way my dad died?"

"As a matter of fact, that particular side of the family did keep its own records as proof of legitimacy and indeed wouldn't hesitate to, shall we say, eliminate the competition. But it is the marriage of your mother and father that has united the two sides of the family, and only you are the correct heir as I understand it. But again, I am your protector. Unfortunately, the news of your miraculous recovery from your head wound and the revelation that you are of royal descent by the press has informed the world who you are. The unfriendly side of the family is aware you exist but not of where you are. Nevertheless, we must be vigilant at all times."

"I wish I could tell Gwyneth about this."

"Have you been able to contact her with your mind?"

"No, I keep trying, but it never happens like before. It gives me a headache, too."

"Try meditating alone and in silence. I will leave you to it, if you like. Let me know if you succeed. It's part of your magic. If you like, I can merge my mind with yours and assist you."

"No, thank you. I'd like to try on my own first."

"As you wish."

Lleus left him alone, and Robin closed his eyes. He suddenly missed Gwyneth and began to think about her. He persisted in his attempt to contact her even though his head began to throb. Then an idea popped into his head. He ran back to his room and looked on his desk for the birthday card she had sent him. It had arrived June 26, the day of his birthday, and he had read it at least a dozen times since. Now if he could just make a connection through her handwriting on the card. Though his head began to ache worse than before, he persisted.

Robin, do you know how hard I've been trying to talk with you? I really miss you!

I miss you, too! Why haven't we been able to talk this way?

I'm not sure, but Myrddin's returned and he said it might be because someone else doesn't want us to.

Someone else? Who would do that?

Lleus Zeifer.

Oh come on, you're not still on about that, are you? You should see what he has helped me find out about the scroll. The information in it is dangerous, you know.

We were supposed to research it together. Robin realized Gwyneth's feelings had been hurt and was suddenly sorry he had mentioned the scroll at all.

Well, we couldn't. I would have if I wasn't so far away, but that's not my fault, is it? I mean, what was I supposed to do, just wait until we were together again? That could be years away for all I know.

Don't say that! Don't you dare say that! Mum and Dad are arranging a trip to Washington now, and we plan to be there in early August. I'll be bringing some T-shirts from the Eisteddfod Festival for you.

You're visiting? That's bloody brilliant! Oh, wow, I can't wait! I'll ask my grandma if you can stay here then, shall I?

No, we don't want anyone else to know, and especially not your grandmother or Mr. Zeifer. That way no one can sabotage our vacation plans and we'll get to see each other. Promise me you'll keep this secret! I really miss you, you know.

I miss you, too. How long will you be here, anyway?

Two weeks, and then back for school.

I can't wait to see you.

That's me, too. Maybe we had better quit for now. I don't want to overtax you. I can tell this is a strain for you, but it's ever so grand talking to you again after all this time. We'll talk again tomorrow if you like.

All right, then. My head is starting to hurt so I think you're right about it being a strain. Until tomorrow.

Robin lay back down until his headache went away. Despite the pain, he was in a good mood since he had finally been able to contact Gwyneth.

Before long, it was time to go to Seattle for the fireworks display. Dr. Dahliwal was almost as excited about the show as Robin was. Lleus decided to go along as well, and provided a limousine for the short trip into Seattle.

The limousine was soon parked near Elliot Bay, where Robin, Lleus, and Dr. Dahliwal walked to the nearest and best vantage point they could find while crowds of people pushed along with them, intent on securing their own space. At last, the fireworks began, and the crowd noisily showed its enthusiastic approval as the children stared up at the display with wide-eyed wonder. Robin couldn't decide which was noisier, the cheering crowd or the exploding fireworks overhead.

Agas Astō Vidātu wore sunglasses as he walked down Alaskan Way toward Myrtle Edwards Park. The briefcase he carried was designed to look and feel like a laptop computer but, despite the logo on the front, it really held a disassembled rifle.

The noise of the fireworks and the people watching were the best cover Agas could have hoped for. No one noticed him as he climbed on top of the public restroom. He kept low and waited for the signal. He breathed slowly to calm himself. His only task was to shoot Lleus in the arm. The boy would believe Lleus had saved his life by having taken the bullet. He needed the boy's trust, and what better way to win it, Lleus had explained, if he was to guide him through his teenage years.

Robin watched as fountains of fireworks sent their spray of sparks two hundred feet in the air from the barge that was anchored a hundred yards off the shore. Mortar shells went spiraling upward, exploding with a dull thud as each shell reached its zenith. The report rattled windows for blocks around the waterfront.

Then, as Robin watched, a tall fountain of sparks erupted from the center of the barge and rose above the other fountains, twice as high. The spray twisted and turned until it resembled a snake. The great head of the snake formed before his eyes, and he knew it was a basilisk. Then the basilisk spread its hood and stared directly at Robin.

"Thou art in danger, Massssster Robin." Robin looked around quickly to see if anyone else noticed the great hissing vision before him, but the rest of the crowd seemed to be entirely ignorant of its presence.

"Only thine eyessss have sssseen me and no other may do sssso. Lissssten to me. Flee at oncssse, little one, for thy life issss about to be forfeit. Do not hessssitate."

"But, what do you..."

"*Flee!*"

Robin felt the electric sensation of adrenalin flow through his body and ran, not knowing in which direction he should go. He ran straight into the arms of Lleus just as the bullet struck its intended target. Robin bounced off Lleus and spun around, only to be seized by Dr. Dahliwal, who roughly propelled him toward the waiting limousine. Before he could react, he was in the back of the limousine, tightly sandwiched between the doctor and Lleus. The car rapidly accelerated as its doors locked the three passengers in.

Agas disassembled the rifle as he lay hidden perched on top of the public restroom at Myrtle Edwards Park. Carefully packed away in its briefcase, it would not attract any undue attention as he made his way through the crowds on Elliot Bay. A bright light shone all around Agas, and he faded from sight.

"You didn't have to be so rough!" Robin exclaimed while he tried to elbow more room between the doctor and Lleus.

"Please forgive me, but your life is being of more importance to me than your dignity," Dr. Dahliwal replied.

Robin stared at him for a moment and then gazed at Lleus, who was leaning back against the seat with his eyes closed, clutching his left arm with a pained expression on his face. Robin felt wetness where he sat. He gasped in horror when he brought his hand up to his face and saw blood.

"*Blood!* Mr. Zeifer, there's blood here!" Robin looked at him and saw even more blood oozing from between the fingers of the hand tightly clamped down on his arm. "You're hurt! Dr. Dahliwal, Mr. Zeifer is hurt really bad! You've got to do something!"

"Please to move to the seat from across you!" Dr. Dahliwal commanded as he moved next to Lleus. "Oh dear! Please, sire, to remove your hand. I am wanting to see the wound!" Lleus removed his hand in silence and the doctor gasped at what he saw.

"Driver, take us to Evergreen Hospital now! Quickly, Robin, hand me my medical bag from under the seat and then come over here! I am needing your assistance!"

"Me?" Robin asked as he reluctantly came near.

"Just do exactly what I tell you to do! No more and no less. Now please open my bag and hand me the scissors!" While Robin searched the bag for the scissors, the doctor quickly pulled on exam gloves. The shirt sleeve was deftly cut away but it had stuck to the wound where Mr. Zeifer had clamped down with his hand. Lleus winced in pain but made no sound as the wound reopened.

"Quickly, put your hand directly where the blood is coming out and clamp down as tightly as you can! Now! Hurry!" Lleus groaned in agony from the renewed pressure.

The inside of the limousine began to spin, and Robin became queasy. He tried to look away from the wound and all the blood, but his own morbid curiosity drew his eyes back to the gory scene. The more he gazed at what he saw, the sicker he felt until he could taste the bile rising up from his stomach. He desperately wanted to control the queasiness and spinning cabin of the limousine, but the more he tried, the sicker he became.

"Look away or you will surely soil the wound," Dr. Dahliwal said. "We cannot afford your being sick just now!"

The anger in Dr. Dahliwal's voice stung Robin, but it also helped to bring him to his senses, and he looked away. While Robin fought the bile in his throat, the doctor continued to work on the wound, applying a pressure bandage to control the bleeding and stabilize it. Before long, he was finished, and Robin released his hold on Mr. Zeifer's arm. He returned to the seat across from the two men.

"There," Dr. Dahliwal said, sounding pleased, "that will hold you until we are getting to the emergency room, and we are almost there now."

"No!" Lleus barked. "No emergency rooms or any other doctors. I do not want any publicity or embarrassing questions! Driver, take us to the house! You may finish treating my wound when we arrive back at the house, where there is more light."

Lleus readjusted his sitting position and made himself more comfortable. He opened his eyes to look at Robin, who was across from him, pale and shaking from the effort to keep the contents of his stomach where they belonged. Robin knew he was about to lose the battle and put his hand up to his mouth.

"Quickly, doctor, the ice bucket!"

Dr. Dahliwal grabbed the ice bucket beside the refreshment center in the cabin and thrust it into Robin's lap just as he emptied his stomach.

"Sorry," Robin mumbled as he cleaned himself up. "I didn't mean to get sick. I'm sorry."

"You have nothing to be embarrassed about, Master Robin," the doctor said. "You should have been seeing me the first day of anatomy class. It was taking a month of those classes before I could hold it down and do the work that was required."

"But why did you continue? I mean that must have been horrible and you must have thought about quitting. I know I would have."

"I continued because I am wanting to be a doctor more than I am wanting to quit. I hated those classes."

"You saved my life just now, Robin," Lleus interrupted.

"But what happened? How did you get that injury?"

Lleus stared at Robin and seemed to be searching his innermost soul. "It is a bullet wound," he said, his voice flat.

"But that means someone had a gun. Why would someone shoot into a crowd like that?"

"The shooter wanted to hit his target more than he cared about his fellow human beings, I suppose."

"His target? What target?"

"Considering the direction from which the bullet came and the fact that you were on my opposite side, you could suppose I received this wound when I put myself between the shooter and you."

"Me? But why?"

"Apparently you are considered to be between another heir and the throne. At least that is what I think has happened. I'm afraid that your life is in danger. That means you must not go out unescorted. Do you understand?"

"Yes, but what are we...hang on...you saved my life. You took the bullet that was meant for me. Why? No, wait, I'm sorry. Maybe I shouldn't have asked you a question like that."

"I did it because of my agreement with your grandmother and because I have become quite fond of you lately. I agreed to educate you and help you ascend to the throne, Robin. With my help, you will become king. But now that I have known you this long, I would do it without an agreement to bind me.

"I did not know what to expect when first I met you, but over the months I have seen in you the virtues I would want my own son to have. You are already a cut above the rest your own age. Now your education will take a new turn, and it will produce in you the qualities necessary to achieve our goals."

"I couldn't even keep my dinner down just now," Robin said. "Someone else would have done better."

"You did more than others would have done, and you did it despite your own stomach," Lleus replied, and then, turning to the doctor, he asked, "Tell me, doctor, is he physically ready to begin the training we discussed? I want to begin tomorrow if possible."

"Yes, I think he is. But that is not the question I would have asked, but rather whether you are being ready! I am not knowing that until I see if the bullet is still in your arm. I know I am working for you, but you are my patient now, sire."

"Then let us go in and let you examine me. We are here."

The limousine entered the wrought iron gates at the entrance to the acreage around the house. They all went in, and both Mr. Zeifer and Dr. Dahliwal told Robin to go to bed, and though reluctant to obey, he conceded that it was late.

Robin slept fitfully, and then he heard Gwyneth call to him. He told her about the assassination attempt, and Gwyneth told him the events in Llangollen that had recently transpired.

I haven't told you about Dewey.

Why, what's he done, gone and beaten some six-year-old up?

That's not funny, Robin. His brother Fred's gone missing, and Social Services has taken Dewey away from his parents.

You're right; suddenly none of this is funny. But why has this all happened?

Apparently you're not the only one ever hit by your own dad. Oh, and you remember that horrid woman your dad brought home that night he, you know, hit you? She was found murdered. The police think it was your dad who did it.

No, that can't be. See, it's this way: if it was him, he would have done it just after we went to Dinas Bran that day. I was told he...he took his own life that morning. When did he have time? Maybe I better tell Mr. Zeifer about this.

I think your Mr. Zeifer knows all about it already.

Just exactly what do you mean by that, Gwyneth?

Don't you think it odd that you were able to leave the country so soon? I think Mr. Zeifer talked to the police. Maybe he bribed them or something, but you would have thought they would have wanted you to stay until they finished their investigation. Robin, you knew your dad was murdered, too, didn't you?

Now that's just wrong! You can't just tell me that and expect me to believe it!

The autopsy said your dad's neck was broken. I know because I overheard Mum and Dad talking about it. Your dad can't have gone and broken his own neck, now can he?

Maybe, but I still say he's not a murderer!

He brought that woman into your house, didn't he? Did you ever think he would do something like that? Did you ever think he would hit you?

So you believe it?

No, actually, I don't. It's just...well...I think Mr. Zeifer had something to do with it. I think maybe he wants to turn you into something you ought not to be.

Ah, come off it, Gwyneth! He saved my life! He took a bullet for me! What more proof do you need? It sounds to me like you're mad at him 'cause you think he's taking me away from you. You don't own or control me, you know, and I've got to do what I'm doing whether people agree with it or not. I've got a purpose now, and I don't know if I ever could have found this purpose without Mr. Zeifer's help. He's a good friend, too. The best.

Okay, I get the picture.

How do you know all this, anyway?

You might not be the only one who can hear other people's conversations from far away.

Really? That would be brilliant if you weren't getting it all wrong!

I can hear you. We're far away. Far, far away.

I'm going to sleep. Good night, Gwyn.

Git.

Robin lay in bed thinking about his conversation with Gwyneth. What if she had been right all along and Mr. Zeifer really was an enemy? If that were the case, then he had played right into his hands. But if he was the enemy, then why would he have taken a bullet for him? And didn't he treat him better than his own father had? Wasn't he the one who was to train Robin now and help him prove his own right to the throne?

His last thoughts turned to his kidnapped twin before he drifted off to sleep. Whether or not Zeifer was an enemy, Robin decided he would ask him about his sister.

Chapter 15
BLOOD OATHS AND CONSEQUENCE

Robin spent the muggy day studying the scroll. He paused to watch the thunderclouds gathering in the foothills when Lleus walked into his room unannounced, his arm in a sling.

"Shall we begin your new training now, my Lord? We can proceed to the daylight basement, where I have set up a gym of sorts."

Robin ran downstairs, barely able to contain his excitement. Once there, he saw a treadmill and weight center and what looked like machines of torture.

"What are those for?" he asked, gaping at the ominous-looking devices.

"Pilates is a holistic exercise program for developing your tensile strength, as well as your core. They are not instruments of torture as one might believe, although some people who practice this method may disagree. We will begin by teaching you to meditate and focus your mind properly first, however. It is a way to exercise your mind and get it back in shape. The meditation will also help you control the headaches that seem to plague you and develop your magical abilities that lie latent within you."

"Magic…I'd really like that! But I'm not really magical, am I? I mean, I've been told that before, but I've never been able to do magic."

"What kind of a king of the magical realm would you be if you were not magical, Robin? Of course, you are magical. When we are through, you will be able to walk through walls and turn invisible to the human eye.

You will be able to create from nothing and you will be able to ride the dragon. All magical creatures will be at your command, and what an army they will make. All will tremble in your presence. Oh yes, you will be king, but first I have a gift for you." He walked over to the wall next to the Pilates machine and brought out two packages that had been concealed, handing them to Robin.

"Open this one first, if you please."

Robin opened the package in front of him and saw what looked like a Samurai sword made out of bamboo. He held it up and looked at it carefully. He turned to Lleus with an unvoiced question in his eyes.

"That is a practice sword. I have one myself, and I will personally teach you the way of the samurai and the secrets of the Ninja."

"But the Ninja are legend and nothing more. At least that's what I've been told."

"Misinformation is what you have been given. In order to guard their secrets, the true Ninja spread the lie that they had no mystical abilities when in fact they actually did. Open the other present now."

Robin opened the next package and found a long samurai sword and a short one. He started to withdraw the long sword from its scabbard.

"You hold an instrument of death. We will begin by practicing with the bamboo sword and then we will use the real one when you are ready."

"But I can already use a sword now, you know."

"Yes, you learned when you and Peter shared one body. Peter's Kampilan sword is clumsy at best compared to this one, and only an expert can handle the samurai sword without unintended harm to himself or to others. Today you begin to learn, and your abilities with the Kampilan will have served only to prepare you for this moment."

Thus began the sessions that would last for two hours every day. Before long, Robin handled the bamboo sword as if it were an extension of himself. As Lleus healed, he was able to spar with Robin. At first, Robin received more bruises than he gave, but it wasn't long before he was the one giving bruises.

One morning before breakfast, Lleus and Dr. Dahliwal waited for him in the basement. After warming up, Lleus asked him to get his practice sword and don his protective gear.

"You will see his amazing progress, today, doctor," Lleus said as Robin prepared. "Today will be the last day to use the practice swords if he has paid attention to his lessons."

Robin wondered who was more powerful. He confidently picked up his sword and bowed, facing Lleus. He imagined himself as all powerful and indestructible. Lleus came at him with blinding speed, but Robin had already sidestepped him by the time the sword came down where his head should have been, and a single thrust between his opponent's outstretched legs sent him sprawling.

"I won't make that mistake twice," Lleus said, slowly getting up. "Are you ready?"

Even as he asked the question, he moved toward Robin again. He feigned an attack to Robin's head and then struck Robin's torso. The blow staggered Robin backwards.

"You seem angry with me, Robin. Use the emotion of your anger and see how much more powerful you will become," Lleus taunted.

Robin quelled his anger. He knew from previous lessons that the unemotional response was always the most accurate. Anger caused one's aim to be off since it clouded the mind. This time, he made a calculated move toward Lleus and feigned a worse injury to his ribs than he actually had. Lleus, thinking he saw a weakness, moved in to strike his ribs a second time. The blow never fell.

Robin's practice sword rose and caught Lleus under his chin, missing his throat just enough to avoid crushing the larynx but enough to cause crippling pain and difficulty breathing. But Robin didn't stop there. He spun around and came down on his opponent's head hard enough to cause bleeding. Robin gasped at what he had done as he saw Lleus trying to breathe and blood dripping onto the gym floor.

"Mr. Zeifer," he blurted out, "I'm sorry. I didn't mean to hurt you like this. I thought you had deflected the first blow. Doctor, help me, please. I didn't mean it. I didn't mean it."

"Look up at the ceiling, sir," Dr. Dahliwal said. "I need to see if the larynx is damaged."

Lleus did as he was told while the doctor palpated the affected area. The doctor helped him up to his feet after a brief examination and turned to Robin.

"There is not serious damage."

"Are you sure?"

"I'm all right, Robin," Lleus said in a hoarse whisper.

"Sorry, I didn't control the blow so well."

Lleus looked at Robin with a smile on his face, but curiously enough, it seemed more malevolent than it ought to. "I am all right, Robin, and I am pleased with you. You were wise enough to not give in to your anger. You were cold and calculating, as you should have been. The fault is mine for doubting your ability as a student. By the way, did you know you levitated just before you struck me with your first blow?"

"I...levitated?"

"Don't seem so surprised," Lleus said. "It is all part of not giving in to your anger and riding the dragon. The dragon snake, or basilisk, to be more accurate, is your totem. That means you share its characteristics, cold and calculating."

"What's a totem?"

"Your animal spirit that lends you its basic character."

"Do you have a totem?"

"I do. It is the red dragon. Both our totems are cold and calculating in battle, and we are assisted by them in that regard."

"I don't want to be remembered as cold and calculating, though."

"Not in all things, just in battle. Levitating is a good talent to have."

"If I levitated once, could I do it again under different circumstances, if I just wanted to levitate and not spar with someone?"

"What a wonderful question! To tell the truth, I was wondering the same thing. Would you like to find out now?"

"Oh, yes, I would! Is it like flying? I like flying, you know."

"It is called riding the dragon," Lleus explained. "Think of it as the meditative state an individual reaches in sleep that allows them to travel astrally. I think you are ready to reach this state without sleeping. You do it by intent, and that is something I think you know about. First, watch me and Dr. Dahliwal."

The two men assumed a sitting posture of meditation, their thumbs touching the middle finger on each hand and each hand resting on their knees.

"Assume this posture as we have, Robin, and calm yourself. Your excitement at the prospect of levitating at will is a hindrance. You must tap into your kundalini and make it rise up through your crown chakra, reaching for heaven. Imagine it as a serpent, or more correctly as a dragon snake. You will find the kundalini at the base of your spine, and the crown chakra is the topmost part of your head."

Robin knelt but found it difficult to calm his excitement. The room was hot from the sun coming in through the windows on the south side of the room, and even with his eyes closed, he could still perceive its golden glow. After what seemed like an unbearably lengthy time, he decided he would open his eyes and give up. Still in the kneeling position, he was terrified to see that he was above the floor and almost touching the ceiling. He fell and grunted when his knees hit the cement floor.

"Well, that will teach you a lesson," Lleus dryly observed. "Next time, don't expect that you can't do it; expect that you can. You will be more prepared for the event. You have become more powerful than I had first believed, Robin. Would you like an explanation as to how it works? It's all very scientific, you know."

"Maybe a new knee, too," Robin said as he massaged his bruised knee and leg. "What do you mean by scientific?"

"It has to do with electromagnetic and gravitational fields as well as atomic structure. In a meditative state, you align your atomic structure and thin it. You are not lighter than air but thinner than air and so you rise up through the molecules that float about you and mingle with them. By using this knowledge, you can align your molecular structure and its electromagnetic field enough so that you can pass through solid objects. Most important, you can dissolve time and bend it and thereby be at any place or at any time without consequence and without aging, as long as you remember that you are a tourist and not a participant."

"Okay, you lost me," Robin said as he looked up from where he was sitting on the floor, still massaging his knee. "Besides, I don't see how one could bend time. You're talking about time travel?"

"Yes and no. First of all, you must understand what time is. Time is a measure of distance and nothing more. However, once an event occurs, there is no changing it. There is no forward time travel because the future changes with every decision made by mankind, both collectively and individually. If you predict an earthquake in two weeks' time and it doesn't happen as you predicted, is your prediction wrong?"

"Yeah, but I think you're about to tell me different."

"Your prediction may have been accurate from your viewpoint two weeks before the event was to occur. Humans petition their god or gods and ask that it not happen, and if the gods are favorably inclined, the event is delayed. Now, notice I said *delayed*. The event will still occur and the prediction is most accurate from that point of view, and the delay may be only a few days or a millennia. Time is the measure of the distance traveled between events, so that means the distance between the prediction and the event was seen as two weeks. If time is bent, the distance is lengthened to a few days or even as much as a thousand years or more. Do you understand so far?"

"But that would mean if one could bend time to lengthen it, then couldn't you bend time to condense it?"

"What a brilliant question, to which the answer is most emphatically, yes." Lleus walked over to a calendar hanging on the wall and tore a page off of it. "Since today is August the first, we shan't need July anymore, so imagine if you will that this piece of paper represents the space our galaxy occupies."

"All right, but then where would our solar system be?"

"How about this corner here?" Lleus indicated the upper right corner of the page and took out a pen, drew a pentagram, and labeled it *Sol*. "Now if I draw seven more stars in the lower left corner, they will represent the Pleiades. There are more stars in this cluster, but we can only see seven of them with the naked eye.

"The distance between these two points is the time it would take to travel between them. A human being would not survive the journey simply because the journey would last four hundred and forty light years, even if we had the technology to travel at the speed of light. Such a journey would be unreasonable unless one could...*fold* time."

Lleus picked up the page and folded the two opposing corners together until they touched each other. Robin looked at what he had done and then he realized what was being taught to him. "It could happen in the blink of an eye, couldn't it?" he asked.

Lleus smiled and leaned down to where Robin was on the floor until his nose almost touched Robin's. "Exactly, and as you saw, it would be as easy as folding paper, once you know how. That is how one would condense time, as you put it.

"You have an advantage since you were in an alternate universe that has already entered the fourth dimension. That event in your life has left you in an altered state, and you will be the first in this universe to be able to use the abilities this state has given you. Some call it magic, but I tell you it is all very scientific. I will also tell you that no other will have as much ability in this area as you will in your lifetime, and I predict you will have a very long life indeed as long as you do as I tell you and learn your lessons well. This is powerful knowledge, and along with this great power must come great responsibility. Will you agree to be responsible for this knowledge? If not, I must discontinue your education, since I will not compromise my principals and produce a possible despot or even what some would call an abomination."

"I'm not any of those things and I don't want to be," Robin declared with some annoyance at the very suggestion.

"Then you must give me your word as I have requested, and we must perform a certain rite to seal the bargain. Do you agree to this?"

"Yes, of course I do! I want to learn all about this, ever so much!"

All Robin could think about was walking through walls and traveling through time. More than anything, he wanted to fly and this man could teach him. Robin was ready to do whatever he had to do.

"The rite is a blood oath. Do you know what I mean by that?"

"Yes, I do, and I'm ready now, please."

"Very well, please stand up then." Robin hurried to obey, hardly noticing the ache in his knee.

"Swear to me that you will reveal nothing that you are about to be taught. Swear to me that you will obey me in all things, regardless of your fear. Swear to me your loyalty and swear to me that you will grant me one request when I have finished your education."

"What request will you make of me?"

"I will tell you when the time comes. Now swear to me you will do these things."

"But, what if..."

"Swear to me!"

"I swear I will do as you ask."

"Now, stand here and wait." Lleus retrieved the short sword from the weapons case on the wall. "Don't worry; the cut will be hardly noticeable. The cut is made by grasping the short sword in your left hand and quickly drawing it through. We will both do this, and then we will clasp our hands together in order for our blood to mingle. Watch how I do it first so that you don't cut your own hand off. Once it is done, we must move quickly so that the loss of blood is minimized. Are you ready?"

Robin nodded and watched as Lleus grasped the end of the blade with his left hand and then sharply draw it through. Lleus quickly handed Robin the short sword, and Robin grasped the end of the blade just as he had seen his mentor do. He gasped in pain as he drew the sword through his left hand and again as Lleus seized his bleeding hand in his own and clamped down so that the two wounds were together.

"Repeat my words and mean them. The promise I make I seal with this blood oath! May we be friends and brothers forever! Should one betray the other, may the blood of the betrayer be spilled upon the ground as he is eaten by the dragon and his soul taken by Lucifer!"

Robin repeated the oath, and then Lleus let go of his hand while Dr. Dahliwal gave them each a supply of sterile gauze pads to stem the flow of blood. Robin kept silent as the doctor bandaged his hand.

"The rest of the day is yours, Robin. When your hand is healed sufficiently, we will continue to work out with the swords. You've done well today, and I am proud of you." Lleus gazed in ostensible affection at him, and Robin glowed when he heard the praise.

"Wait, I've got another question."

"Just one?"

"Well, yeah, for now, anyway. It's something Grandma told me. She said I had a twin. You don't know anything about that, do you?"

"Your grandmother told you that? I shall have to see what I can find out."

"You don't know, then?"

"It's time to clean up now, Robin. I'll get back to you on...a twin, you say." Lleus paused for a moment, seemingly distracted. "Well," he said at last, "up you go to your bath."

Robin ran up to his room to change out of his workout clothes. His hand ached, and he took the gauze pad off to inspect it and to put a proper dressing on. Intent on the task, he didn't notice Kat-sidhe watching him.

"What happened to your hand?" she asked.

"Hey, don't sneak up on me like that. I cut it, is all."

"Want me to look at it?"

"No thanks; I can manage."

"Let me see."

"It's nothing. I can do it."

"Let me see." This time Kat-sidhe had moved to his hand and, with a wave, forced Robin to show his palm.

"Hey, knock it off!"

"Don't talk to me that way! What have you done?"

"I...I just m-made a promise is all."

"You are in league with the enemy and have made a fool of me. You've become an abomination! I want nothing to do with you!"

"No, wait, I'm not an abomination!"

"You are a fool if you think that!"

"How have I been foolish?"

"Your twin is right about you. You are most dense, even after you were warned about Lleus. I will speak with Mother Lilith, and we will see if the injury has afflicted your brain."

"But he saved my life!"

"No, he made it look like he saved your life. I've been waiting to tell you this, but only now have I had the opportunity. Robin, I never dreamed you would take a blood oath with him. He wants you to become king and so do I, but not an evil king."

"I'm not evil." At least he didn't intend to be, he thought, but what if he had made a mistake? Surely it would be all right to make a mistake as long as he learned from it.

"Should I just leave you and not come back? Should I let your life play itself out so I am not to blame for your stupidity?"

"I'm not stupid!"

"You've made a bargain with Lucifer, Robin! What would you call it?"

"I'm not stupid!"

"Were my words in a different language? Let me be blunt! Lleus Zeifer, Lleus Zeifer, Lucifer, *Lucifer!* You have taken a blood oath with Lucifer himself!"

"Can't you at least show me what to do?" Robin asked, near tears.

"Watch carefully and do this."

Kat-sidhe disappeared without a sound, and Robin was left alone in his room, staring up at the ceiling where he had last seen her. He wondered who Kat-sidhe meant when she said his twin had tried to warn him. Brigid was his twin in Peter's universe, but Peter was sort of his twin soul, or was it Gwyneth? It was Gwyneth who had always said not to trust Zeifer, but she wasn't his twin in this universe. She was just the neighbor's daughter.

Maybe he was supposed to be emotionless and make decisions like he would in battle. But more than ever, he felt like crying. Then it occurred to him he should disappear just like Kat-sidhe had. But how? he wondered.

Sleep escaped Robin that hot sticky night. The sweat on his forehead mingled with the tears in his eyes, and the salt made them sting. Robin felt shame as he had never felt before. Maybe if he tried to talk to Kat-sidhe again he could say he was sorry or anything, just so he could make it better. He muttered her name as quietly as he could. If Lleus Zeifer was really Lucifer, then it certainly wouldn't do to have him know he had been found out.

Fairy dust exploded all around him. It didn't cheer him up to see her return, however, since his recent actions were all too painfully on his mind. Kat-sidhe hovered like a humming bird just in front of his nose so that he had to cross his eyes to see her properly.

"Was there something you wished to discuss?"

"I've done something horrible!" Robin managed to say between sobs. As much as he wanted to control himself, the more he tried, the more difficult it became. Kat-sidhe reached her hand out and touched him where his heart would be.

"Peace, I speak peace to your heart." Next she touched his throat and said, "Speak your truth to me and have no fear of reprisal. Besides, confession is good for your soul." The lump in Robin's throat disappeared immediately, and he found his voice.

"Gwyneth tried to warn me, you know. Everything she said about him haunts me now. Oh, Kat-sidhe, what have I done?"

"I think I know why Myrddin was detained now," she finally said. "He was taken prisoner by the orcs just after you returned to this universe. Our kingdom is at war now. It began when you left our universe. It distracted us so much that we weren't able to help you like we should have. Perhaps I am the one who should apologize for that and my outburst."

"But it was my decision to allow him into my life even when I was warned. I should have known better. Gwyneth certainly did."

"You are not entirely to blame, Robin. Stronger men than you have been seduced by his shadow. All of humanity is to blame for his presence among us, and all of humanity is responsible for resisting him at all costs, not just you."

"You came back and that is enough. What am I gonna do?"

"Listen to me! Regardless of the blame, we must take steps to repair the damage. Say and do nothing to reveal you know who Lleus Zeifer is. If he wishes to continue your training, then do so. I would imagine that he has trained you properly up to this point since his seduction is to give the truth and buy your trust with it and then he will persuade you to use that knowledge for ill."

"But I can't trust him."

"No, of course you can't. But he mustn't know that he can't trust you anymore. Trust no one that is in league with him. I must go now and confer with Myrddin and Mother Lilith. I will return as soon as I can. Have courage and do not be so hard on yourself. If you are finished feeling sorry for yourself, you can now begin to correct what has been done. I leave you with hope, for together we will conquer this evil."

Fairy dust exploded around him again and Kat-sidhe was gone. He lay back on his bed, staring at the ceiling wanting the pain in his heart to go away, but it stayed until he could scarcely bear it any longer. A thought occurred to him, and the terrible idea made him shiver with fear.

A time would come when he would have to sever his relationship with Lleus, and that would not be a pleasant event. He had neither parents nor adults in his life to whom he could go with any confidence. Maybe this was exactly what Zeifer had wanted. Robin shivered again.

Chapter 16
THE CONFRONTATION

Gwyneth muttered under her breath as she tried to loosen the seatbelt on the British Airways airliner as it approached Kennedy Airport. She looked at Dewey as he drooled unconsciously onto his pillow.

She looked across the aisle at her mother and stepfather and again at Dewey napping beside her. She wrinkled her nose when she smelled his sweat from the long flight and the overly stuffy cabin. She supposed that they would all need a bath before the trip ended but wished Dewey had taken one before they boarded.

She wondered why some boys seemed to care more about their cleanliness and appearance than the others. When he took the time to clean up, Dewey wasn't so bad looking, she thought. She decided to switch seats with her stepfather for the second leg of their flight, once they were Seattle bound.

Dewey opened one eye and looked at her.

"You're drooling," Gwyneth commented.

"Wha...oh, sorry. Get any on yeh?"

"Here," she said and handed him a tissue with a not-at-all-amused look on her face.

"Thanks. I dreamed about yeh. Well, Robin, too."

"That's nice."

"Robin were a king, and we was all grown up. We was bes' friends. I were 'is general. You and I was real friendly like, too."

"How friendly? What..."

"Oh, yeh know, jus' friends. Robin gave me a medal for bravery, and the army were all magical creatures. Robin and I was bes' friends in me dream. Do yeh think 'e 'ates me still, or do yeh think 'e'll let me be 'is friend when I see 'im again?"

"I'm friends with you, aren't I? He doesn't know how much you've changed."

"I've never had any real friends before."

Gwyneth wondered what Robin's reaction would be when he saw Dewey. She had meant to tell him at first, but decided against it in the end since she was afraid he wouldn't let them visit. Robin couldn't know what had happened to Dewey and how he had changed into a completely different person from the bully he had once been. Fred, on the other hand, was even worse than before and had run away from home.

Gwyneth sat next to her mother on the connecting flight and glanced over at her stepfather and Dewey sitting together in the next row. They were both playing cards, and even though she wished to join in, she was nevertheless grateful to be next to her mother and away from the annoying smell. Still, she thought, a game of cards would be nice, and Dewey did have a nice sense of humor. She thought about Robin and couldn't help thinking something very wrong had recently occurred.

She tried to contact Robin, and when they were about an hour away from SeaTac Airport, she burst through the wall. She gasped audibly and immediately clamped her own hands over her mouth to prevent anyone else from hearing and asking questions she didn't want to answer.

Robin, why haven't you let me talk with you? I've so much to tell you and I missed you loads.

Just busy, I guess. Robin was on his bed staring at the ceiling when Gwyneth burst through.

Listen, I don't have a lot of time, but we are landing at SeaTac in an hour. I can't wait to see you. We are getting a hotel room first and then some rest, but tomorrow my dad says he will call your grandmum and ask to visit.

You're here? Brilliant. I really missed you, you know. I've loads to tell you, too, but it's occurred to me that this telepathy thing might not be as secure as we thought. You and I aren't the only ones with this ability.

All right then, we'd best be careful what we say. Have you been all right lately? I mean, nothing bad has happened, has it? It's just I've had an achy feeling in my heart since this afternoon, and I was just wondering.

I'll fill you in when you get here. But so you won't worry, I'll survive. We better quit for now, I don't know who might be listening, and if they are...well, I'll explain when you get here. I can hardly wait, Gwyneth, I missed you lots and more than I realized. See you soon.

Wish we could talk more, but it's good to hear you just the same. Bye for now.

Gwyneth's mind went suddenly silent and she wondered if Robin experienced the same sensation. The seat belt signs came on, and the pilot announced that they were making their final approach into Seattle. Gwyneth stared out the window next to her and thought the clouds looked like they did when they flew out of Heathrow Airport. She knew that they wouldn't be able to see Robin soon enough and despite his reassurance that he would survive, she worried even more than she had before.

⌘ ⌘ ⌘

Robin stayed in his room most of the day. He decided to get up at dusk and get a snack from the kitchen. As he approached his bedroom door, he heard a soft knock and a voice whispering to him.

"Who's there?" he asked as he leaned closer to the door.

"Shhh, not so loud, young master. It is I, Dr. Dahliwal. You and I must be speaking before the hour is getting later."

Trust no one, Robin thought, but he knew he had to maintain the illusion that everything was still the same. He quietly opened the door and let the doctor enter his room. Dr. Dahliwal took a quick furtive glance down the hall before he walked through the door. He sat in the chair by Robin's computer desk and stared at him for a moment before speaking in a whispered tone.

"I must inform you of the terrible news, my Lord. I am most sorry for your loss, but I was told to inform you in the morning and not tonight. I am risking my life and my family to do this now and not as I was told. Do you understand?"

"What's happened?" Robin whispered.

"I am terribly sorry, but I am doing all that I could. It is your grandmother. It seems this afternoon she is laying down for a nap and she is not appearing for her tea. I was told to wake her, but I could not. She is passing away in her sleep, and it appears it was most peaceful. I am most terribly sorry."

Robin was stunned. He was more alone than he had first thought. Then a question occurred to him. "Who didn't want me to know about this? Tell me!"

"Please, kind sir, do not be angry with me. Mr. Zeifer is not all that he seems to be, and I am usually not inclined to disobey him, except for this one time."

"Oh, wow!" Robin exclaimed. "I've been so stupid! But why are you telling me, then?"

"It is for some time now that I am attending to you and your grandmother as your most personal physician. Before, I was only an intern working in the emergency room at Cardiff General Hospital. It was there one day they are bringing a young boy in who was mortally wounded in his head. By some miracle, he is living and he stands before me today. Mr. Zeifer was there on that day and persuaded me to quit my employment with the hospital and become your physician. I, too, took a blood oath that I would serve you and Mr. Zeifer, but now I am afraid his true nature is being revealed to us." The doctor held up his hand, and Robin saw a thin scar running diagonally across the palm.

Robin stared at his own hand and asked, "You don't really believe that a blood oath carries an invisible curse, do you?"

"Where I am coming from, my family is Hindu in their beliefs," the doctor said. "We do not believe in the Christianity of the Church as you do. We do believe in a good and evil concept that can manifest in many ways. You and I have the same thing in common. We have both taken a blood vow with evil manifest, and we are both invisibly bound by it. I am an adult and responsible for my actions. You, on the other hand, have been taken advantage of as you are only being a child yet. This fact is allowing you more hope than I have."

"Hope of what?"

"Hope that you may not be bound by an oath that an adult is bound by since you are a child and not to be held accountable for certain actions. You are not at the age where all agreements between you and another can be binding. If that explanation is satisfactory, there is something else I must tell you."

"I understand it well enough."

"In case you didn't know it, Mr. Zeifer is having someone to shoot a gun and make you believe the bullet is being meant for you." Dr. Dahliwal's eyes bored straight into Robin, making him feel uncomfortable. "It is also possible that your grandmother is dying by the hand of another."

Robin sat in brief silence and then looked up at the doctor and said, "But that doesn't make sense."

Dr. Dahliwal sighed. "Mr. Zeifer is wanting to create a bond between himself and you. He is wanting to adopt you and raising you to be most molded into his own image. In the end he is having a puppet who sits on the very throne that he is wishing to destroy. He is wanting you to trust him so much that you will allow him to own you. I am risking my own life to protect the boy to whom it is happening and I would be killing the man who tried to do that to my son. I am a worthless man if I do any less."

"How can he destroy the throne if he puts me on it? It sounds like he is preserving it, not destroying it. Besides, it doesn't explain why he would take the bullet for me, even if what you say is true. I also helped to save his life, you know."

"I'm afraid you are wrong about some things, Robin. First of all, he was in no mortal danger, but he is making it appear as if that was the case. He is meaning to take the bullet and you are thinking he is saving your life. There are few bonds stronger than the bond of those who are saving each other's lives. You are being obligated and would do anything to fulfill that obligation to the one you are owing your very life to. For instance, you would be inclined to be taking a blood oath. Is it not so?"

"Yes, it is so," Robin said after careful consideration. "Now my grandma is dead and I'm on my own, aren't I? I have to decide what I'm going to do. And if I'm the crown prince, then I must rule from this day forward, mustn't I?"

"Yes, but I am thinking you should not be in a hurry to claim your throne at this time. Instead, you should be concerned with the oath you are taking and how to break the chains it is creating around you. You are obligated to evil itself, and you must be resisting the wishes of this evil. I personally can do no more other than what I have done, and what I have done may very well be costing me my life. I must go now before I am being missed or else Mr. Zeifer will know you are being warned. Whatever you are deciding will be better than giving in to Mr. Zeifer and what he wants, but whatever you are deciding, you must decide this night. Farewell, Prince Robin, and know that from this day forward I am taking the stance that will save my family. As for myself, I am beyond redemption and am no longer being trusted from this moment on."

Robin watched Dr. Dahliwal as he quietly opened his bedroom door and stealthily walked down the hall. In a flash, Robin grabbed his gym bag and packed a change of clothes. Then he went to the kitchen to find enough food to last for at least a day or two.

He packed away the supplies and then remembered the swords in the basement. As quietly as he could, Robin stole his way down to the gym. Leaving the lights off, he carefully groped his way to where the swords were kept. He reached for them in the darkness and felt them to make sure he had not picked up the practice swords by mistake. He pulled the long sword part way out of its scabbard and felt the edge nick his finger. He grunted with the sudden pain. Just as he opened his gym bag to pack away the swords the lights came on.

"It's all right, Robin," Lleus said with a smile. "If I were you, I would be sneaking down here to see those magnificent swords as often as I could. That is what you are doing, isn't it?"

"Oh...yes, sir, just a quick look," Robin stammered. "If we start practicing with them, though, isn't there a danger that one of us would get hurt?"

"Yes, of course that danger exists, but you have demonstrated proper control, and I have complete confidence in your abilities. What about you, though? Do you have complete confidence in my abilities with a real sword?"

"Yes, I think so. I should have confidence in you, shouldn't I?"

"I have an idea," Lleus began as his smile broadened. "Why don't we test our confidence out with each other? Prepare yourself while I do the same."

Robin watched Lleus pick his own sword up. He knelt down on the floor, closed his eyes, and began to meditate. Robin did the same.

"Begin!" Lleus shouted.

He was upon Robin before he finished the second syllable of the word. Robin rolled to his right and parried before the blow fell. Quickly, he regained his feet and faced Lleus while the sweat on his brow trickled into his eyes, making them sting. Lleus was already levitating, but so was he. Robin trembled from the excess adrenalin coursing through his body and the fear of being in over his head.

"You could have done this before, couldn't you?" he said as he watched Lleus floating in the air.

"Long before, as a matter of fact. Would you like to see what else I can do?"

As soon as he posed the question, Lleus's image split in two so that Robin had to move his eyes back and forth to watch him. The awful truth now visible, Robin struggled to keep his fear in check.

"Now, tell me, Prince Robin, which one is the real me? If you choose wrong, I will run you through before you can react to the real one. Choose soon. I am about to attack."

Robin wanted to wipe the evil smile off Lleus's face. But which one was he? How was he supposed to tell the difference? Then he saw it, or rather didn't see it. One image had no shadow. Robin faced the one with the shadow as both of them closed in on him rapidly as a striking snake. Robin rolled toward the shadowless image and parried successfully.

"*Good boy!*" Lleus shouted. "You did that well. Shall we try again?"

"You were just playing with me all this time, weren't you, *Lucifer?*" Robin asked, hoping to delay the next attack.

"What if I am? Think of the confidence you have gained along the way. Did I tell you your grandmother died early this evening? It's true, you know, and the throne is within your grasp."

"What if I don't want this throne?" Robin asked.

Lleus lowered his sword and gave Robin a curious look. "You won't have a choice, you know. I am not the only one who knows you are the crown prince now that Lady Morgana has passed on."

"But how can my grandmother's death bring me the throne? I thought it passed to the first-born male—you know, from father to son."

"Your grandfather, whom you never knew, was a prince related to Dagobert, and the child your grandmother bore was your father, William Glen Gilman."

"What did you need me for, then? Why couldn't my dad have been king?"

"You misunderstand. He *was* to be king. He would rule until you came of age and abdicate in deference to you. Most people would sell their souls to be a king, even if only for a brief moment in their miserable lives. He was unappreciative, however, and was already beginning to abuse his power. You, like your grandfather and father before you, are also a prince. This made you a threat to your father. He secretly made plans to murder you when he learned it was you I wanted, and not him, to become the king. The title passed to you upon your father's death, and your grandmother became your regent."

"But why me? If my father was as bad as you say, isn't that what you want me to become?"

"Never. Your father made no secret that his heart was corrupted by his absolute power. You, on the other hand, remain true to your good and kingly principles. I need you to be good and kind, Robin, not abusive as your father was."

"But why kill Grandma?"

"Queen Morgana taught your father to be abusive and would have done the same to you against my wishes, and I am not used to being disobeyed."

"But you called her Lady Morgana before, not queen."

"Right you are. I persuaded the Chamber of Peers to confer upon her the title of queen in secret. But you do not inherit the throne through her, since it can only pass from male heir to male heir. You inherit the throne through your father. You were born in France, did you know? It's where your mother and father met on holiday. The first five years of your life, you lived in Berlin, and this means you are a French king of German background and exactly what Nostradamus predicted.

"The family tree is traced through the mother, but only the first-born male is the heir. Your grandmother is related to the House of Capet and that is the French side, but the Gilmans also came from France during the time of the French Revolution. They were Huguenots. Being queen meant everything to your grandmother, and when she agreed to my terms, I made her queen."

"Am I the first born, or was it my twin? And what exactly do you mean by terms?"

"Your grandmother never should have told you about your twin. But for the sake of the argument, without the existence of your twin it no longer matters whether you were the first born or not. It is you, Robin, and you alone. You are the only male heir there is.

"I am now your regent until your eighteenth birthday. As regent, I will rule in your stead, having the rights to vote at the Chamber of Peers with all powers of attorney on your behalf. You will be first in line within the Capetian Monarchy and your power within the Chamber of Peers would be second only to the president of the Chamber. Your grandmother helped to persuade the Chamber of Peers to automatically confer the office of president of the chamber upon whoever is your regent and those were the terms."

"You are my regent now?" Robin glowered. "You tempted her with all the power and authority of a queen in exchange for being my regent? Is that why she came to Wales and took me away? How long have you been planning this?"

"I have watched you ever since you were born. We could take this one step further if you like. I could adopt you as my son. Would you like that?"

"You don't want me as your son! You want me to be your puppet! I won't be either one!"

"Curious choice of words, that. So, you won't be my puppet. Will you be king then and make me your puppet?" Lleus Zeifer, though he spoke near to laughter, had no amusement in his eyes. Robin began to think he derived enjoyment from torturing souls, especially his.

With his bulldog jaw grimly set, Robin pronounced, "I will be a king for the people of my kingdom, if that's what you mean. I'd rather you weren't a part of that kingdom though, thank you."

"Curious thing about being a regent, you know. It means I have custody of you. It was all automatic, you see. That means you are under my care as if I was your father and have the right to make decisions that will affect the outcome of your life. Adopting you would only be a formality. And when this body I use for this brief moment upon this filthy planet expires, then you will allow me full possession of your younger and more vibrant body. This is the one request I make, and you are bound by the blood oath to allow it."

"I won't let you do this!"

"Calm yourself, dear boy; it's not as bad as you might think. This way I have become your surrogate father. I am now someone who will help you and guide you along the way as well as someone who will be there for you when you need until the time comes when you are ready to assume the full responsibility of your station."

"You had my father murdered, didn't you?"

"Your father was a despot and I couldn't use him as such. He was blinded by his own ambition, and in blindness he resides within the belly of the dragon. I wanted someone who has strong moral and ethical values. I want you. Your goodness will become legend, and your state of innocence will cause the world to view you as the new Messiah.

"I can give you the power to cause major earth changes and rain terror down upon its inhabitants. But instead I would have you use that power to save the world, and all will bow before you and call you God."

"I don't believe you! I want to talk to Myrddin and you can't stop me!"

"Myrddin has been, shall we say, unavailable for quite some time now. It would be a mistake to believe I am a liar, Robin, and I have always and I will always tell you the truth."

"I want it undone!" Then Robin held up his scarred hand. "*I want this undone!*"

"Even if I was inclined to do so, neither is possible," Lleus stated. "Besides, where would you go and what would you do with no one to look after you?"

Although he was terrified, Robin managed to grimly reply, "I'm prepared to do whatever it takes, and I can look after myself just fine!"

Lleus studied the small boy who defiantly stood before him. He smiled and said, "So, you've packed your bags already, have you? You won't get very far. This estate is surrounded by a high wall, and the razor wire I had installed is very sharp. There aren't many ways to escape this compound without serious injury. Did I also mention that the area inside and out is patrolled by orcs? I would have Dr. Dahliwal confirm this for you, but it seems he has recently met with a most unfortunate accident, you see."

"What have you done to Dr. Dahliwal?"

"Actually it would be more accurate to ask what he has done with himself. He chose to violate our blood oath. This resulted in his soul becoming forfeit. I found it a most delicious soul even if it was a bit spicy for my taste."

"What...spicy...what do you...please tell me you didn't..."

With a very displeasing smirk on his face, Lleus finished the sentence for Robin. "Eat his soul? Indeed, that is precisely what has happened. He now resides within the belly of the beast and is part of the dragon that pursues. This is where all blind souls go who choose to violate their blood oath with me."

Robin's blood ran cold as the implications became clear to him. He frantically considered running for the only door to the room but quickly dismissed that possibility since Lleus would be upon him before he had crossed the room halfway. The inevitable became clear to him, and he steeled himself to get ready for the impending battle.

"Perhaps you require proof that I have eaten the good doctor's soul? Gaze then upon his disembodied head!" Lleus manifested the bloody head of Dr. Dahliwal in his left hand and threw it at Robin's feet.

Robin staggered away from the horror that was Dr. Dahliwal. Fighting revulsion and nausea, he struggled to keep his own panic at bay. He trembled and broke out into a cold sweat as the eyeless sockets of Dr. Dahliwal's head opened and gaped at him. Robin cried out in terror.

"Forgive me, Robin," spoke the head. "It seems I am no longer being in a position of assistance to you. I am thinking now that you are fleeing this place and finding your way back to Llangollen. Once there, you should seek out Dinas Bran. It is your only hope. Tell my family that I love them and it is for their protection that I am violating my blood oath."

Revolted, Robin held both hands to his mouth and dropped his sword. His peripheral vision caught sight of Lleus moving in with his sword raised to strike. Robin dove for his own sword just as Zeifer's sword came down. The sword missed its mark entirely, and now Robin was between the door and Lleus with his own sword in hand.

Fairy dust and light brighter than the sun exploded all around Robin just as Lleus's sword came down a second time. Robin parried and the sword glanced off, slicing deep into his left thigh. Robin cried out in both pain and terror. Grimacing and rolling around on the floor, he held his leg tightly, trying to stem the flow of blood. He gathered his wits and quickly stood despite the pain. Myrddin and Kat-sidhe stood between him and Lleus.

"How fortunate for Robin that you chose to return at this exact time," Lleus said with a sinister laugh. "Your light has caused me to miss my mark and his leg remains attached. You know you have no right to interfere now that the blood oath has been taken. The boy is mine by spiritual law and the law of free will. Neither of these laws may you or any other violate!"

"The boy is a child and not yet responsible for certain actions or foolish decisions! Be gone, evil one! Be gone and be damned!" Myrddin's voice filled the room, and Robin felt the power emanating from him.

Kat-sidhe flew to Robin's ear and whispered, "When I tell you, run for the door and I will open it. Do not hesitate, but prepare yourself, for I will speak the word sooner than you think."

"You are wasting my time," Lleus said as he rose into air, smiling malevolently. "I fear the time has come to end this interruption."

He moved rapidly toward Myrddin, closing the distance between them in less than a heartbeat. Myrddin set himself for the attack and raised his oak staff to point it at his descending enemy. Robin grabbed his gym bag by its handle, hoping Lleus wouldn't notice.

"Run, Robin!"

Kat-sidhe flew directly into Robin's chest. Amidst great clouds of fairy dust, he was propelled through the door, crashing into the wall across the hallway outside.

Robin's heart beat madly against his chest, and sweat soaked his shirt through, pouring down his brow and into his eyes. He ran despite the pain in his leg and his desire to see what had happened to Myrddin. His aching sides felt like they were splitting apart, but on he ran. He heard the voice of Lleus cry out in anger as he climbed the stairs, and then there was only dread silence.

Robin burst through his bedroom door, and the doorknob caught his injured leg as it rebounded from the force with which it had been pushed, making him cry out in pain. He desperately grabbed the Holy Grail from under his bed, stuffed it into his gym bag, and tossed everything out onto the roof just beneath his bedroom window. He stepped out into the cool night air, frightened and all alone.

What he saw next made him scream out in panic despite his best effort not to. There, level with his own head as he stood on the edge of the roof, was the head of the most strikingly handsome man he had ever seen. His impression was that the head was disembodied much the same way as Dr. Dahliwal's head had been. As he peered below to the ground, he saw that the man was indeed whole and fourteen feet tall. What was most amazing, however, was not the stature of the man or the long, flowing, white hair that reached down to his waist or even the shockingly indigo blue eyes that looked as if they were made of porcelain, but the fact that he had white wings.

Chapter 17
A BATTLE JOINED, A PLOT REVEALED

The giant man smiled and gazed into Robin's eyes while his wings expanded and contracted. He held out his enormous hand and said, "May I help you down?"

Robin took the hand that dwarfed his own and floated gently to the lawn. His bags and the Holy Grail were next while Robin watched the strange winged giant. He was dressed in golden armored breastplates that covered silver chainmail reaching down to his knees. He wore brass bracers and greaves that covered his shins. His metallic armor was as flexible as if it were the giant's second skin.

The front door of the house burst open, and Myrddin flew through it, closely pursued by Lleus. There was no longer an evil smile but instead an expression of violent rage on Lleus's face.

"Will you excuse me for a moment, Prince Robin?" the giant calmly asked.

The giant flew towards the ugly confrontation, drawing a magnificent double-edged sword. The giant settled between the two assailants, and they lowered their weapons to regard the new intruder. Lleus bowed ceremonially to the giant man, and the giant returned a bow in kind.

"Hello, old friend," Lleus spoke at last with a hint of genuine affection. "How have you been? I've missed speaking with you these past few millennia."

"And I with you, old friend," the giant replied.

"You are interfering here, you know," Lleus continued.

"I do so on the behest of the Mother Goddess Azna."

The giant sat cross-legged on the ground. Lleus did the same.

"Have you considered that you might be in violation of spiritual law in your zeal to fulfill Mother's request?"

"Perhaps, but do not forget that it is Mother's prerogative to interfere in the interest of enabling a higher spiritual law than the one to which you refer. Tell me, old friend, how is it we have become adversaries when once we were the best of friends? This saddens me."

"You know the reason! I was ready to claim my inheritance and it was denied to me! I have a right to it despite what you so-called loyalists believe! It was you, in fact, who expelled me from Father's presence! But you are not here to discuss that matter, are you?"

"No, I am not. I am here to divide right from wrong. I am here to unite that which never should have been divided. Please put away your hatred and help me to make the parallels one, my brother."

"One of the parallels is mine by right of inheritance! I created it! It is mine! I shall take both of them should they be united, but I will let the other to co-exist if I am allowed to inherit the universe I created for myself! It is you who should help me, Michael! Join me now and I will seat you at my right side!"

"I am deeply offended by your effort to tempt me," Michael calmly replied. "You and I have a destiny together even as much as this boy has with us. Release him from his blood oath and allow him to find his destiny on his own and not the fate you have trapped him into. It is destiny we must ultimately achieve and not some fate forced upon us against our will by deception."

"The oath was taken of his own free will! He is mine now, and you are interfering! Be gone and gather your forces for the coming war. I would rather confront you there on the battlefield, as it should be between two warriors, and not here like this."

"If that is your wish, then I will bargain for the life of the boy by agreeing to meet you on the battlefield as you say. Release him from the blood oath now if it is a bargain!"

Michael no longer smiled, and his wings beat furiously, causing him to rise off the ground while dust swirled all around him. His magnificent sword glowed and emitted an ominous drone. Lleus stood, smiled, and bowed.

"I will consider your offer, old friend. I cannot decide now, but I will release him into your custody for the time being. Keep him close and guard him well, for I may yet claim him by my right of the blood oath. Besides, it is a whole human I want on the throne, not one without a soul. I leave you without harm to anyone."

"Then I allow you to leave without harm. I will not allow this should we meet again. Our final destiny fast approaches, my old friend, and the grace you receive today is the last you will receive in this universe." Michael bowed in turn, and Lleus was gone in the twinkling of an eye.

Michael's expression quickly changed to one of impish amusement as he turned his indigo gaze upon Robin. "The bugs will set up housekeeping inside your mouth if you continue to leave it open like that."

Embarrassed, Robin quickly closed his mouth and asked, "Who are you? Are you an angel?"

"Indeed, I am an archangel. My name is Michael. You, of course, are the high prince Robin Gilman, but I think we should have someone look at that injury now, wouldn't you agree, Myrddin?"

"Whoa...this is really cool!" Robin burst out before Myrddin could reply.

"Kat-sidhe informs me that we are temporarily safe," Myrddin said, "but the area will soon be swarming with orcs. We need to leave now before the vile creatures arrive, and then we can seek medical attention for Robin's injury."

"Where would you take the young prince, then?" Michael asked.

"To where his twin awaits. Transportation will be a problem, since I doubt Robin will be able to concentrate long enough to fly the entire journey. Not with that wound."

"I will transport the prince then," Michael stated.

Michael gently picked Robin up, cradling him in his great arms. Robin felt as if he had just been picked up by clouds. A feeling of well-being and security such as he had never known before engulfed him.

"But I thought you were a warrior angel?" Myrddin asked.

"I am, as you say, a warrior angel, but for this one I make an exception. Besides, I will need to speak with his twin, and I might as well carry him along the way."

"Wait a moment!" Kat-sidhe said. She wrapped Robin's leg as rapidly as she could. She worked so quickly that to the others she was a blur of motion. "There, that will stop the bleeding until we get him proper attention."

They rose in the air and flew toward the west. Kat-sidhe's personal guards brought Robin's belongings, following close behind. Robin was amazed at the silence around him, thinking that Michael's enormous wings should surely make more noise.

"Their design is exactly like that of the barn owl, you know," Michael stated.

"Excuse me," Robin stammered, "are you speaking of your wings?"

"Isn't that what you wished to know?"

"Well, yes, but I hadn't asked any questions, at least not out loud."

"It's an angel thing," Michael laughed. "You know, answering questions before they are asked out loud. All angels do that. And in answer to your next question, I am your chief guardian angel, and I am assisted, or rather you are assisted, by several Seraphim and two Cherubim."

"Whoa, this is really, really cool!" Robin beamed. "But why haven't I ever seen them? I mean, I see you so I should be able to see them, shouldn't I?"

"We do not often appear except under the most extreme circumstances. We normally stay out of sight to avoid giving our charges a false sense of security."

"How's that?"

"If you had known I would suddenly appeared to assist you, would you have run when Kat-sidhe told you? I think not. You would have stayed to fight thinking that my presence made you invincible, and Lucifer would have won."

"But you could have saved me, right? Even if I hadn't run."

"I could have, but I would not have been allowed."

"But why?"

"Because of the blood oath, and because your decision to run was also a decision to distance yourself from him and his influence. By running, you took an action that rejected the possibility of allowing him to possess you. I know, for instance, that for a moment you doubted that he was evil and would have allowed him anything, including access to your own mind. He was trying to possess you and almost succeeded."

"So if I had decided to let him, you wouldn't have saved me?"

"Free will. Guardian angels whisper in your ear all the time and warn you of the dangers you could face. But if you decide not to heed those small inner voices, not even God himself will interfere with that, although he very easily could."

"Thanks—for helping me, I mean."

"No, Your Highness, thank you for making the correct decision."

Despite his aching heart and throbbing leg, Robin's troubles seemed to disappear as he spoke with Michael. The Edgewater Inn looked wonderful to Robin as they flew near. He would see Gwyneth as soon as they were in the hotel room with the Reynolds family.

Then they were inside the hotel room, without Robin remembering going through the lobby, and lights were turning on while everyone began hugging him, which made him uncomfortable. Gwyneth grinned from ear to ear despite still being sleepy from having just awakened. She held Robin tight. Dewey stood awkwardly in the doorway and waited for Robin to notice him.

Robin pried himself loose from Gwyneth and turned to shake hands with Tom. "Thank you for coming," he beamed. "I missed all of you lots."

"And we missed you, Robin. Shall I tell him now what our plans are, Myrddin?"

"What are you doing here?" Robin asked.

"Pardon me?" Myrddin asked.

"Not you; him!" Robin pointed at Dewey.

"Robin, please!" Gwyneth pleaded. "You don't understand! We invited him!"

"You invited him? Why, is he your boyfriend now? What are you playing at, anyway?"

Tom's arm went around Robin's shoulders and forcefully propelled him toward Dewey. "The two of you have a hatchet to bury, Robin, and I will not allow this sort of dissension within my family. Dewey, it's time you said to Robin what you came here to say." Tom, though gentle, was not to be denied.

"I-I'm sorry for the way I treated yeh before," Dewey began in a barely audible voice. "I...I never meant for it to go as far as it did. I only meant to scare yeh, not 'urt yeh."

Then he wiped his eyes to see Robin better. Robin was astonished. He had never expected this from Dewey, and now that it had happened, he was at a loss for words. The two boys stared at each other for a few silent moments more. Robin stumbled through his mind trying to find the right words. Robin felt as if he had been trapped into being somewhere he didn't want to be.

"Robin, you can't just stand there!" Gwyneth's interruption made them both jump.

"But...I...I don't know what to say. Okay then, I accept your apology. But you better not try it again and you better not ever think of hurting Gwyneth either!"

"Yeh 'ave my word on it," Dewey solemnly said.

Both boys extended their hands and briefly shook. Robin seized Dewey's left hand just before he released his right. There on the palm was a thin scar.

"What's this, then?" he asked even though he knew the answer.

"A stupid mistake," Dewey said. Robin held his own hand up for Dewey to see, and they silently regarded each other.

"Where's Fred, then?" Robin asked.

"I don't know just now. 'E ran away from 'ome just after, and no one's seen 'im since. I tried to find 'im once and thought I saw 'im, too, but 'e doesn't much want to speak with anyone, I guess, so 'e ran the other way when 'e saw me."

"He ran away? But why? He could have come here if he'd wanted."

"Our dad got pretty upset and started knockin' us round. Fred could never take it as well as I could, and 'e just ran."

"You mean your dad, you know, hit you?"

"'E always 'as as long as I can remember, but 'e did it more to me than Fred. After you were 'urt and we were in trouble with the p'lice, then it was all over the telly and 'e seemed to take it all out on Fred. Fred just couldn't stay anymore."

"That's when social services came for Dewey," Gwyneth added. "Mum and Dad took him in as his foster parents."

"Wow, that was really nice of them. Especially considering how Dewey attacked you and me."

"We was paid to do it, you know. I think that's 'ow Fred is survivin' all alone, especially considerin' that me share of the money went missin' the night 'e disappeared."

"You were paid? Who paid you? Why?" Anger began to well up inside Robin again.

"Some man named Lleus Zeifer."

Chapter 18
THE WONDER IN HEAVEN

The next week was spent allowing Robin time to heal. The evenings were his favorite since he and Gwyneth studied the ancient scroll together. Though Robin had a difficult time staying on task, he persisted as long as Gwyneth wanted him to. They traced Robin's family directly to King Arthur.

"Pendragon, that's the name you are connected to," Gwyneth stated. "We can trace that name back as far as we can or we can trace that name all the way forward and confirm everything. Which do you think we ought to do?"

"Maybe we should do both and see where it leads us. We've got to confirm what we've found anyway, and I'd like to see who the Pendragons descend from out of curiosity. I'd rather like a break now if you don't mind, though."

Robin was weary, and his eyes itched from all the strain. They had been at it for several hours while Myrddin spoke with Darla and Tom in hushed tones and Dewey occupied himself at the hotel's complimentary play station.

"I'm getting tired of this, too," Gwyneth returned. "But we can start again in the morning."

"Yeah, well it's easy for you, isn't it?" Robin groaned. "I've always had a difficult time with my studies, you know, and I am trying to stay with it as much as I can. I need a chance to get out for some fresh air."

"It's what we have to do, so you don't have to be such a git about it!"

"Then how about a journey to Yggdrasil?" Myrddin interrupted.

~ *Gilman's Parallel: The French King* ~

"Really?" Robin beamed. "Do you mean it? Will I get to see Mother Lilith again? Can Gwyneth go, as well? What about Dew…"

"Calm down, boy, calm down," Myrddin chuckled. "Yes to your questions, and Tom and Darla will be going along, as well. We have some business to discuss with Mother Lilith, and Kat-sidhe has already gone ahead to secure the way."

The wait to depart for Yggdrasil seemed to be extraordinarily long. It was only a few minutes, however, before Robin was flying once again. Dewey, wide-eyed with terror, gazed continually at the ground, wishing his feet were there instead of up in the air. Fairies flew all around him, desperately trying to cheer him up, but Dewey could only think he would plummet to the ground in a dreadful heap at any moment. Robin knew Dewey would soon come to terms with the flying.

Gwyneth flew next to her parents, pointing out certain landmarks while Myrddin led the way, watching purposefully ahead. Robin could see Dinas Bran below and knew they were nearing Yggdrasil. Suddenly, he saw movement. Orcs were everywhere, tearing Dinas Bran apart. The ancient ruin was nothing more than an unrecognizable pile of rubble.

"Gwyneth," he shouted, "look below!"

"Yes, I see them! What do you suppose they are looking for?"

"This!" Robin called holding up the scroll. "*Oh, no!*" he yelled as it slipped out of his hand and began fluttering to the ground.

He longed to turn back the hands of time so he could relive the moment when he had decided to take it with him to Yggdrasil. If only he had left it behind. Now it was fluttering in the wind toward Dinas Bran and the orcs below. He dove after it, but the more he tried, the more it seemed to have a will of its own as it stayed just out of his reach.

"Robin, no!" Myrddin shouted in horror.

Myrddin pursued Robin, trying desperately to reach him before he was seen by the orcs. Robin plummeted on, frantically trying to catch the scroll before it hit the ground, not realizing that Myrddin was close behind him. Robin wished he had worn goggles as his eyes watered from the wind forcing its way between his half-closed eyelids, but on he sped toward the havoc below. With Myrddin only inches away, Robin finally seized the scroll.

"Gottcha! Ow!"

Myrddin roughly grasped Robin by his collar, quickly pulling him away from the chaotic scene below. An orc screeched an alarm, and an arrow flew by, just missing them as they struggled to gain enough altitude to be out of range. Another arrow followed the first, and then many more were sent their way. One lone arrow struck the scroll, forcing Robin to drop it a second time.

"Oh, no you don't!" he cried out as he broke free of Myrddin's grip.

Robin heard Myrddin cursing and swearing behind him and could only assume that the wizard was once again trying to catch him. The scroll came to rest near the orcs, and they swarmed over it. They began fighting over it, each wanting to be the one who would present it to their dark lord, Lleus Zeifer.

The orcs were now distracted, and Robin reached for his sword, hoping to use the advantage of surprise and his sword skills to retake the scroll and get cleanly away. But the sword wasn't there. Too late, he remembered he had never considered there might be danger along the way to Yggdrasil and had left it behind. Now his only hope was complete surprise and quick reflexes. If the orcs continued to fight over the scroll, he knew he could snatch it away before they could react.

He ignored his own fear and Myrddin's voice shouting to turn around and rammed into the squirming pile of orcs. Amid the fierce shrieking and outrage, he held onto the scroll as he sped away. Despite their dull-witted intelligence, the orcs regrouped sooner than Robin thought possible. Two of them attached ropes to their arrows and sent them up. Robin was just breathing a sigh of relief when he felt one of the arrows stick in the leg of his jeans with its barbed tip.

Bracing themselves and holding on to the other end of the rope, the two orcs violently pulled back on the cord just as it went taut. Robin cried out in pain as his previously injured leg jerked in the opposite direction, pulling him down.

Dazed, he desperately held onto the scroll as the orcs ran toward him from all directions. Four of the orcs each grabbed a limb, pulling him out in four different directions.

"Myrddin!" he screamed out, and as quickly as he called out, the violent tug-of-war ended.

Robin, careful not to put any weight on his throbbing leg, stood slowly. Myrddin pointed his oaken staff at the grumbling horde of orcs, and Kat-sidhe flew between him and the orcs.

"Want Grall! Give Grall now!" the nearest orc cried.

Bleak and Gloom, the two traitors, suddenly appeared and hovered for a moment from above. They both screeched a war cry that sounded like a thousand banshees and charged straight at Robin. Robin gritted his teeth as a most unpleasant shiver went through his body.

"Stop!" Kat-sidhe yelled. The magical power behind Kat-sidhe's voice caused Bleak and Gloom to halt, though they stayed in motion, circling about the trio, maintaining their distance.

"We are more powerful now, Your Majesty," they said together as one voice. "We are now two become one in separate vessels, and our collective consciousness has made it so. You will not survive our attack, but we will give you this one chance to live. Place the Holy Grail upon the ground and you may leave unharmed."

"Power such as you refer to is in the eye of the beholder!" Kat-sidhe returned as she bravely stood her ground.

It was then that several things happened all at once. Myrddin repelled several orcs with a simple wave of his staff. Next, Kat-sidhe yelled her own war cry, harshly piercing Robin's ears. A violet light from Myrddin's staff filled the evening sky so bright that Bleak and Gloom and the orcs were blinded for a moment, but it was that very moment that Kat-sidhe needed.

Kat-sidhe charged straight at Bleak and Gloom and set their wings on fire as she passed by. The cries of pain and anguish from the two traitors filled the air, adding to the noise and confusion. Dewey surprised everyone. He came from behind Robin, yelling at the top of his lungs and brandishing a fallen tree branch that resembled a golf club.

"No, Dewey, no!" Gwyneth screamed.

Before anyone could stop him, Dewey was upon the orcs, swinging his terrible club with remarkable accuracy and deadly force, scattering the orcs that moments before had circled like a pack of wolves. The first orc was caught on the temple and collapsed in a heap, and then another and another, each rapidly decomposing before their eyes. Those that were lucky fled down the slopes of the tor, too frightened by this strangest of attackers to collect themselves and regroup.

Robin suddenly found himself feeling curiously useless. He stood still and gaped at Dewey as he made his attack on the terrified orcs. Myrddin took advantage of the distraction and seized Robin by the collar. Kat-sidhe, along with several of her personal guard, grabbed Gwyneth and Dewey.

They flew the rest of the way to Yggdrasil in silence and were soon at the giant mountain ash, exhausted but safe. Robin's leg was throbbing with so much pain now that he could scarcely concentrate. He looked down at his leg and saw that his jeans were soaked with blood.

"That's goin' to leave a scar," Dewey remarked as he hobbled over to where Robin sat propped up against Yggdrasil.

"What happened to you, then?" Robin asked.

"Oh, er...I turned me ankle when I 'it the ground back at Dinas Bran. Do yeh know 'ow annoyin' those fairies are? They were tryin' to stop me from goin' down and 'elpin' yeh, but I managed it anyway. And Gwyneth... yeh should 'ave 'eard 'er! She's almost as annoyin' as me mum, the way she was carryin' on." Dewey changed his voice to sound as much like Gwyneth as he could and in mocking tones said, *"Oh, Dewey, you could've been killed! Why ever did you do it for? You gave me such a fright!"*

"Actually, it's a good question, that," Robin said with a broad grin. "Why did you do it?"

"Well, can't 'ave the future king's 'ead on an orc pike, can we now?"

"Er, thanks for that," Robin said, feeling awkward. "You sure scattered them! Do you have that club with you still?"

"What...oh yeah! Quite the mashie, that." Dewey held it up for Robin to see, "You scattered some orcs, too, yeh know, and without a weapon. If I 'ad seen yeh doin' somethin' like that before, I never would 'ave picked on yeh like I did 'cause I would 'ave been too afraid. What was that 'orrible smell they made after I 'it 'em? It was like they rotted away into nothin'."

"Oh, they don't die like we do. They just sort of rot away where they stand, all at once really. First time Gwyneth saw it happen, she threw up and passed out."

Both boys laughed at this but didn't see Gwyneth until Dewey looked around for her. When his eyes met hers, he stopped laughing.

"I'm...not...*Brigid*!" She said as she stomped off toward where her parents were engaged in a conversation with Myrddin.

"Now we done it!' Dewey remarked as he watched her march away.

Robin suddenly felt a most uncomfortable feeling in his stomach, and a lump formed in his throat. Then he realized he was feeling Gwyneth's anger and hurt feelings, just as if they were his own.

"It is because you are an empath, Robin," Mother Lilith said.

"Whoa!" Dewey exclaimed.

"It is really good to see you again, Mother Lilith," Robin said as he knelt before her.

"I have much to discuss with you, especially concerning Lleus Zeifer and a certain blood oath you have taken."

Robin suddenly had difficulty breathing and his eyes blurred, but still he spoke. "I am sorry for what I did. I never knew! I just want it undone!"

"Hush, child, I am here," Mother Lilith declared as she put her arms around him. Robin felt the same peace and security and the same sensation of being held by clouds that he had felt when Michael had first held him.

"I tell you now that in this time I have been given special dispensation to assist all those who would dare break their blood oath with the evil one. It is you I will help first and then the others who would dare. You are not the only one, you see, who wishes his mistake to be undone, nor are you the only one who is willing to defy Lleus Zeifer."

"I don't even want to talk with him ever again. I still don't understand though. He asked me to let him merge his mind with mine and..."

"I am pleased you did not allow that to happen."

"But, if he's really Lucifer, then what he wanted would be like possession."

"Yes, but only if you had allowed it by your own free will. The prophecy would have then been fulfilled."

"Prophecy? You mean I was supposed to let him because of some prophecy?"

"You were to be the Mabus, the last and final Antichrist."

"You knew this? What else aren't you telling me?"

"Lucifer wants to raise up a priest king who would be viewed by all of Earth as its messiah. He will call this person his own son and will bestow upon him many of his special powers. It was already foretold by the seer Nostradamus that a king of French descent would claim his throne during the end of time and during a period of world war. It is upon this child king that Lleus set his sights. What better revenge than to turn one of the Creator's innocents into the son of the beast."

"You should have told me!"

"Your anger is inappropriate. We had to try and help you to make the decision only you could make. We had to hope you would not choose to be the son of the beast."

Robin sat hugging his knees close to his chest while he rocked back and forth. He thought about how every decision he had made lately had turned his life upside down. Each decision had propelled his life to this one point but he wondered if this was the point he truly wanted to be at. Robin slowly stirred and sat up.

"Is that what I was supposed to be, the son of the beast?" he asked the others. "Well, it's not what I want to be. I just don't know if I can do this alone."

"But you don't have to do it alone!" Gwyneth burst out. "I'm here to help you!"

"I'm not lettin' you do this alone either!" Dewey emphatically stated. "I like a good fight, anyway, and I bet you're gonna be in loads from now on."

"We are all here to help, Robin," Myrddin said. "I know you were left on your own for a time, and I apologize for that, but I was detained by the orcs, and I believe Kat-sidhe was there when you needed her most. You had to pass the test of being tempted by Lleus, and with that decision we were forbidden to interfere. I will be there when you need me as long as I am able, and to that end, I have dedicated my life."

"Our home is now your home, Robin," Darla said as she put her arms around him, and though he felt uncomfortable, it was still nice to be held. "In case we neglected to tell you, we have had adoption papers written up, and you will be living with us from now on until you are ready to leave."

"In Llangollen? Do you mean it? Mr. Reynolds, is it true then? But how? I thought…"

"Darla and I have worked with Social Services as foster parents for some time now. After we applied to be Dewey's foster parents, the paper work for you was approved straight away."

"But you can't have had time."

"Myrddin came to us just after you left with your grandmother. That's when we first met him. We all came to realize what could happen in your life, and we drew up the paper work."

Fairy dust exploded in his face as Kat-sidhe flew at him, trying to hug him, which was almost impossible considering her size. He held out his hands palms up so she could land and he could see her up close.

"If you ascend to the throne and stand against this ancient evil, the Ellyllon Tylwyth Teg will live on. We have everything to lose if you do not do this and everything to gain if you decide to take the throne on the side of good, as is your right. But even if there was no reason such as this, I have grown fond of you and would spend my life to save yours."

"Thank you, all of you," Robin managed to say. "Kat-sidhe, could you do me a favor, though?"

"Anything, my Lord."

"Is it possible for you to not make so much fairy dust?" Robin asked as he waved his hands, trying to clear the air around him for what seemed the umpteenth time. "It always gets in my nose." Kat-sidhe giggled, and her laughter infected the others. Their somber mood disappeared.

"Let me see your hand, and yours, as well, young man," Mother Lilith said. She took Robin and Dewey's hands in hers and looked down at the thin scars and then into their eyes.

"You are both forgiven for your transgressions, and only the scars need to be removed at this time. You have both learned from your mistakes and have made the momentous decision to change what was wrong with your lives, and that says an awful lot about the both of you. Shall we proceed?"

They solemnly nodded their assent and steeled themselves for whatever would come to pass. Lilith kissed the scarred hands of each boy. First they felt their hands grow pleasantly warm and then the warmth spread throughout their bodies, settling in their hearts. The warm glow they felt made them feel at peace with all that had happened, and then they felt happy inside, something neither had felt for a long time.

Chapter 19
THE CHOOSING

"What do we do now?" Robin asked Mother Lilith.

"We prepare for war," Mother Lilith pronounced.

"War? With Zeifer? He still can't make me become his puppet king, can he?"

"Only if you allow it. He has caused certain prophecies to come to pass, and he has taken steps to eliminate your competition for the throne. But you have defied him, and all he has worked for has gone up in smoke, to say the least. He is angry and will have his way or he will cause another to usurp your throne if he can. By eliminating your competition, he has also eliminated any possible ascendants that he could turn to his evil purpose, save one.

"Do you know what I mean about forgiveness? The Creator has forgiven you for the blood oath you took, and you must never again give it another thought, but you must forgive yourselves also. After that, you may forgive each other for your actions against each other and for wishing the other harm. This way, you two will be friends forever, and today you will begin a bond that will be stronger than any evil that could possibly come your way. Gwyneth also is a part of this bond, and the three of you are a triune power."

"What does that mean?" Dewey asked.

"The three of you are individually powerful, that is true. Together and united by this bond of friendship, you will act as one and your power will be three times three. Now, Dewey Wilkins, I wish for you to meet someone wonderful. This one will teach you to prepare for war."

"But isn't war wrong? I like to mix it up, really, but war means that many will die. I'm not sure I want to be at war."

"None of us want war, Master Wilkins, but if we are to be attacked, we will certainly need to know how to defend ourselves. Besides, a man who has nothing he believes in that he would die for is not really a man." Michael stood behind Dewey, and when Dewey turned around and saw who was addressing him, he nearly fell over. "Martin Luther King, Jr. said that. He was one of my best trained warriors, you know."

"Whoa!" was all Dewey could say.

"You are also a mighty warrior and lack only proper training. I will be honored to train you if it pleases you."

"Whoa! I mean, will yeh let me use a sword like the one yeh 'ave?" Dewey couldn't take his eyes off the magnificent sword. "I wonder if I could see it closer. Could I...please?"

"Certainly."

Michael handed the two-edged sword to Dewey. Robin gaped with envy. He silently wished he had asked to see the sword earlier. He watched as Dewey's hands lovingly stroked the weapon.

"I like this sword," Dewey said. "It's looks 'eavy, but it's light. This would be easy to wield, I wager." Dewey handed the sword back to Michael haft first, but Robin saw he had a puzzled look on his face.

"Mighty warrior named Dewey Wilkins, I am Michael the Archangel. Of all those whose lifetimes involved being a warrior, you were among the mightiest. Does that answer your question?" Dewey was surprised that Michael could know what he had not asked, but Robin knew that for Michael this was nothing unusual.

"Whoa! Yer Michael the Archangel and it's yeh wants to train me? Whoa! Yeh mean it? Will I 'ave a sword like Robin? Could I 'ave a sword like yers? Am I dreamin'?"

Robin thought he saw tears in Dewey's eyes but decided to keep his observation to himself. Dewey had never been happier than he was now, and Robin correctly perceived the tears he saw were there for that reason.

"I shall never mislead you. You will have a sword much like mine, and with Robin's help, you will soon be well trained in its use. I need good warriors like you. Robin has need of good warriors, also. Now I must speak with Robin and answer the questions he has."

"Sorry," Robin said, wishing his mind wasn't so easy to read. "I didn't mean to interrupt, really."

"War is coming, and it is inevitable. The orcs are under Lucifer's command. He is also amassing a vast Nephilim army as we speak, and these two armies are what you and Dewey will be concerned with. I will be there to help, as will the armies of the Fairy Kingdom. There is one thing both of you must not do, and I must have a solemn promise from the both of you on this matter. I do not want either of you to confront or otherwise physically engage in battle with Lucifer when he is the dragon. I will deal with him, and only I shall do this. Do you both agree?"

"Yes, sir!" both boys said at once.

"But I don't understand," Robin blurted out. "If anyone has a reason to fight with him, it's me, since he's the one who did all this to me and he killed my—"

"Robin," Michael gently said, "it is a mistake to believe evil can be overcome by physical means. Lleus Zeifer is not called the red dragon because the color red is considered lucky by some. He is called that because of the blood he has shed while in the guise of the dragon. Mark my words, he will be known as the dragon pope, and when he faces me, he will be the dragon and will not appear human to those who see him. I am the only entity to ever face him in battle and live. Please give me your word you will not seek him out. Please, Robin, I insist."

"You have my word," Robin solemnly swore. "But I'm not sure Dewey and I could face an army of orcs and evil Nephilim by ourselves, either. Surely you don't think we could do that?"

"You are correct, and that is why you will have all the help you need," Michael explained. "Kat-sidhe and I will be choosing one hundred and forty-four thousand of her elite troops, and they will be the first to answer the call to arms on your behalf. There are also men who would dare defy the dragon, but their number is unknown at this time. All men must make the same decision to defy evil that you and Dewey have made, and only then will they be fit to join our ranks. Because of your decision, Robin, a ripple effect has caused the hearts of some men to do just that. I am sure many more will follow."

Robin and Dewey exchanged a knowing glance between them, and as one they asked, "How much time do we have?"

"Much of that depends on the outcome of certain events that have yet to occur. I will tell you, however, that the time is short and the first battle will be fought before any of us would like. We must, therefore, gird ourselves spiritually and physically for that moment, and we must do this now so there will be enough time. The war I speak of could last for many years, and its outcome is dependent upon the will and courage of those who would resist the dragon."

Robin suddenly felt dazed by what he heard and, after careful consideration, he asked in a hushed voice, "You're talking about Armageddon, aren't you? The Church teaches that we will win because of you. But you're saying that we might not win, aren't you?"

"The future is completely dependent upon man's free will, you see."

"But we have to win! We can't just let Lucifer have it all! The Bible says we'll win!"

"It also predicts an Antichrist that will suffer a severe head wound and survive with the whole world witnessing the event. You suffered a severe head wound and survived, Robin. It was on the...what do you call it...oh yes...the television that event was internationally broadcast. You survived, much to the amazement of the whole world, and now people say you are a miraculous boy who will do great things. But you turned from the fate of becoming the Antichrist, and now the outcome has been changed because of your decision, Prince Robin, heir to the throne of Jerusalem. That took an enormous amount of courage, and it has affected the entire world. Lucifer must devise a contingency plan that no longer involves you. He means to eliminate anything or anyone who stands in his way. That means war."

"But why war?"

"If he wins the war, he could put you in a position where you couldn't possibly refuse him possession of your mind. What we need to do is go to the Princes du Sang before Lleus does and have them confirm you as the crown prince."

"How will that help?"

"Lleus had the only other possible heir, your father, assassinated shortly before he murdered your grandmother and Dr. Dahliwal. The Princes du Sang will have no other choice than to confirm your right to the throne. The president of the Princes du Sang, however, is Lleus Zeifer, and he is already named your regent."

"We should go to them now and explain what happened! I know they'll understand!"

Michael stared directly into Robin's eyes, waiting for the new information to sink into his brain. Then Michael spoke again after the brief pause.

"Lleus Zeifer wields the power that should be yours."

The truth hit him in the groin almost as if Dewey had kneed him like he had in Llangollen. Robin found himself wishing he was in Llangollen, in early spring. Those were happier times, he thought, even if Fred and Dewey constantly beat him up. Now it seemed as if that time was long ago and a memory in blackest night. His leg, throbbing with pain all during his conversation with Michael, suddenly began to hurt even more.

Two fairies were cutting away his pants leg before he could protest. The renewed bleeding that had begun when he struggled with the orcs had almost stopped, but the wound itself was now deeper than he had imagined. When he saw it, he almost swooned. The fairies magically bandaged his leg, and the pain went entirely away. Though he still limped, it was easier to walk.

"I've got to fight him, Dewey," Robin said matter-of-factly as he watched the two fairies tend to his wound. "I've got to win! I must be king, and I must protect my kingdom and all who are in it! I can't let Zeifer win!"

"You're wrong, you know," Dewey said. "*We* can't let 'im win! Besides, since I'm not thrashing yeh anymore, I suppose I need to start thrashing someone, and it might as well be 'im!"

"It's a war we could lose, you know."

"Right then, it's a war, and I'm in!"

"And I'm in!" Gwyneth declared.

"Thank you," Robin said. "Gwyneth, I'm sorry Dewey and I poked fun at you."

"Yeah, sorry, Gwyn," Dewey added.

"I guess I was a bit sensitive," Gwyneth said. "You forgot one thing, though, Robin. I'm not like Brigid, who passed out at the first sight of blood. That was in the other universe. I won't give up on you and expect you to rescue me. I can rescue myself. I can fight and I mean to."

"Well, if you say so," Robin said.

"I do say so! Besides, you'd still be a useless git if you and Peter had not exchanged cellular memories. Say, do you suppose they're fighting their own Lleus Zeifer in their universe?"

"What did yeh say?" Dewey asked incredulously. "And who's Brigid and this Peter guy?"

"They're our parallel lives in the other universe," Gwyneth began.

"And I'm s'posed to believe that," Dewey said. "I'm not gormless, you know. 'Ang on..."

"What is it, Dewey?" Gwyneth asked in an alarmed voice.

"He's thinking what I'm thinking!" Robin said as he stoically set his bulldog jaw.

"'Ow do you know what I'm thinkin'?"

"If I'm heir to the throne," Robin continued ignoring Dewey's question, "here in this universe, then Peter is heir to the throne in the other universe. If Lleus Zeifer turns Peter, then he could turn me despite my decision to defy him when the universes and all parallel lives merge as one. Mother Lilith, am I right about that? Is that possible?"

"I wish I could tell you that you are wrong, Robin," Mother Lilith responded. "This is something I told Gwyneth to keep secret from Peter. Peter, you see, is more susceptible to being evil than you are and could possibly take the blood oath you took, but Lleus would not have to deceive him as he deceived you. You have come to the same conclusion that we came to, and we believe this is exactly what Lleus plans. If he turns Peter into the Mabus, he could possibly turn you when the universes merge. In the meantime, Peter and Brigid are in danger and need your help."

Robin shuddered at this and quickly stole a glance at Gwyneth. If Peter was susceptible and gave in to Lleus, then what would Brigid do? he wondered. Could she see through him the way Gwyneth had?

We'll have to figure a way to help her see through Zeifer, then, won't we? Gwyneth, you heard my thoughts!

Yes, of course I did. The real question is what if she can't talk some sense into him? Oh dear, Robin, what if she can but he chooses differently than you?

"I'm not as free of the blood oath as I thought, am I?"

"Unless you are strong enough to be the dominant part of your soul when it merges with its other half," Myrddin said, "then your assessment is most unfortunately correct."

"This gives me more reason to confront him than I had before! Michael, why didn't you explain this to me before I promised you?"

"Please understand that if you confronted Lleus and lost, then the other half of your soul would be the only part of your soul left in either universe. Lleus would slay your vessel and free your soul. It would merge most definitely, but it would not be allowed to be the dominant part of Peter's life since his vessel would be the only one physically left functioning."

"Let me understand this. You're saying that if I'm killed, my half of my soul will merge with Peter, but Peter will be dominant. If I'm alive when the two universes merge, I might become the dominant half of my soul if I am strong enough. Maybe, that is, if I'm lucky. What happens if he wins when you confront him?"

"That's never happened before," Michael replied.

"Never happened before? How many times?"

"Well, when I confront him in this universe, it will be the second time."

"You've never considered defeat before, have you? It could happen, you know. It's just me, if you lose. I'll have to confront him then, won't I?"

"If it comes to that, yes, you will have to confront him. For that reason, you must guarantee me you will not do so until there is no other choice, and I will guarantee that my attention will not be divided when I do confront him."

Robin saw the black bird first as it circled down from the sky, and when it was near enough, he recognized Powys Fadog. It looked as if someone had singed his wings. Puzzled by the crow's injuries and presence, since it belonged near Dinas Bran and not at Yggdrasil, Robin addressed the bird before it could land.

"What are you doing here? I thought you always stayed near Dinas Bran? Who did this to you?"

"Dinas Bran burn!" Powys Fadog screamed out. "Crows die, not live! Dragon comes! Run hide! Run hide! Dragon wants child!"

The dragon announced its presence with a roar and moved its seven giant heads in Lilith's direction, spewing fire that was so blistering Robin thought his flesh would surely peel away. Robin immediately put himself between Lilith and the dragon. He could smell his own hair burning as fire enveloped him a second time.

"Go away, Zeifer!" Robin bellowed.

"Come with me and I will go away!" the dragon hissed as it belched more flame, stinking of sulfur.

"Go away, dragon," Michael said in a calm and peaceful voice. "Lilith is no longer in this place. Pursue her if you must, but sooner or later you and I will confront each other, and I mean to put an end to this." Robin looked around for Lilith and discovered that indeed she had gone.

"I will find her with a flood from out of my mouth! A flood of fire! *And I will destroy you as well, Michael!*"

The dragon suddenly swelled and reared back, shooting flames out of its seven mouths, burning everything in its path, including the mighty giant mountain ash, Yggdrasil. The stench of the acrid smoke filled the air, making the others gag. When the flames subsided, Michael was unharmed. Though Yggdrasil no longer had any leaves, it continued to stand.

"You don't want to face me now, old friend," Michael said as if nothing unusual had happened. The dragon's eyes blazed with hatred as it regarded Michael.

"I concede that fact, my brother," the dragon declared. "I will return when I am more assured of my goal. Lilith cannot hide from me forever, nor can you conceal her forever."

The dragon then looked directly at Robin. It bowed its seven heads and spoke once again. "You will be mine, Your Majesty, once I have possessed the mind of your parallel counterpart. Unless you would face me now, we will face each other then."

"Don't you dare touch Peter or Brigid!" Robin yelled.

"Honor your blood oath to me, and I shan't touch them! Honor it not, and I will pursue your parallel counterpart for my revenge!"

Dewey yelled and ran straight at the dragon, brandishing his war club menacingly above his head. Michael was in front of him in an instant. Dewey ran into him and was repelled backwards by the force, onto his back, so that he was staring dazedly up at the sky. Robin made a move forward but Michael's hand restrained him before he took the first complete step.

"Have you forgotten your agreement with me so soon, Robin?" he asked.

"I will face the boy and force him to defend himself soon, my old friend," the dragon said. "You will not be around when this happens. Hopefully, he will remember that he promised not to face me and hesitate just as I move in for the kill. For that reason, I am most grateful for your assistance with his future fate, mighty Michael the Archangel! I go now! I leave you unharmed, but not in peace."

The dragon roared, and fire belched out of its seven horrible mouths. Robin looked around to see if Gwyneth was all right and saw Dewey was already with her, holding her as she trembled with fear. When he turned his gaze toward the spot where it had been only moments before, the dragon was gone. Kat-sidhe flew over to Michael and they spoke briefly. Their conversation ended almost as quickly as it had begun, and Michael turned to Robin.

"The dragon has just declared war, and I must leave now to select from Kat-sidhe's elite. You are all safe for now and will be protected by my Seraphim. When next we meet, Robin, you will be back in Llangollen. Until then, you must certainly know you can defend yourself if you are cornered. But again, I beg you, do not seek out a confrontation with the dragon. That is for me to do and no one else. Do you understand?"

"Yes, I understand."

"Now I must go. You will all be safe until the war begins. That is when I will return. I leave you all in peace."

He was gone before Robin could finish blinking. How could he stop Lleus from turning Peter into the Antichrist unless he indeed faced the dragon? Robin was careful to keep this thought to himself.

Chapter 20
THE WAR IN HEAVEN

December in Llangollen brought freezing weather and a brief snow storm that left the landscape swathed in blankets of white. Tom and Darla were certainly wonderful foster parents, but Robin often found himself wishing they didn't always say he should continue to be normal. Their idea of normal was that everyone should go to school, do chores, and then homework in the evening. Even though Robin had to admit that this was normal for most families, his life wasn't so normal anymore, and besides, homework was not what he did best. Now he worried mostly about the future but hadn't heard from Myrddin or Kat-sidhe since he returned to Llangollen.

Most of the house had gone to bed while he had stayed up in his room struggling with an English essay that he didn't really understand. He listened to the sounds that seeped through his bedroom walls and began to identify them one by one as his weary mind wandered. Dewey slept in the bedroom next to his, and Robin thought that if he could hear him snoring now then it must be deafening inside the room itself. He felt a chill blast of air from his open window and got up to close it. He wondered why he didn't remember opening it in the first place as he pulled it down. Then out on the snow, he saw movement.

He watched, holding his breath. Dressed in white robes that blended with the snow, Myrddin removed the cowl that covered his head. Robin gasped and threw open the window again.

"Myrddin," Robin whispered, "is that you? Come up; it's awfully cold outside."

Myrddin nodded his head but held a finger up to his lips to indicate silence. Then he was in Robin's room in a flash. Robin quietly closed the window and turned to see Myrddin brushing off snow. His stare made Robin feel unsettled, and he braced himself for what surely must be disturbing news.

"What is it?" Robin whispered, full of dread.

"You've been studying the scroll for a long time now, haven't you?" Myrddin asked as he sat down in the chair across from Robin's bed.

"Yes, sir," Robin sighed. "It's all rather tedious, you know. Gwyneth keeps me at it for hours sometimes."

"Does she really? Good, good for her. Found anything of interest?"

"Well," Robin began, "we were tracing some of the Huguenot family histories during the French Revolution. There was some Protestant minister that helped them flee to Wales, and since they were being hunted, they changed their names to avoid detection. The new names are recorded in the scroll, and because of that, I can trace all the way back to King David of Israel."

"So could Jesus."

Robin started to speak, but Myrddin held his hand up to his lips and pointed to Robin's bedroom door. Myrddin rose from the chair and grasped the knob gently with his right hand. The door was open in a flash, and Gwyneth stumbled through, nearly knocking Robin over as she desperately tried to keep her balance.

"Hey!" Gwyneth protested. "What did you do that for?"

"Forgive me, Gwyneth," Myrddin said as he steadied her, "if I had known it was you, I wouldn't have acted so cautiously but would have graciously invited you in. This discussion involves you, as well."

"You mean the scroll?" Gwyneth asked, still trying to catch her breath.

"Yes, I do. What have you discovered?" Myrddin asked her.

"Oh...well...it seems Robin is directly related to the kings of Israel and perhaps beyond."

"Hang on," Robin exclaimed, "you heard all that? Through the door? Can everyone else hear that well through that door?"

"No, silly, but I can because I was listening to your thoughts, and Myrddin's, too."

"You can hear my thoughts?" Myrddin asked in surprise. "Your talent has developed more than I expected. That could come in handy some day. But I came here to discuss what all of this means. It is now time to present you to the Princes du Sang."

"Myrddin," Gwyneth began, "why is Brigid my double? I mean, if Robin and Peter are doubles and yet the same family then why not me and Brigid? Why couldn't I have been Robin's twin in this universe?"

"But you are both in the same family now. All things work out for the best."

"You mean we're both in the same foster family now. I never knew my real parents."

Robin stared at Gwyneth. She noticed and drew her robe tighter. The more he looked, the more uncomfortable she became.

"Stop it!" she hissed when she could stand it no longer.

"Stop what?" Robin answered in obvious confusion.

"It's not a gentlemanly thing to do, Robin," Myrddin instructed.

"Oh, sorry, but it's just…well that means…it's a bit of a shock to find out like this. Sorry, Gwyn."

"Git! I suppose you would rather we weren't related then?"

"No, oh no! I meant…I think…oh wow!" Robin sat back down on his bed, holding his head in his hands. "I think it's rather brilliant, really. I mean, your mom and dad adopting me makes us stepbrother and sister. Myrddin, is there more?"

"Well," Myrddin slowly began, "it's rather difficult really. You are both of royal heritage and in line for the throne with no kingdom. Robin is first in line, but Gwyneth is next. A queen has never sat on the throne, but if something were to happen to you, Robin, then it is Gwyneth who would have to assume that position."

"Is Gwyneth in danger? Please tell me, because I think we have a right to know if someone wants her eliminated."

"I think we all have a right to know, Myrddin!" Tom Reynolds interrupted. Darla was standing just behind him with an anxious look in her eyes.

"What's goin' on?" Dewey asked, rubbing his eyes trying to get the sleep out of them.

"Well," Myrddin said with a twinkle in his eyes, "I needed a private conversation with Robin first but I do apologize for having awakened the entire household."

"Don't mention it, Myrddin," Tom said. "I had to get up and see who was speaking so loudly from Robin's bedroom. What are you skulking around for, anyway?"

"Ah, well, do you know anything about Gwyneth's lineage?"

"I'm not sure anyone does. We only know we adopted her after she was left on the doorsteps of a church in Toulouse near the Canal du Midi. The nuns there didn't know anything or else they weren't saying."

"Tom," Darla interrupted, "are you sure this is the best time to be so open?"

"Why not?" Gwyneth asked.

"You see," Darla said, "now we've upset her. Darling, we love you as if you were our own. Surely you know that."

"Of course, I do. But you must know I wonder about it."

"I wonder about it also," Myrddin said. "I could tell you what I think, but until I know the facts, we still wouldn't know anymore than we do already. I'm not sure that would do you any good."

"But I want to know who my parents were. Why did they leave me? Why did..." Darla put her arms around Gwyneth and glared at Myrddin.

"Oh dear," Myrddin said, "I really did mean to be more tactful. It's why I was skulking about, as you put it, Tom. Forgive me for being such a bumbling old fool."

"You should have realized she would have questions," Darla accused.

"Mum, it's all right. But I do want to know. No more keeping things from me."

"Speaking of keeping things from us, why are you really here?" Robin asked.

"Let me first explain what has happened today," Myrddin said. "As you know, the pope was assassinated about the time Robin was leaving for America with his grandmother. The new pope was named today and confirmed. The new Pope is Lleus Zeifer, and he is now known as Pope Draconis Lleus DeVyla the First. The reason it took so long to confirm him at the conclave was because some did not wish to break from tradition and start a new line of popes. Lleus can be very persuasive, and in this case, he was aggressively so. There are now two cardinals that need to be replaced at this time, and he is the one to name them."

"He's the pope now?" Tom asked. "That's just not right! That's just downright unsavory!"

"More important, it gives him more power with the Princes du Sang," Myrddin continued. "I met with the Legitimist Committee in secret, however, and showed them a copy of the scroll. They wish to confirm Robin before Lleus has time to interfere and foil their attempt to be rid of his influence."

"But they can't crown me king just yet, can they?" Robin broke in. "I studied the way it's supposed to work, and they have to name a regent in my stead, and Lleus is already regent."

"Very good, sire," Myrddin beamed. "The Princes du Sang wish to name Tom and Darla as co-regents in his stead. All of this must be done with the utmost secrecy, and done immediately. Lleus will be enraged when he finds out. We must all leave for Paris. By the way, you do practice the Roman Catholic faith, don't you, Robin?"

"I never went to church much, if that's what you mean. I was baptized and I guess we did go to Mass once in a while. Why is that so important?"

"The king must practice that faith and, once crowned, will carry the title Eldest Son of the Church. All French Kings have done so since the Merovingian Kings. We should leave for Paris at once."

"When do we possibly have time for that?" Darla interjected. "These children need their sleep!"

"Time is escaping us as we speak, in fact," Myrddin softly replied.

"What do you need us to do, Myrddin?" Tom asked.

"Stand where you are and do not move. I will attempt the rest. Now I must summon the dragon."

"I've seen enough dragons, thank you," Robin mumbled to Gwyneth.

"I heard that, sire. I am about to summon a different dragon than the one you suppose. Now quickly, Robin, the scroll. We'll need it."

Then Myrddin spread his arms out, and with his cloak still about his shoulders, Robin thought he looked a bit like Michael.

"*Anail nathrock, uthvass bethudd, dochiel dienve! Cum saxum saxorum in duersum montum oparum da, in aetibulum in quinatum...Draconis!*" Myrddin spoke the chant three times. The room grew silent. The lights dimmed until they disappeared altogether. They were in Paris before the winter sun appeared over the horizon.

No one paid any attention to Myrddin and his peculiar entourage as they made their way through the streets of Paris and entered a large government building. They entered through massive oak doors and found themselves in a cavernous, opulent hall with stairs ascending to a second landing, where they could see offices and conference rooms.

They entered one of the conference rooms, where a round table surrounded by thirteen red-satin-covered chairs was situated. An altar overlooked the table, and along the walls were paintings and photographs of kings. Robin gaped in wonder as Myrddin stood behind him.

"Most of these kings are of the house of Bourbon. Now this one," Myrddin explained as he pointed to a particularly ancient painting, "is Arthur Pendragon, King Arthur that is. The Pendragons were of French descent, just as you are. You are descended from him."

"How long have you known that?"

"Long before I first met you, actually."

"Why tell me now?"

"Because now is the time that the king of French descent must take his throne, and the king must understand his ancestry. I never told you before so that you would study the scroll and learn about it on your own."

"I hate studying! You could have told me sooner, you know."

"Then you would not have been considered worthy, despite your credentials," a tall, balding man with a pencil-thin mustache said.

"Hugues Capet, my old friend! How are you this fine morning?" Myrddin beamed at the man as they embraced and kissed each other on the cheek.

"I am tired, cranky, and a bit apprehensive. Lleus does not yet know that we meet. If the vote is even, he will still be the president of the Princes du Sang and it will be his vote that breaks any tie. We are assembling now and should be seated."

Hugues indicated two chairs drawn up and placed on the altar. What was extraordinary to Robin was the presence of a throne that had been placed between the two otherwise ordinary chairs. Myrddin guided Robin to one of the chairs on the altar and took the other for himself, with the throne between them. Twelve men standing behind the chairs at the round table stared at Robin, making him very uncomfortable.

"As vice president of the Princes du Sang, I call this conclave to order. Each of you has a copy of the credentials in question and the lineage they prove. The boy who would be king sits at the altar and awaits your adjudication. I will now entertain motions from the floor."

It was moved and seconded that the vote should be taken immediately. Discussion was called for and one lone man stood up. Recognized by Hugues, he looked at Robin.

"So, you believe you are the heir with the right to the throne?"

"Yes, sir," Robin mumbled.

"Do you have the scroll?" the man asked.

Robin took it out of his shirt and handed it to him. The other men at the table began whispering amongst themselves. Myrddin smiled.

"Do you know who I am?" the man continued. "I am Henri Chambard. I am loyal to the true church and the pope, and loyal to the only true throne that I believe we in this room should recognize. I tell you all that it is a mistake to confirm this child to a position that does not exist. This is a committee that should only be concerned with real kings and not someone's wild imaginings that this child is king. I will not play this game."

"May I remind my esteemed colleague," Hugues said, "that our charter specifically details that we are to consider all legitimate cases that arise concerning the French monarchy as well as the throne of David? This boy claims the latter, and he has provided proof. We are mandated to vote on this matter. Surely you have spoken with your loyal constituents, Henri, and surely they have pledged their votes according to your wishes. If you have evidence that refutes the boy's claim, then present it. Otherwise, the question must be brought to a vote."

"Lleus is not present. We should wait for him." Henri's eyes were blazing.

"Lleus is unavoidably detained. But then you knew that, didn't you? There are twelve present, and if there is a need, then we will wait for his vote."

"Call for the question!" the other men began shouting.

The gavel rapped so sharply that it sounded like a thunderclap to Robin. Silence echoed in the room, and Robin suddenly began trembling.

What are you trembling for?

I don't know. I'm really nervous, though.

Maybe it's adrenalin. What if they don't confirm you, Robin?

Don't say that!

I didn't, actually!

"You will each receive a white marble and a black one," Hugues began as he held up a blue satin bag with marbles inside. "I will then pass the bag around, and each of you will indicate your vote by placing the white marble inside the bag if you are for and the black if you are against. The tally will be taken, and the votes will be kept secret."

First the marbles were handed out to each member, and then the bag was somberly passed around. Each member placed his vote in the bag as it reached him, and at last the bag was again in the possession of Hugues. A shallow box was brought to Hugues, and he emptied the bag into the box and displayed its contents to all the members.

"Please, for your viewing, witness that there are exactly twelve marbles. This guarantees that all members present have cast one vote and one vote only. Henri if you would be so kind as to assist me with the validation of the count?"

Henri reluctantly stood beside Hugues as he counted the vote out loud. The vote was eight to four in favor of confirmation. Henri groaned in protest.

"I still believe this vote is illegal!" Henri stormed. "Lleus will not be happy!"

"Why do you still call him Lleus?" Hugues responded. "Even I have enough respect for his new office not to refer to him so familiarly."

"You have no idea what you are doing, Hugues! We must take this vote again and only when the pope is present!"

"No, we now must name regents," Hugues declared. "If it pleases the council, may I introduce to you Tom and Darla Reynolds, who are the only candidates for this office."

"The pope is already regent and was so named when we still all referred to him as Lleus. And you are fully aware of that fact!"

"Sit down, Henri! You know full well that being the pope presents a conflict of interest, and besides, the boy needs parents, as well, not just regents."

Henri sat down, still glaring at Hugues. The vote was taken as before, and once again the vote was eight to four in favor. The conclave was then adjourned, and each member greeted Robin and introduced himself to him, bowing as he made way for the next man in line. The last to speak to him was Hugues.

"I am Hugues Capet, as your Royal Highness already knows. Congratulations and may God speed."

"Thank you, sir," Robin managed to reply. "That man, Henri Chambard, he's loyal to Lleus Zeifer?"

"I think you may already be aware that he is not the only one here loyal to the pope. I could offer my opinion, but I'm not sure that would do any good since I perceive you may have already formed one of your own. N'est-ce pas?"

"I know who *he* is loyal to, but there were four votes against and that means there are three more who may be loyal to Zeifer. I was wondering who *they* were?"

"But why, your Royal Highness?"

"I must be about the business of being king."

"You are confirmed as the heir apparent, but you are not yet crowned king. You will not be crowned until your twenty-fifth birthday. As to you being about the business of being king, as you put it, you are wise to find out who your enemies are, but wiser still to find your friends."

"May I then consider you a friend?"

"Not only a friend but a loyal subject as well. I pledge my life to you, your Royal Highness, if it pleases you."

"Pledges and oaths can be hollow at times, Robin," Myrddin interrupted. "I can assure you, however, that Hugues is the genuine article and means every word he says and indeed will give his life defending you, as I will."

"Thank you, but I hope that won't be necessary."

"Yes, it will! Your life will be mine!" Lleus had entered the room unseen and unnoticed. Now he was standing before them in all of the regalia of the office of the pope. His eyes were boring into each of them, and Robin thought he noticed the hint of red in his eyes. In his right hand he held the scroll. Henri Chambard slipped through the exit and was gone.

"Your eminence, how wonderful to see you. We were disappointed that you missed our conclave," Hugues said. "May I present his Royal Highness, the Crown Prince Robin Peter Gilman?"

Hugues rose in the air, grasping at his throat, unable to breath. His legs began kicking as he struggled violently to free himself from the unseen strangler. A wet spot appeared, dampening his pants, and beneath his kicking legs a small puddle formed. Then his body became still before it fell back to the floor, limp and lifeless.

"Do you see how undignified it is to die, Robin?" Lleus quietly said as he gazed at the lifeless form before him. "The human body eliminates its waste just before the soul exits, you see. Shall we see if your body does the same?"

Robin frantically searched the room for someone who would help him, but everyone was motionless like statues. He reached out to shake Myrddin, thinking the powerful wizard was only dazed, but even Myrddin's robes were as hard as stone. There was no life in any human present. *And soon*, Robin thought, *there will be no life in me.*

"What would killing me accomplish?" Robin asked in an attempt to buy time.

"If you die, then Peter will be the dominant half of your soul. It's you I wanted first, Robin. I can still teach you. It is still not too late."

"No! I will not be your evil king!"

"Perhaps the life of another could persuade you," Lleus said as he walked over to Gwyneth.

Robin watched in revulsion as Lleus put his hand beneath her unmoving chin and cupped it while he smiled malevolently. He turned his gaze to Robin with glinting eyes.

"Leave her alone!"

"You took a blood oath. Abide by it!"

Push him, Robin! It was Gwyneth. Lleus gave no sign that he was aware that she had communicated to him.

He's too big! Robin thought back to her.

Not with your hands! Use your mind! Robin, please!

Knowing there was no time to argue, Robin concentrated with all his might and pushed out by intent with his mind. Even though he had hoped it would work, it was still shocking to see how violently Lleus flew backward through the air. His body struck the nearest wall and slumped to the floor, momentarily dazed.

Now push Myrddin!

Again Robin pushed, but Myrddin barely moved.

That's it, keep trying!

You've got to help! We've got to do this together! Now!

The strangest sensation permeated his very soul. It was as if he and Gwyneth were one person, if only for just a brief moment. It was during that moment that he knew she was his twin. She was the one kidnapped long ago, and they had found each other again. It was wonderful.

Dewey! Help us! Push! Both Robin and Gwyneth invaded Dewey's mind with their thoughts.

Though shocked by the newness of it, Dewey used his own mind, and together all three pushed. Together they moved the wizard until he was free. Myrddin stumbled forward, shaking his white hair and beard, trying to clear his befuddled mind. Lleus stirred and regained his feet.

"Monster!" Myrddin shouted when he saw Hugues's body on the ground and the others in their frozen state.

"Fool!" Lleus retorted. "You should have stayed in your Druid version of heaven where you belonged!" It was Myrddin's turn to fly through the air, striking the far wall with a sickening thud. A thin groan escaped his lips, and his face momentarily turned blue.

Robin felt a vicelike grip around his neck and was lifted off the ground the same as Hugues had been. Panic rose in his throat as he fought to breathe. His head became dizzy as he sensed his trachea being crushed by the unseen fingers of the ghost hand that held him high in the air. He could hear Gwyneth screaming and people shouting his name. The room grew darker, and before he passed out, he thought it would be nice to take a trip to the restroom as soon as he could. Darkness overcame him, and he dreamed of flying.

When he awoke, Michael stood over him, beating his wings in rhythm to his breathing. Robin gulped in the air as if it were water and the desert were all around. He sat up, but Michael's giant hands kept him from standing.

"Not just yet, little one. Catch your breath first," Michael said. Robin coughed and sputtered as his throat burned with each inhalation.

"D...do...don't call me that!" Robin said as he looked down at his pants, looking for telltale dampness. He was relieved to find he was dry.

"Little one? Forgive me, but all humans are little ones to me. I meant no indignity." Michael smiled.

"What happened? Where's Gwyneth? Where's Myrddin? Where's everyone else?"

"We are wasting time!" Dewey said.

"Dewey! How could you?" Gwyneth raged. "He almost died, you know!"

"Not while I'm here he won't!"

"Enough, little ones. You are safe in the keeping of my Seraphim," Michael admonished. "None of you will do any more fighting this day. But if Dewey wishes to observe and learn, I will have the Seraphim take you to a safe viewing locale."

"What are you talking about?" Robin said.

"There is about to be a great battle such as the world has not seen for many millennia," Michael instructed. "To understand, you must first know that Kat-sidhe presented her elite guard to me, and from among her best I handpicked one hundred and forty-four thousand troops. These chosen will be under my command as we go to repel the orc hordes and Nephilim under the command of the red dragon. Dewey has chosen to pursue the destiny of a great warrior and, for his edification, must witness the strategy of this battle. He will not be a warrior of the physical realm but of the magical, and this war is magical in nature."

"Where is everyone else?" Robin asked. His eyes darted around and discovered they were at Dinas Bran.

"Myrddin has returned them home, where they make preparations to leave for a safer environment. War is upon us."

"Let's just get goin'," Dewey said.

"But it's dangerous!" Gwyneth protested.

"Do not worry, beautiful lady. The three of you will be safe," Michael answered.

Even as Michael spoke, Robin felt himself lifted by the irresistible force that felt like clouds. They were soon standing high on a mountaintop in the Pyrenees. Despite the snow and cold, a roaring fire and heavy fur wraps kept the bitter wind from chilling them to the bone. The cold was not on Robin's mind when he looked from their perch and saw the orc hordes below advancing toward the French troops.

Dewey walked over beside him and handed him a pair of field glasses. The two boys grimly watched the ominous proceedings below them.

"Gwyneth, don't you want to see?" Robin called.

"No! I'm cold and I'm staying here by the fire. Besides, I've seen enough violence, thank you."

Dewey tugged on Robin's arm and pointed toward Michael. Kat-sidhe had slipped by them and was engaged in animated conversation with the Archangel. A vast cloud of fairies hovered behind them as they spoke. Their wings sounded like angry hornets, not the gentle flutter Robin had become used to, and their fairy dust had changed from brilliant gold to deathly green.

"Look-it that!" Dewey exclaimed tugging on Robin's arm. "The orc machines are weird."

"Catapults, they're using catapults!" Robin said.

"I 'eard in ancient times that the Romans would 'eat rocks and throw 'em with the catapults. The rocks would explode, and if that didn't work, they'd fling animal skins filled with 'ot oil followed by flamin' arrows." Even as Dewey said it, they saw a single arrow arcing through the air, followed by an eruption of flames. Then screams rent the night from far below.

"They're screaming. Can you hear them, Dewey? They're screaming."

"But why aren't they shootin' back?"

"The weapons of war that mankind uses have been rendered useless by the Nephilim," Michael said, startling both boys so that they almost dropped their field glasses. "That dark magic must be overcome if we are to win this battle. Stay here, both of you, and do not stray! You will be safe as long as you do as I ask. I must join the battle."

"But where are the Nephilim?" Robin and Dewey said at the same time.

"They wait behind the front lines for the orc hordes to sacrifice themselves and will appear only when they are assured of minimal loss," Michael replied, his expression grim.

Michael rose in the air, spreading his magnificent wings, and plummeted down the mountainside. The one hundred and forty-four thousand fairies flew in formation behind him. Orcs scattered in their horrible wake, and wherever the fairies flew, green death followed. A roar that sounded like hissing and screaming all at the same time announced the presence of the red dragon.

Acid that melted metal and flames that burned flesh spewed out of the seven mouths of the dragon, killing the humans and leaving the orcs unharmed. Screams from both sides could now be heard.

"This could be a stalemate," said Dewey.

"It's the dragon," Robin replied as he continued to watch, "If Michael can stop the dragon, then we have the advantage."

"What if it goes the other way?" Dewey asked as he looked at Robin.

"But that's not how it's supposed to happen. Michael's supposed to win. All the prophecies say so."

"Myrddin said the prophecy was you were s'posed to turn evil and become the Antichrist. I'm glad that prophecy didn't come true, but it also means that other prophecies might not come true. Maybe we should do somethin'."

"You better not!" Gwyneth shouted. "Michael said only he would fight the dragon and you two weren't supposed to!"

"But what if Michael loses because we played it safe? What if the prophecy 'as changed? I mean, it already 'as. What if we are s'posed to do somethin' to help 'im win? What if by doin' nothin' 'e loses?"

"But what if you die in trying and then we find that it all wasn't necessary?" Gwyneth cried.

"What if we don't have to leave this place to do what Dewey suggests?"

"Huh?" Dewey and Gwyneth spoke at the same time.

Robin gazed through his field glasses at the battle below. He followed the troop movements of the French, who were now being joined by another army far off in the distance. His idea had come to him in a flash, and the concept was brilliant in its simplicity.

"You showed me how, Gwyneth, when we pushed Myrddin with our minds."

"But this is beyond that, Robin!"

"No, I don't think so. Now listen, illusions are easy to form. We could create one that might distract the dragon just enough to give Michael the upper hand. We could do this together."

"But what am I s'posed to do?" Dewey said.

"Michael said you were a magical and spiritual warrior. I know an illusion will help, Dew, but what I don't know is which one is best. Besides, if you're everything Michael says you are, then you have the ability to help create an illusion same as Gwyneth and me."

"I don't know. What are you plannin', anyway?"

"Gunfire! Cannons! Bombs! None of our conventional weapons are working. If we give the illusion that they've started working again...if we make it *sound* as if they are, the dragon will be distracted. It's the dragon that must be stopped. It's the dragon that makes the dark magic, so we have to make him think that his magic has failed!"

"Sound...I never would have thought of that in a million years," Gwyneth whispered.

"All right, then, there's three of us and three sounds. I'll take gunfire."

"It's cannons for me, then," Gwyneth volunteered.

"Cool...bombs!" Dewey grinned.

"Maybe we should form a circle and hold hands," Gwyneth suggested. "Okay, everyone, concentrate!"

They formed a circle, clasped hands, closed their eyes, and concentrated on the sounds they wished to produce. The sound of distant gunfire reached their ears, followed by the occasional cannon fire. Robin and Gwyneth concentrated on their sounds but secretly listened for bombs. None could be heard.

After a moment, Dewey groaned in frustration. Robin and Gwyneth opened their eyes and looked at him.

"Well, I 'aven't 'ad a lot of practice like yeh two, now 'ave I?"

"You have to use your imagination," Gwyneth urged. "Imagine the biggest bomb you can and watch it drop to the ground. When it reaches its target, *hear* it blow up!"

"We can't stop now. Keep trying," Robin urged.

Again, three pairs of eyes closed, and three pairs of hands clasped together. Gunfire was all around and getting closer. Cannon shells could be heard roaring through the air and exploding as they found their targets. Then the ground shook, and a blinding light illuminated the night sky until it was as bright as day. Waves of heat hit them next, and Robin thought he could smell his hair burning.

Robin and Gwyneth opened their eyes in terror. Dewey grinned.

"Not that big!" Gwyneth's voice quavered with fear.

"No, that was brilliant!" Robin argued. "Keep it up! One or two more like that and the dragon is bound to investigate!"

They concentrated, and again the sounds of conventional weaponry filled the air. The ground shuddered beneath them, and a fireball came so close it threatened to engulf them. Three Seraphim appeared, and though they did not speak, it was obvious they were alarmed. One of the Seraphim appeared inside the circle the three friends had formed and stared at Robin with anger.

"Oops, sorry," Robin mumbled. He automatically knew that the Seraphim were angry because he had interfered.

"*Duck!*" Dewey yelled.

They ducked just as the dragon flew at them. The Seraphim flew back at the dragon, causing it to wheel and turn to avoid a collision. Trumpets sounded so loud that they thought their ears would burst. Angels with wings the color of shadow appeared and engaged the Seraphim in hand-to-hand combat.

The dragon landed directly in front of Robin, and fire mixed with its acid saliva spewed out of its great maw. Gwyneth screamed, and Dewey could be heard shouting indistinguishable words as Robin fell to the ground, engulfed in flames.

"Coward!" Michael shouted. "Face me now if you will! It is time!"

Robin frantically felt his clothes, his hair, his face, running his hands all over his body to see if it was still there. To his surprise, he was completely intact. It was as if nothing had happened. Someone hit him from behind and bowled him over just as Michael rose in the air and shot like an arrow, straight at the dragon. Gwyneth screamed hysterically, holding him down and hugging him so tight he thought he would suffocate. Dewey raged at the dragon, calling it every foul name he could think of.

"Get off! I'm all right!" Robin shouted through the noise and confusion.

Above them, fairies began to amass and rained their deathly green fairy dust down from the mountaintops upon the orcs. The three Seraphim, although pursued by the angels of shadow, collected each of them and sped them away to a safer vantage point on a large rock that overlooked the scene of the battle. It was war in heaven, thought Robin as he watched and trembled.

The dragon roared and met Michael head on in an enormous impact that sent tremors all through the ground. Michael cut at the dragon with his two-edged sword, gashing its left flank as if it were paper. Immense gouts of black dragon blood flew through the air, but the dragon seemed hardly wounded. It snapped its teeth and ripped one of the wings away from Michael's body. Michael fell far below where the orcs were frantically trying to fight off the attack of the fairies. The orcs fell on Michael before he could regain his feet and bore him down.

"No!" Robin screamed. *"Fight with me you son of—"*

A hand clamped down on his mouth. Robin swung his arms and broke free to see Dewey behind him, holding his nose where Robin had hit him.

Robin turned and ran at the dragon, and Dewey followed. The dragon landed on the ground, its seven heads smiling at the boys as they charged.

"And with what shall you fight me, my prince, more illusion?"

"I know you're Lleus! I'll fight you any way I can!"

"How brave! How heroic! Humans will write songs and poetry about you for this act of stupidity! Very well, it will be as you wish, your Royal Highness." The dragon disappeared in a red mist, and Lleus stood in its place, his left thigh bleeding profusely from where Michael's sword had left its mark.

Robin shook with fear. He could hear Gwyneth screaming somewhere behind him. To his left, Dewey grimly waited for what would happen next. Dewey looked back at him and nodded, showing that he was there to fight along with him. Two swords materialized at their feet. One sword was double edged like Michael's, and the other was Robin's samurai sword.

"I have given you your weapons," Lleus sneered. "I will face you both at the same time and in human form. That should level the playing field since, after all, I am Lucifer the Son of the Morning, the Bright and Shining Morning Star! I am Sorrow! I am Death! I am the Eater of Souls! Defend yourselves!"

Robin and Dewey picked up their respective swords and stood side by side. Both boys were sweating, and both trembled with fear and loathing for the monster that stood before them. Blood was still pouring out of Dewey's nose where Robin had accidentally hit him.

"Now you've done it!" Dewey said.

Robin glanced at him with a thanks-a-lot-for-that sort of look. Lleus grinned and brandished his own sword. Both boys steeled themselves. Michael blazed before them in white light that made them turn away.

"Did you miss me, Lucifer?" Michael asked. He laid his sword down on the ground before his feet. "Father offers you clemency and forgiveness for all your misdeeds. He wishes to have his prodigal son returned to the family. Will you accept what Father offers?"

"*Never!*"

Lleus charged Michael, and the two-edged sword, which was only a moment before lying useless on the ground, cut him in half before he could take more than two steps. Lleus stared at Michael with a look of surprise.

The top half of his body slowly toppled as the sword came down a second time and cut his head off clean at the shoulders. The head rolled down the mountainside and out of sight. The two halves of Lleus' body disappeared in a red mist, leaving no evidence that it had once stood before them.

"You're hurt," Robin finally managed to say to Michael after collecting his furious thoughts.

"It will repair itself. For now, you are still in danger. The orcs are ascending the mountain and will be upon us soon."

"Take Gwyneth and go!" Dewey shouted. "I'll 'old 'em off!"

"*Haven't you two learned anything at all?*" Michael was so terrible in his rage that both Robin and Dewey were struck silent. Then, more gently, the Archangel continued, "You will both have an opportunity to fight, but only if we are caught by the pursuing orcs. Kat-sidhe and the one hundred and forty-four thousand will keep them at bay and eventually destroy them all."

Robin felt someone touching his shoulder. He turned to see a distraught Gwyneth staring at him with pleading eyes. Reading her thoughts, he knew she wanted him and Dewey to leave now and not stand and fight. He nodded to her and sheathed his sword. Dewey did the same.

"Now, listen, all of you," Michael cautioned. "I will not be with you. It is not often that an Archangel needs rest, but this once I must do exactly that. Kat-sidhe and my Seraphim will guide you back to the Reynolds' house. Myrddin will be there waiting with further instruction." Michael's breath came in heavy gasps.

"Michael," Robin asked, "is Lleus dead? Will he be back? Will you—"

"Peace be unto you, little one," Michael soothed. "Lleus has left this universe, never to return. There is a possibility that he may still find a way to accomplish his objectives, however. For now, you are safe. As for me, I will heal and I will face him again, but not in this universe. Your world is now free of his influence."

The Seraphim appeared and gathered the children in their arms. Golden fairy dust exploded all around them, and Kat-sidhe appeared before Robin with the most serious look on her face he had yet seen. Michael's image faded away. As they rose in the sky, the orcs charged over the rise and began shooting their arrows at them from the hill where they had only moments before been standing.

Chapter 21
THE KINGDOM OF MAGIC

Darla hugged all three children at once, and Tom, looking stunned, listened to them explain what they had seen and done. Kat-sidhe and Myrddin talked quietly in one corner of the room. Someone had left a radio on, and the early morning news anchor announced that the pope had disappeared and a member of the French parliament had been assassinated. Then the news turned to the war.

The devil-like creatures had been overwhelmed by the strangest aerial assault force ever witnessed in the history of mankind. Only their ancient-looking weapons of war had been left behind after the battle, and no trace of the dreadful creatures could be found. Eyewitnesses, however, gave the story credibility. The Spanish and French forces were mopping up along the foothills of the Pyrenees.

Robin was suddenly riveted to the radio when he heard the last story of the day. The news anchor explained how a young prince had been confirmed as the heir to an obscure throne that many thought no longer existed. The identity of the prince was not being revealed for his protection, according to a spokesman for the Princes du Sang, which was described as the governing body for the ascendancy rights of all royal heirs. What the news did report as fact was that this young prince was of French descent and would become king when he was of age. What kingdom he was to rule or even if it existed, however, was unclear, the newscaster reported.

Robin sat in silence, pondering what had happened to him as the others continued their animated conversations. *We should all be tired*, he thought, but excitement was still coursing through his veins. He needed to talk to someone and thought of Myrddin but decided Lilith would know more about what he intended to ask.

"Myrddin," Robin approached, "I'd like to go see Mother Lilith, please."

"Oh my! Robin, I'm sorry but that's not possible," Myrddin responded.

"But I don't understand. Why not?"

"Yggdrasil has been destroyed."

"How? Who did it? Where's Mother Lilith gone?"

"The dragon destroyed the tree so that the way to the other universe would be sealed. Even Kat-sidhe cannot go home. We have been discussing our options and, unfortunately, we seem to have none at this time."

"But we can't just stay here!" Robin blurted out. "I have to get to Peter and warn him about Lleus! He's in danger! You've got to figure a way to the other universe!"

"Robin," Kat-sidhe said, "please understand, Yggdrasil is destroyed. It was the only way back that we know of, and it is gone."

Tears ran down her face. Robin thought his heart would break when he saw Kat-sidhe weeping. Then a thought came to him, and he smiled.

"Yggdrasil was very old. I wonder what it was like when it was first planted. I wonder if it produced seeds. I wonder how fast it grew and how long it took for the doorways to open once it was mature enough. You wouldn't happen to know, would you, Kat-sidhe?"

"It was planted before my time. What did you say about seeds?"

"Yes, it might work at that," Myrddin said as he stroked his beard, lost in thought. "But we need to make it grow as rapidly as possible. Are some of your fairies of the forest available, Kat-sidhe?"

"There are sixteen thousand of them!" Kat-sidhe began flying around the room, bouncing off the walls and scattering fairy dust everywhere, infecting the entire room with her hysterical laughter. "There are sixteen thousand!"

Robin had to cross his eyes to see Kat-sidhe as she flew to him and kissed him on the lips. Crystal blue light bathed the whole room, but what Robin did at not first understand was that the light was emanating from him. Robin felt his face redden. It puzzled him that Kat-sidhe's kiss would affect him that way.

"Well, what are we waiting for?" Myrddin said.

"Don't you ever sleep?" Darla protested. "These children are exhausted, and so are we."

"Darla is right about this one, Myrddin," Tom added.

"Forgive me, but this can't wait. Once it is done we will certainly all rest."

Tom shrugged his shoulders at Darla, who was about to open her mouth. Darla sighed and nodded her head in agreement. Before they could collect their thoughts, everyone was at Yggdrasil, gazing in wonder at the beauty all around contrasted by the ugly, burnt-out stump of what was left of the magnificent mountain ash that had commanded the center of the glade.

"Robin, Gwyneth, Dewey," Myrddin ordered as soon as they arrived, "quickly now, go find as many seeds as you can and bring them all to me. Make sure the seeds you bring have all been in the fire that destroyed the tree."

"Seeds, seeds, we must find seeds!" Kat-sidhe shouted to the sixteen thousand fairies of the forest.

Even Tom and Darla joined in the search, acting like they were two children on an outing. Soon all the seeds they could find were at Myrddin's feet.

Robin watched in wonder as each forest fairy seized one seed and planted it in the ground. The sound of thunder could be heard in the distance, drawing closer. Dark clouds gathered in the green hills around them. Fat rain drops hit Robin in the face, and he opened his mouth to try and catch one, but instead a raindrop went straight up his nose, making him sneeze and cough.

"That'll teach yeh a lesson," Dewey laughed.

"I got one!" Gwyneth shouted. She too had tried to catch a raindrop but was more successful than Robin.

The forest fairies encircled the group and began chanting. The entire circle moved first two steps forward and then reversed one step, ever advancing counter clockwise to a primal rhythm. The others soon joined in, forming their circle inside the fairy circle that surrounded them. They danced the encircling dance of the fairies as they repeated the chant. On and on they danced in the rainstorm and long into the night.

It was early morning when Robin looked down at the ground and saw mountain ash sprouts. First, two leaves unfurled and then there were four, eight, sixteen, and more and more until young saplings surrounded them, all full of life and vigor. The chant stopped unexpectedly, and only the falling rain could be heard. Then the rain ceased as abruptly as the chant.

"My forest fairies will tend to the saplings, and one will be chosen from them all to replace what was destroyed," Kat-sidhe joyfully explained. "There, where the forest begins, is a place beneath the canopy of the trees prepared for all of you to take your well-deserved rest. You will be safe here from all harm."

The weary travelers made their way to the edge of the forest and found beds surrounded by fairies. Each bed floated in the air and when Robin lay down, it was like floating in the clouds. He didn't know how long he slept or when he first fell asleep, but when he awoke, he was looking straight up at the night sky full of stars.

He quietly arose so as not to awaken the others. He wandered back to the edge of where the saplings began and watched the forest fairies as they tended each one with their special loving care. Myrddin sat down beside him.

"I like the fairies," Robin said. "They're brilliant, and I wish they could be here forever. It's sad they can't go back home."

"This universe was once their home, too, you know," Myrddin replied.

"How long do you think it will be before we can cross over to Peter's universe?"

"I don't know, Robin. I don't know."

"I've learned to do some pretty amazing things. Do you think Peter can do these things, as well?"

"Those amazing things are proof you have magic inside you. Peter lives in the universe of magic. I believe he is just as magical as you are and only needs to learn how."

"Who will teach him? You?"

"I wish I could, but we can't cross over."

"Lleus?"

"Maybe."

"Michael said that we were free from Lleus's influence here. But I wonder if he went to where Peter is."

"I think that is a strong possibility."

"Do you think he might try to deceive Peter the way he did with me?"

"Maybe."

"I took a stand and broke my blood oath. Do you think Lleus will make a blood oath with Peter?"

"Maybe."

"Do you think...do you think...Peter will take the stand I took?"

"Maybe."

"If Peter goes bad...you know, evil...do you think Lleus might win?"

"Maybe."

"The universes are supposed to merge. I'm supposed to merge with Peter. What if he's gone evil and I haven't? What will I be when we merge? Please tell me that I won't be evil, 'cause I want to know if I can change whatever happens. It's why I want to get to Peter and warn him. He has no idea what he is about to face."

"I don't know." Myrddin put his arm around Robin.

"Then I have to know. I have to know how to be the strongest if Peter gives in to Lleus."

"Yes, that part I do know."

They sat in silence, watching the saplings grow. Robin felt comforted knowing that there would soon be a new Yggdrasil. Soon they would be able to help Peter and Brigid.

Robin, where are you?

Hi, Gwyneth. I'm just here watching the trees grow.

I need to tell you what Lilith said.

Thought you did.

She said we're twins. But I don't get it. You don't think...

No, I don't think you are my twin; I know you are. My grandma told me you were kidnapped and never found. We've got to find out why, though. I mean I'm sure Lleus had something to do with that, but he had a reason, and that might be a good thing to know.

You're right, about us being twins, I mean. He didn't want us to be together or be able to talk the way we are now. Maybe it's because he knew I would help you resist his evil.

You're strong that way. It's pretty cool, really. Maybe Brigid will help Peter resist. We've got to figure a way to tell them, Gwyn. We've just got to.

Shut it, yeh two. I'm tryin' to get some sleep 'ere.

Dewey?

LOOK FOR ROBERT W BOYER'S NEW BOOK:
GILMAN'S PARALLEL
THE DOPPELGANGER

Robin knows he has to find a way back to Peter's universe and try once again to thwart the plans of Lleus DeVyla Zeifer. The future of the world depends on it.

Made in the USA